D.1

Weathered

Storms

<u>Acknowledgments</u>

First and foremost, I would like to thank God for planting the seed in my soul of creating my first novel. I have always wanted to become a writer; it started out with me scribbling kiddie songs in my notebook to jotting down poetry as a teen. Now a vigorous adult woman, right before my eyes, my dream has come true. I would like to thank my husband, Stefan Parker, for being so patient and so willing to listen to me read passages of my story to him and giving me his best feedback. My husband is definitely my biggest supporter. I love you, babe, and I appreciate you along with our beautiful son, Liam aka "King". You guys are my heart and soul. I also would like to thank my Pastor, Artura Faison; you have been a great role model, spiritual Mom, mentor, counselor and best friend. I thank you Pastor for believing that I was capable of doing anything I put my mind to. Thank you for seeing past my flaws and teaching me to see all the incredible things in me I once couldn't see. I would like to thank my editor, Marcia Fingal, for implementing her editing skills and helping me make this novel into a masterpiece... You're the bomb girl!

I want to thank my mom, Ms. Tanya Hayden, for her unconditional love and for also believing in me and all my dreams, whether you thought they were crazy or not. Love you, Momma. Special thanks to all of my other family and friends, Lashanda Vest, Elizabeth Sterling, Alexis Robinson, Akirra Outerbridge, Latoya Gadsden, Ramona Reyes, Janet Badia; Geneva Potts, Nicole White, Sabrina White, Lorraine Boyce, Murial Alston, Ellen Onja Brown, Curtis Brown, Rosemarie Reeves and Gloria Lattimore. My siblings, Silvia Knight, Ali Knight, Kareem Knight, Cory Potts, Yolanda Potts, Natasha Wiggins, Melvin "June-bug" Washington, Jonathan Washington and Lohattis "Tiz" Hayden. As well as my massive amount of cousins and my church family, the "BCCPF" clan; I love all of you guys to no end. Your girl did this... Now watch me soar beyond my limits.

This book is for all my sisters and brothers, but mainly my sisters. Have you ever felt like life was so complicated that you didn't know what to do or who to turn to? If you did turn to someone, it seemed like they weren't listening... judging you when you weren't asking to be judged. Maybe you've felt sick and tired of the drama and found yourself constantly asking "Why me?" You may have even thought you should just give up and end it all. Well take a walk with Shenelle Patterson, a young woman who journeys along a stormy road in her life. I assure you, you will no longer feel alone. Here's her story...

Prologue

I don't know what happened! One minute I was transfixed in a photograph of my life, and then the next minute I was at a maternity ward. After the long process of agonizing pain and different colors ripping from my inner flesh, I watched as the nurse disappeared with my baby. All I could feel at the moment was bitter coldness from ventilation. The presence of a deadly shadow was somewhere lingering in my room. My mind was unsettled as I heard cries near my bed; it was guttural and eating away at my emotions. I couldn't deal with facing again the man who I considered the love of my life, sitting beside me. He was uncontrollably upset. There was no explanation for why things had to be this way. I just knew our love child was taken from us and would be away forever.

My hands gripped the bars at the sides of my bed; it angered me how things changed so drastically. I thought everything was done right, minus one flaw that was now left for questioning. A name was picked out, a nursery was in need of a small human being, and unisex clothing was still embalmed in gift bags and pretty boxes. Our child's gender was supposed to be a surprise, but instead their arrival ended in a surprising departure. A part of me wanted to run and look for my baby to hold once more, if only the epidural injection wasn't keeping my lower body paralytic. Love-of-my-life grabbed my cold, shaky hand. He caressed it, telling me everything was going to be alright. It was a lie. I knew I would never be alright again, and neither would he. The doctor came back into the room empty handed. Her face looked perturbed as she instructed me to wait six weeks for my body to heal... What about my mental healing? Childbirth was supposed to be one of the best experiences anyone could live for, but for me it was one of the worst experiences I have ever lived through.

Chapter 1

Months Later...

It was a Friday afternoon, extremely sunny for a day in February. I sat out on the balcony, covered in a fleece blanket as I smiled at the little kids running around, dressed in their warmest attire. They were throwing snowballs at each other from the big storm the day before. They seemed happy the sun was out. It was always freezing at this time of year. I was bored sitting at home and watching the interaction between the children made me reminiscent of my own childhood. I remembered those days, when my mother would tuck my shoulder length braids inside my hat and bundle me up in a snowsuit, real tight. I could barely breathe. My two brothers and I would go outside, make snow angels and play for hours. Afterwards, we would run to the store, each with a dollar given to us by daddy and buy a bag full of candy we knew we had no business eating. That's what we did every single winter until we were pre-teenagers. It was a tradition for me and my siblings. But that was back then... the time when family love was more valuable.

I was stuck in memory lane for a while when I thought about my best friend Alicia. She's been my ace boon coon ever since the first grade. While most friends who grow up together eventually go their separate ways, Alicia and I were different. Alicia was that friend who you ate lunch with at school on a daily basis and sat next to in every class you had together. That friend, who came over to your house on the weekends and painted your nails, combed your hair and talked about which R&B singer she had a crush on. The girlfriend you would run and call on the telephone to tell all the juicy details about your first date. She was also there when the tears fell from your first heartbreak, and more than likely she would be crying right along with you. What any girl could ever want in a true friend, with no questions asked that was Alicia!

People who knew us well even said we looked a lot like each other. We shared the same mocha complexion, bright almond shaped eyes and thick, long black hair. Both of us were born to African American parents, but it was obvious some of our qualities were complimentary to our Native American heritage. Whenever I spoke of Alicia or even thought of her, I couldn't help but be appreciative of my dear friend and our close knit friendship that has all the more flourished as we've grown. Alicia was definitely more than my best friend, she was my sister.

Thinking about Alicia took me back briefly to the conversation we had a few days earlier. I was supposed to have given her another call by now, but I couldn't. I would only tell her what she didn't want to hear. She had been ringing my phone off the hook and I avoided her like the plague. I knew she was just being the concerned friend she has always been, but I was hardly ever in the mood to hear her wrath that's been awaiting me. First for not calling her, and also once I tell her the news I know would be a disappointment to her. My guilty conscious must have triggered some kind of electric power surge because my cordless phone rang and flashing across the caller I.D was

Alicia Daniels. At first I was hesitant to pick up the phone, but I couldn't let ole girl strain her head over me any longer, so after the forth ring I answered.

"Hello."

Alicia gasped sarcastically, "OMG, She-She, you're alive!" She-She was the name Alicia gave me when we first met, short for my actual name, Shenelle. "Hey, Leece," I responded dryly.

"Sis, where in the world have you been? I've been calling you for four days. Why haven't you answered me, better yet why didn't you call me back? You know that you were supposed to!"

"Yes Bestie, I know. But you also know me well enough to realize exactly why I haven't called you back or answered your calls."

It disgusted me when friends or relatives played the question game as if they didn't already know all of my motives. I was a very stubborn person and I only moved how I wanted to move. There will always be those few people in your life who ignore the facts and still consistently press you because they don't want to embrace your barriers. In my world, that was on them. People such as Alicia, our other best buds from college, Natari and Hannah, and a couple of my relatives, they all knew better than that.

"You're right, She-She. I do know you that well, so I take it you didn't even go. Did you?"

"I went, but I only stayed for five minutes." I could tell by the sudden silence that Alicia was shaking her head disappointed. I know she really wanted me to do what was necessary to get myself together, but I always fought it.

"Shenelle, why do you keep doing this to yourself? You have to get this help so you can get well. You'll start to see a difference in your life and feel a whole lot better as time moves on. It's been almost a year now, how much longer are you going to keep holding all that stuff in?"

I rolled my eyes to the back of my head and slowly allowed myself to drift away from Alicia's lecturing, even though all she was trying to do was keep it real with me. I thought back to the kids looking happy, playing in the snow, and then quickly my mind went to that horrific day and the events that took place. It kept replaying in my head since it first happened and I couldn't stand how it made me feel. Tears filled the brims of my eyes as I clutched the lower part of my belly. I didn't want Alicia to know I was crying again for the hundredth time, so I quickly swallowed the fully formed lump in my throat and stifled my tears.

"Leecy, I'm going to go I promise."

"Shenelle, you promised me like twenty times already. It isn't easy to get these appointments." Alicia sounded frustrated. After all, she did travel across the nation just to sign me up for a doctor's appointment.

"Well this time, I'm serious. I swear between you and this dude, I can't figure out which one of you is worse." If there was one thing I hated among all other things, it was being pressured into doing something I didn't want to do, even when it was for my own good.

"You already know that I love you, She-She, you're closer to a sister to me than my real sisters. You're like my Siamese twin and you always have been. If you hurt, I hurt and I don't want to hurt anymore, so I really need you to get better and be you again. Darryl really loves you too, Shenelle, as if you were his rib in spite of all that has happened between you two." The sound of Darryl's name gave me chills that made me cringe. Then the instant replay of that day came again; the distressed look on Darryl's face and the hurt in his eyes was tormenting in remembrance. I seriously needed to get some immediate help, but I needed even more to get off this phone.

"Alicia, I have to go! I want to hang up so I could call and set up an appointment for Monday." She grilled me in an overbearing motherly tone. "She-She, are you telling me the truth? Are you really going to try and do it this time?" I responded with a little bit of enthusiasm to hopefully get her to back off with her pestering. "Yes Leecy, I'm really going this time and I'll stay until it's my turn to go in."

"Good, that's my girl! You better call me afterwards, before I'll have to break into the confines of your home and whip your butt."

I chuckled.

"I'm serious, Shenelle. Do not play with me!" she warned.

"I will call you, Alicia! I love you, bye now."

"I love you too, Shenelle. Talk to you later." After I hung up the phone from Alicia I did exactly what I said I was going to do. I called to set up an appointment for the following week. Then I turned on the TV and watched a lifetime movie until I dozed off.

***

Fifteen minutes passed as I sat in the waiting area for my name to be called. It has been almost ten years since I last met with a psychologist and I was a nervous wreck. One would've thought I'd be a champ at this type of position by now since I already had a year of the experience. I couldn't stop fidgeting as I surveyed the room and eventually became attentive to the headlines of a spread of magazines that was perfectly organized on top of a high class model coffee table. I had the last appointment, so I was the only one there. The jittery feeling in my bones made me imagine how a promiscuous teen might feel as they waited for the results of an H.I.V test, or a chain smoker after being screened for lung cancer. I wanted to leave so badly, but I promised Alicia I wouldn't. It was only right for me to do this if I wanted the flashbacks to go away.

I kept looking at my cellphone to keep up with the time. Never mind the very visible, big, round clock hanging on the wall above the secretary's desk. It was 5:15pm and it was getting dark outside, I wish my boyfriend Darryl was here with me. I hadn't seen him in three days. I knew he had to work or else he would be sitting right beside me, holding my hand. Although I had been speaking with Darryl over the phone the three days, I missed him something terrible. In fact, it was him and Alicia who stood in support of me and suggested I get the help I need, for my sake and for the sake of our relationship, but more so for my sake.

Sitting for so long, I was becoming less patient by the minute and starting to get annoyed by the popping sounds of the water cooler near me. I looked at the time on my phone again. It was getting closer to six and I was beyond done waiting. I stood up, smoothing out my clothing, readying to leave and right then, the door to Dr. Pauline Mayes' office opened up. I was shocked when I saw a man walk out. He was young, appeared to be about twenty one years old. What really caught my attention was the brightness in his Mahogany colored face. It seemed as though the entire universe had been lifted off his shoulders, like in a renewal form. I must've been staring at the man for a while and didn't realize it, because Dr. Mayes had to break me out from my concentration.

"Ms. Shenelle Patterson, would you like to come inside?" I turned around to face a pleasant looking, middle aged woman. She smiled and I felt a twinge of embarrassment, like a school girl caught in the act.

"Yes, Ma'am. I'm sorry." I bashfully walked past her without making eye contact into the room. She shut the door and extended her hand smiling. "I'm Dr. Pauline Mayes. It's nice to meet you."

"Nice to meet you as well." I shook her hand and I don't know why, but as soon as my hand touched hers all of the nervousness I felt vanished.

"Well for starters, I would like to apologize for keeping you waiting. Some of my clients tend to speak longer than they mean to. Your patience is greatly appreciated." I laughed on the inside. Aside from her not knowing how impatient I actually was, the real deal was that waiting my turn wasn't really much of an opted conclusion. All day different people came with their tall tales of misery to filter out, so a long wait after being on an even longer patient list just to be seen. It was a nuisance, but it was necessary.

"No worries," I casually replied. Dr. Mayes smiled again and I wondered if her being so cheery was one of her ways of breaking down the walls to my misery. She politely offered me a seat.

I looked over at the furniture setting that was a décor of an espresso brown, suede love seat with beige and brown accent pillows and a club chair with an ottoman. Dr. Mayes had a nice and welcoming demeanor, I liked that. I could feel from her vibe that I would be able to talk to her about anything and she wasn't the hypercritical type; she seemed very humble and down to earth. I also couldn't help noticing how well kept she was. She wore a sleek taupe pantsuit, with an off white, high collared blouse, and pumps that matched to the tee. Dr. Mayes was a pretty woman; she was about average height and medium built. Her pixie cut hair had a burgundy tint to it which complimented the red hue in her Cinnamon brown complexion. She didn't wear much make-up, just a light brush of lipstick that boosted her smile. As I looked at her I thought she resembled Judge Lynn Toler from *Divorce Court*. I sat down on the love seat and she took a seat behind her desk.

"So Ms. Patterson, what brings you here today?" I couldn't answer her right off the bat. I really didn't know what to say or where to even start. I just knew all the years I've been on this earth, I felt like I was hanging off the toenail of hell. I said the first words I could think of.

"*Life* is what brought me here." Her face was impassive, nonetheless still inviting.

"Okay, well how about you start off with telling me what's been bothering you the most? What exactly made you want to seek professional help?" I became nervous again as I reviewed my life inside my head.

"That's the problem; everything bothers me. I've been through a lot, like ever since birth and… The list goes on." I watched as Dr. Mayes' facial expression changed from delicate to concern.

"Hmm, so let's talk about it. What are these things that enter your mind? How are they affecting you?" There was something about Dr. Mayes. She was different than what I expected from a psychologist. Other therapists would have been quick to pull out a pen and pad and start jotting down information, making just enough eye contact to get an answer to any of their questions. Dr. Mayes was the total opposite; I had her undivided attention.

"I've been having these flashbacks from my past; bad things that has happened to me. No matter what I do to keep my mind off of them, they just keep coming back and it's driving me insane." I quietly exhaled to let go of the breath I'd been holding in while I was talking. I knew that telling Dr. Mayes about my problems was normal and her listening to me was the whole point of her job, but I was still afraid. I didn't want to appear crazy to her.

"How often do these flashbacks return to your mind, Ms. Patterson? Is it okay if I call you Shenelle?"

"You sure can. The flashbacks come constantly, on an everyday basis, and I can't eat or sleep. If I eat, my food won't digest properly and I regurgitate; as far as sleeping..." I huffed again, but louder this time and shook my head in anguish. "When I do sleep, even if it's just ten minutes, the flashbacks come in my dreams and wake me. I can barely hold a conversation without being interrupted by these bad memories." By then Dr. Mayes had on her reading glasses and was writing on a pad little by little.

"So have you been feeling depressed? Have you thought about hurting yourself or felt like you've wanted to hurt someone else?" Before she could come up with another question I blurted out, "All the time!" She stopped writing and popped her head up.

"All the time what, Shenelle?"

"All the time I feel like hurting someone!" I wasn't going to dare tell her about the few times I actually attempted suicide. I just wanted some help I wasn't trying to get sedated.

"Who have you felt like hurting?"

I desperately wanted to tell her, but I felt like it was too soon and little did she know, there was more than one person I felt like hurting. "There's nobody in particular. It's just..." I paused, I was starting to think I should quit while I was still ahead and just leave. Forget about this therapy thing.

"Just what?" Dr. Mayes softly asked. I could see the eagerness in her face of wanting to know more about my demons, but I couldn't bring myself to tell anymore.

"I don't know." I put my head down, feeling discomfited.

I wanted to get out of that office and run. I was in the midst of telling this person who doesn't know me from the Garden of Eden, things I hadn't even told my friends and never had any intensions of telling. I definitely wasn't ready for this, I wasn't ready to open up and disclose my skeletons, and more than likely, end up being admitted into a mental institution once I was done. I looked at the time on my cellphone. It was 6:30pm; I already had a long day and was fatigued.

"Dr. Mayes, I really should get going. I have an early day tomorrow. Can we reschedule this for another time?" She half smiled at me. I knew that she knew I was making an excuse to get out of telling her more things and leave her office.

"Of Course," she said. I anxiously stood up as she pulled out her agenda to set a date at her convenience.

"Is a week from today at 5:15pm good for you?"

"That'll be fine." Dr. Mayes got up from her chair and walked around the desk over to me.

"Okay, Shenelle, I will see you next Tuesday at 5:15pm sharp. It was a pleasure meeting with you today."

"Thank you and likewise," Dr. Mayes opened the door for me and I walked out. I kept walking and never looked back as I heard her make one last statement.

"Get home safely!"

When I got home it was a little after eight 0' clock. I hurriedly stripped out of my clothes and hopped in the shower to wash off the subway bacteria. I wasn't in the tub for five minutes when the flashbacks began. There I was, in the hospital bed crying hysterically. I couldn't believe I had just pushed out a baby boy, a son I would never bring home, put in his basinet and watch him sleep. A son I would never know, tell how much he meant to me and just how much I loved him. To see his tiny, lifeless body in his father's arms was heart wrenching. I backed up against the wall, slid down in the tub and wept. I felt so betrayed, how could I have created something so beautiful, just for his life to get cut short so soon. Sometimes I wonder if I am being punished for something I'd done, something I wasn't aware of. I could not understand it for the life of me and wished God would have taken me instead. I almost jumped out of my skin when I heard a knock at the bathroom door. I figured it was Darryl.

"Just a second!" I yelled out. I let the steaming water hit my face hoping I would appear flushed to disguise my crying, but Darryl being Darryl, he walked in the bathroom anyway and pulled back the curtain.

"Darryl, I told you to wait a second." I had my back turned to him, trying to hide my face.

"Shenelle, look at me!" Darryl knew what was up, we had been here before.

"Shenelle, mama, look at me." I didn't budge, so he turned me around and looked into my bloodshot eyes. "Aw, baby," he murmured and grabbed my soaked, wet body. I buried my head into him and sobbed even harder.

"It's happening again. Shenelle, please tell me you went to see the therapist today, like you promised." I didn't respond and just held on to him, keeping my face nuzzled against his shoulder. He turned off the shower water and let me go just enough to reach for my bathrobe that was hanging on a hook at the back of the door. He patted me dry with my towel and helped me into the robe. We went to the bedroom and sat on the edge of the bed.

"Did you see the doctor, Shenelle?" he asked again. I was a little bit calmer and rubbed my throbbing eyes, feeling sleepy.

"Yes I did."

"And, so what happened?"

"Nothing happened. I told her about the flashbacks and then it was getting late, so we had to reschedule."

"Alright, but you better go to the next one. When is the appointment scheduled for?"

"Next Tuesday." Darryl nodded, pleased with the arrangement. "Good, I can't wait until you get better, babe. I hate seeing you like this."

I looked away, also feeling abhorrent of my situation. "I know you do."

Darryl was my heartthrob, undoubtedly one of the most gorgeous men on the planet. From the first day I saw him I was smitten as if put under a hypnotic trance. To accurately describe Darryl was a cross between NFL players, Victor Cruz and Chad Ochocinco, but if asked I'd say neither one of the two looked better than him. Darryl stood up from the bed; his six foot two muscular frame towered over me as I remained sitting in my robe. He looked at me and I felt so small. Our eyes were locked for what felt like ten minutes, telepathically communicating our love for one another.

"Are you hungry?" I nodded my head in response. Darryl walked to my dresser and pulled out one of his huge t-shirts and a pair of my night shorts. It was something he always did since our college days, back when we lived together in a cozy little town house not far from campus. He tossed the clothes at me. "Here Ma, put this on and try to rest while I fix you something to eat." I quietly dressed, lied down and closed my eyes. I felt Darryl peck my forehead and whisper, "I love you."

Because of my many restless nights, it wasn't surprising I would fall out within seconds. It's clear I love Darryl. He hasn't changed from the heartwarming, genuinely loving man he was from when I first met him. The routine with Darryl was the same, whether I was sick, sad or angry. He could always somehow make my day better or at least try to. The sad thing was regardless of how much I loved Darryl, going back to my session with Dr. Mayes about me wanting to hurt people, he was the main person I wanted to hurt.

A couple of hours later, I awoke to Darryl gently shaking me. He led me by the hand to the dining table. I couldn't help but blush as I saw the table was nicely set up with two gold, taper candles, two plates with ground turkey over whole grain spaghetti, Texas toast, and a side of mixed salad. He also had the nerve to top it off with a bottle of Merlot red wine, chilling in a tin bucket of ice. I was smiling as I sat down in the chair he pulled out for me.

"Wow Darryl, you really went all out. This is nice. Thank you!"

"Anything for you, babe. You're welcome."

As I was eating, I noticed Darryl was staring at me. "Why are you looking at me like that, Darryl?" He shrugged. "Nothing baby, I've just been worried about you. I'm glad you were able to get some kind of rest. Usually you're up after fifteen minutes. I checked on you periodically and you were comatose. I guess the lack of sleep finally caught up to you, huh?" He took a bite of his garlic bread.

"Obviously, I'm glad I got some sleep too." I sat my fork down, suddenly losing my appetite. "I wish all of this would just go away." Darryl looked at me with empathy in his eyes.

"It will, but the length of time is up to you, babe. Hopefully the therapist can get to the bottom of what you're going through and help you find a solution." There were no lights on in the dining room but the burning candles. The flickering flames illuminated the room and the glare that was set upon the love of my life's face made him appear ten times more handsome. I loved having romantic moments like this, but I wasn't sure how many more of these moments we would have. I watched as the hot, melting wax drip down the candle to its holder, slowly shrinking it until there was nothing left. It reminded me of how my issues were slowly burning away my soul, soon leaving me to be nothing but worthless remains.

"I hope so too," I sadly replied.

After dinner, I helped Darryl clean up the kitchen. I brought two pieces of key lime pie for dessert into the living room and joined him on the sofa. He was shuffling through the selection of movies on Netflix. "Alicia called earlier. She wanted to know how your session with the therapist went. Since you were asleep, I told her that everything went fine and you'll holler at her tomorrow," Darryl informed.

"Thanks, I appreciate that; I meant to call her when I got in. She was probably a little upset, wasn't she?" Darryl made a face like I had two heads. "Naw, you don't know your friend by now, Shenelle? Alicia isn't like a lot of these other girls out here, she understood."

"I know, it's just I promised her I would call her as soon as I hit the door. She already got on me because I didn't call the last time." Darryl smacked his lips and waved his hand at the situation.

"She's good money and if she really is mad don't even sweat it. She'll get over it." I smirked at Darryl's comment. It was funny to me when it came down to Darryl and Alicia; it was because of Alicia I met Darryl. When we were in high school, she and I promised each other that we would go to the same college. If it wasn't for her dragging me to that frat party years ago, Darryl probably would've never existed.

***

The next day after work, I met up with Alicia at the gym to tell her about my visit with Dr. Mayes. When she saw me, she practically ran to me like a little girl who hadn't seen her mother in days. "She-Sheeeee!" Alicia jumped onto me squeezing the life out of me; I hugged her back just as hard. It had been a little while since we linked up with each other.

"Dang Leecy, how long has it been again?" I joked.

"It's been three freaking months!" Alicia playfully punched me on the shoulder after every word. She took a few steps back and looked at me, cheesing as she admired my figure. "Look at you, Sis, you still look good and that's a blessing." I raised my left eyebrow. Because of my unbalanced eating habits, I knew my weight had changed a lot and I hardly looked the same.

"Really? That is a blessing." We both laughed. I hopped on a treadmill and Alicia took the one next to mine.

"So girl, how have you been?" she asked with much concern.

"I've been okay. Hanging in there the best way I know how. How are Rondell and my two pretty nieces?" Alicia began to run on the treadmill like she was training for a marathon.

"Ron is good, working hard at the firm and being super dad. As for the girls, honey, I'm about to send those two little 'pains-in-the-butt' to your house and let you and Darryl raise them." The thought of raising two little girls made me smile. I could imagine Darryl spoiling them rotten and giving them unlimited piggy back rides until they were worn out.

"Hey, Darryl always did say he wanted to have a daughter, but what makes you say that?"

"Well, your little Erica thinks she's grown wanting to run around the house all day with her play make-up on from that set you bought her last Christmas. I had to deal with her temper tantrum this morning because she wanted to wear it to school. I started to tear that little snooty behind of hers up too, but lucky for her I had to get to work. Tori, she's good, only that it's so hard to get her to go to sleep.

All she wants to do is play and watch cartoons all night long."

"Well, you already know how little girls are. We were the same way when we were their age."

"Um Sweetie, Erica is only six years old. There was no way in hell I was able to even dream about debating with my mother on wearing lipstick and eye shadow to school at her age." I raised my eyebrows in accordance. "Yeah you are right about that."

Alicia's mother, like mine was as strict as they come. Alicia and her sisters knew not to play with Ms. Sheila because she'd take them down in a heartbeat. In fact, when we were kids, I remember Alicia getting smacked by her momma so hard, she had symptoms of whiplash for a week. Yet still, her mother was one amazing woman who I loved dearly and she loved me just as much in return, like I was one of her own. Every now and then, she would proclaim her admiration of the special bond that I have with Alicia. Especially since her two other daughters often gave Alicia a hard time, mostly because they were jealous of her and her success.

"Leecy, how are Mom and Poppa doing by the way?"

"Oh, they're doing fine. Mom is mom and Daddy's leg has healed miraculously after the car accident, so he's back on the road, traveling back and forth from South Carolina trying to keep up with the uncles. But enough about my life, Shenelle; let's talk about you now."

I sighed. I was hoping she'd forgotten about the whole therapy thing, because I really wanted to talk about other things, anything but that. "I'll tell you what. Let's get out of here and find some place more comfortable to talk and I'll tell you how it went from there."

"Okay, let's do Red Lobster then."

"Fine!"

When Alicia and I arrived at the restaurant on Times Square Avenue, I was shocked it wasn't packed from the floor up. Any other time, everybody was in there flowing heavy for the hankering of all you can eat shrimps and crab fest. We sat at a two seated booth; I looked over the menu while a waitress welcomed us with a basket of their famous biscuits and two glasses of iced water. Alicia made the decision for both of us to skip the appetizers and went straight to ordering drinks. Then like there was no tomorrow, she started with the questions.

"Alright Shenelle, no more getting around the subject! How did the session go with the therapist yesterday and what's her name? Is it a woman?" This chick really wasn't going to let this thing go.

"Yes, her name is Dr. Mayes and it went okay. Honestly there's really nothing much to discuss. I went to her office and spoke to her for about an hour, telling her about my flashbacks and that was basically it." I picked up one of the biscuits and started pinching bits and pieces off, attempting to bird feed myself. Alicia huffed and rolled her eyes, signaling that she was getting impatient.

"Shenelle, please stop playing with me!"

"Leecy, I'm being serious. I told her about the flashbacks and the affect they were having on me and…" I stopped talking, observing Alicia's face. She looked like she wasn't even trying to hear it. I put the biscuit down, giving up on any effort to eat it. I switched over to my tall glass of legal toxin with the intention to consume every drop of it and just told everything exactly how it went.

"Okay look, I went and told the therapist what I could summon the courage to tell her. I did not tell her everything, more like nothing because I got nervous. You know it's been awhile since I've seen a professional and I just couldn't do it. I mean I don't know this lady…" Before I could even finish my statement, Alicia exclaimed, "Shenelle, what do you mean you don't know her? You're not supposed to know her any more than what she is there for. She's not losing out on anything if you don't tell her what's been going on with you, but you will if you do not stop being so damn stubborn. I don't understand what it is that you're so afraid of. You act like you haven't done this before."

I curled my lips and gave Alicia that eye. "Yeah, and you know how that turned out!"

"Okay, but all therapists aren't the same and you know that, so that's not an excuse, Shenelle. I mean it's not like I haven't tried to get you to have sessions with Hannah, but you wouldn't even meet with her either." Alicia shook her head aggravated with me and took a big sip of her Kahlua.

Hannah was Alicia's former college roommate; she and Alicia clicked from the first day they met. She wasn't the average prissy little girl with dirty blonde hair. She was rather mellow and real cool, but when tried was a tough little Virginian cookie. She had this hood spunk to her as if she was raised straight out of the ghetto. Alicia had been begging me to see Hannah for counseling since she graduated with a Ph.D. in Psychology, but my answer was, no. Hannah had even offered to counsel me for free, at home and on Skype, so I wouldn't have to travel. While that all might've sounded well and good my answer was still, no.

Again, Hannah was cool as the breeze from the trees. I dug her enough to hang out with her from time to time, engage in conversations about how pathetic some men could be, and bug out with her and the rest of our girls in the house while we caught up on our favorite shows. I didn't dig her that much though, to want to sit and get up close and personal with her like I did with Alicia. So alternatively, Alicia searched and found some agencies for therapy online.

She and I gazed at each other for a moment and the same waitress came back to take our orders. We decided we'd take our meals to go. Alicia started back in on me, "Your skull is too thick, sweetie, you don't listen to nobody! You really have to stop being the way you are! You need the help, Shenelle!" Alicia looked away for second and bit her bottom lip; she looked back at me with tears in her eyes. Her voice cracked as it was turned down to a little above a whisper, "I love you, She-She. You got to get this help. I'm afraid that I'm going to lose you one day to you doing something that cannot be fixed and that thought is making me sick. You have to talk to this therapist, Shenelle. You need to wring out your soul from all of the impurities, so that you can be free to move forward and never look back." By that point I had my face buried in my hands and was silently crying myself. Alicia had always been on point with everything.

Ever since we were kids, she could read a person just by the scent of their clothing, which would explain her bachelor's degree in Sociology. I hoped to God she wouldn't tell our partner-in-crime, Natari about our little conference. The three of us were Bronx bound chicks and out of our trio, Natari was roughest one. She was two years older than Alicia and I, so we considered her as the big sister of the crew. I wasn't afraid of her because I was just as feisty as she was, but if I thought Alicia and Darryl were working my nerves about my situation, I seriously didn't need to face Natari. I felt Alicia touch my hand.

"Shenelle, you are going to be alright. I have faith in God and you're in my prayers twenty four/seven. You're going to be fine, okay?" She used her other hand to wipe my wet cheeks. Alicia intertwined her fingers with mine to comfort me. "Let's go, I'm driving you home."

***

I made it to Dr. Mayes' office right at the edge of time, it was a good thing Darryl let me drive his jeep or else I probably would've been late. At exactly five fifteen, Dr. Mayes came out for me. I walked into her office and sat down on the comfy love seat. The softness of the cushion gave my tense muscles a sense of relaxation that allowed me to breathe a little easier. Dr. Mayes sat down in the club chair and this time had her pen and pad on hand to take notes.

"So, how are you feeling today?" I nonchalantly replied, "I'm okay." Dr. Mayes smiled as she jotted down her decoded version of what I said.

"Good. Can you say the same about this past week?"

"Yes, everything has been pretty good this past week."

"Okay and how have you been eating and sleeping?"

"It's been a little better."

"Okay, good!" Dr. Mayes put her pen and pad down, removed her glasses before looking at me and jumped right to the point. "So, Shenelle, this is the situation. I looked over my notes and it's to my understanding that you have symptoms of a mental illness called PTSD; it has also been known as *"Shell Shock"*. Have you heard of this?" I thought back for a few seconds and remembered Hannah mentioning something like that to me when we were in college. "I've heard of it, but I'm not too familiar with what it really means."

"Okay, well the proper medical term for it is called *Post Traumatic Stress Disorder*. It's when an individual experiences traumatic events in their life; like witnessing someone being violently hurt or murdered, or you yourself having been physically hurt or mentally hurt."

Dr. Mayes eyeballed me as she talked. "This person may have recurring memories of the incident, be it nightmares or what you are experiencing now, Shenelle, flashbacks, lack of sleep, loss of interest, and poor appetite. Some may over indulge in food, alcohol, sex, drugs, gambling, all just to fill a void. It is also likely to become agitated very easily. One minute you can be up and the next minute, because your mind has converted back to a horrific event, you can be down. Sometimes it can be difficult to stay connected with the world, and function in the present day because your mind constantly goes back to the past."

I was letting Dr. Mayes diagnosis sink in. The entire time I thought I was just severely depressed. Now that I knew there was a name for what I was experiencing, all I wanted to know next was what could be done, so I won't end up losing my sanity completely. "Dr. Mayes, what would be the solution to all of this? What do I have to do so that it could all end and I can be normal again?" I watched her forehead crinkle as if I was crazy, a look I've been receiving from people a lot lately.

"Shenelle, you are normal. You're just mentally disturbed which could be triggered by anything and it can happen to anyone even me, but about what you can do. You can start by telling me everything that has happened to you. You said that you've been having problems since you were born, right?" Dr. Mayes gave a look that said she was insisting on an accurate answer.

"Yes."

"Okay, so the only way I can help you get to the root of your issues, is if you let out all of your skeletons and allow me to enter into your world. Tell me the story about Shenelle Patterson." I sat quietly for a while. I felt like I was about to be put on blast, but I knew this was all for my own good. I had friends and family who needed me to get well. I released an invigorating breath and sat up straight, locking eyes with Dr. Mayes. I nodded my head as though I have found my inner strength.

"You want my story? Alright, here it goes…

<u>Part 1</u>

The

Beginning

Chapter 2

April 19, 1984 was the day I was born. I was my parents' only daughter and the youngest of three children. My eldest brother, Jeremiah once told me that before I came along, my parents always stressed how much they wanted to have a little girl, especially after having two boys. As I became of age, I learned it was my father who really wanted me and not my mother. The only people I was close to in my household, was my father and my eldest brother. My other brother Timothy and I, we just did not click. We loved each other like any other siblings, but we hated each other all in the same breath. In his mind, I was a spoiled, annoying, little brat which is how he described me to anyone who asked. In my mind, he was an arrogant, self-centered bum. He never wanted to do anything, but start squabbles with everybody, and bring all different kinds of girls to the house every day, just to use them and then toss them. He was nothing like Jeremiah, who I called Jere for short.

Jere was a good boy. He always catered to Mom's and Dad's needs; he was an honor student in school, and he worked and handled his business like a man. He also was very protective of me. Everybody loved them some Jeremiah. Damn near all of my girlfriends wanted him, along with every other woman. When I really thought about it, Jere was like our father, all the way down to his good looks. Now, my relationship with my mother was another story of its own and the very beginning to all of the madness I have experienced in my life. Otherwise we were a small family, living in a private house in a quiet part of the Bronx.

I wouldn't say we were like the Huxtables from *The Cosby show*, but my parents certainly did try their best to keep our family stable. We celebrated the traditional holidays as a clan each year, whether it was Easter, Thanksgiving, Christmas or New Years. My mother would cook these massive feasts and we would party and get our grub on. Every once in a while, we would do our family outings and have fun together. When it came to birthdays, my parents were up on it at all times and the day as I recall, never ended in a disappointment. My father was a hardworking man who worked two jobs as an MTA Bus driver and a school custodian. He took care of the bills and made sure that his wife and kids didn't want for anything. My mother didn't work, but she was that woman who spent most of her time going to church.

I remember the old, big, rusty bricked building that was up the hill from our house, *the House of Praise* was what it was called. I personally called it the *"House of Craze"* because everyone from pimps to drug addicts walked into that building, and then two hours later walked out as crazier pimps and drug addicts. I could look out from my bedroom window and see people from the neighborhood, dressed in their Sunday best walking to that church. I can't believe my mother used to actually roller set my hair with those giant, pink, sponge curlers and dress me and my brothers up to go to that anti-religious jungle. I remember sitting in the pews, sweating out my curls; my skin glistening from the concoction of perspiration and Vaseline.

The preacher's big mouth would bellow a verse from his sermon and disturb me whenever I dozed off. We always sat towards the front row of the congregation in order from biggest to smallest. Since I was the smallest, I had to be squished between my brother Timothy, and some old lady who wore a humongous hat that blocked the lighting like an eclipse. She constantly smelled like she bathed in perfume and it would make the food particles churn in my stomach during the entire service. She hummed every time the pastor testified and made suckling noises trying to dissolve a peppermint. To say this lady was a real pain would be an understatement. My mother participated in all of the activities the church offered; putting up the biggest front like she was the most wonderful mother and doting wife. I found the whole thing to be comical because my mother wasn't on any scale a saint. If anything, I'd say she was more like a she-devil in angel's clothing. I had to give it to her though for going so hard to make such an impression. Anyways that was my family, the first people in my life who I loved dearly.

(1990)

The complications began when I was six years old; at home the ritual every day was simple. In the morning, my mother would tap on the footboard of my bed, waking me for school. She would have my uniform ironed and neatly hanging in my closet. My hair would already be done the night before, so all I would have to do was bathe and brush my teeth; after my brothers had taken turns using two thousand hours' in the bathroom. Breakfast was always ready on schedule and my father was usually the first one at the table. After getting dressed, the first thing I would do was run downstairs to my father as he was leaving.

"Good morning, Daddy!"

"Hey, baby girl! Good morning to you," he said as he adoringly swooped me up in his arms. I wrapped my arms around his neck and hugged him tight. I could see from the corner of my eye my mother was staring at us as she put a spoonful of grits in her mouth.

"Have fun at work."

"Thank you, sweetness, and you do your best at school, okay?"

"Kay!" My father put me down and I ran over to my mother and grabbed her neck. "Good morning, Mommy!" She halfheartedly hugged me back.

"Morning, go sit down and hurry up and eat your breakfast so you won't be late for school."

"Kay!" Just as I was about to sit down in my favorite chair, the one that was in between Jere's and my father's seat; Timothy sat down in it.

"No Timmy, that's my chair!" I was trying to ease my way onto the chair and he pushed me away. "Move! This is not your chair. Your name is not on it."

"But, I always sit here," I whined as I struggled with him to regain my seat. He pushed me again. "Move girl! Mom, can you tell her to move?"

"Shenelle, knock it off! Nobody has any assigned chairs here. Sit right there and hurry up and eat your cereal, please!" My mother yelled pointing her long finger at Timothy's seat.

"Shenelle, here you can have my seat," Jere said. He was about to get up from his chair when my mother stopped him.

"NO! I want her to sit right there! Shenelle, sit down!" I began to sob. My mother snatched me by my shirt collar and warned through clenched teeth, "Girl, you better be quiet before I give you something to really cry about."

I sat down and quietly ate my Lucky Charms. Afterwards I got my book bag, jetting out the door without saying goodbye to my mother and waited for Jere and Timothy to walk with me to school. It was my first day starting the 1st grade at P.S.93 and I couldn't wait to get there and reunite with all of my friends. I loved when I was at school; it was my outlet from being at home. I got to be around other kids my age and it was a place where I was happiest.

***

When my brothers and I made it to the school yard, Timothy walked off and got on line with his class. I was about to run off when my brother Jere stopped me. "Shenelle hold up! You know if any of those booger nosed punks mess with you to come and get me on the sixth floor, aw'ight?"

"Kay!" He gave me a hug and watched me walk safely to my class before he went to his own. I got on line behind my friend Tiffany from my kindergarten class.

"Hi, Shenelle," Tiffany said. I greeted her with a friendly bear hug. She played with the colorful beads that dangled at the ends of my long braids.

"Guess who's in our class?" she exclaimed.

"Who?" She pointed at the front of the line. "Stupid and ugly Kevin!"

"Ewww, aw man, I hate Kevin!" Kevin turned around as though he heard us; he saw me and twisted his face. He crossed his forefinger along his neck indicating I was dead meat. Although he tormented me, I wasn't scared of him because I had two brothers who could give him what he gave me. I returned the gesture right back, rolling my eyes and crossed my arms.

Kevin Parker was my nemesis ever since we were in day care and the world's new production of Dennis the Menace, I hated his guts. He was a fresh, annoying, little boy and ugly wasn't even the word for him. He was bald headed with crooked teeth, pudgy, and cockeyed; then to top it off, he had the nerve to be bowlegged. I swore if all of those qualities weren't the saddest combination in the world, I couldn't think of what could be worse. I've seen water bugs in my backyard that looked better than he did. Kevin picked on me non-stop. My father once told me that whenever a boy picked on you, it meant he secretly liked you. In the beginning that sounded cute and exciting, but Kevin killed it for me and made that statement very hard to believe. He chased me around every day and other girls, lifting up our skirts. My brother Jere had warned him on many occasions to leave me alone, but it just went through one ear and right out the other. Jere had even made Timothy beat him up and still no change at all.

The principal blew a whistle for everyone to quiet down and made an announcement over the bullhorn as the teachers went to their assigned classes. My teacher was Ms. Thompson; she was a young white woman who probably just got her teaching degree and starting her career. She had a carefree attitude to her and seemed like she would be an easy kick in the sand. We went to the auditorium, said the pledge of allegiance, sang the national anthem and then went up to our classroom. As if the day couldn't get any worse since the episode at home with my mother, I was seated right next to annoying behind Kevin at the back of the room and ten desks away from my buddy, Tiffany. I pleaded with Ms. Thompson to change my seat, but she refused because my name was already taped to the desk in alphabetical order. I didn't get thirty minutes into my first lesson before Kevin began to kick me under my desk. We went into a kicking match until I eventually gave up.

"Stop it, Kevin! Ms. Thompson, Kevin keeps on kicking me and won't stop!" Ms. Thompson made Kevin stand in a corner of the classroom and moved his desk next to hers, so she could supervise him.

"Aw man! I didn't even do nothing to that girl," he lied. I was relieved he was far away from me and went back to doing my school work.

At recess I had a ball; I played tag, hide and go seek, and played Patty cake with my little posse of friends. I got a star sticker on my worksheet for excellence and just knew I was due to make student of the month before the school year was over. The day didn't turn out so bad after all, and it was even greater that I went home with no homework and a lollypop. I truly believed the lucky charms I had for breakfast must've done the magic that was advertised on the commercials. When I got home I didn't get the chance to show my parents my worksheet because they were too busy reprimanding Timothy for fighting in school on the first day. I just did the usual, washed my hands and changed into my house clothes. My brother Jere did the honors and fixed him and me a snack which was usually either PB&J and a Hi-C juice box or a chocolate pudding cup.

We went into the den and Jere turned the TV on to *Muppet Babies*. It was surprising I didn't have to beg him; Jere never liked to share the TV. He felt since he was the oldest he should have the first choice of everything. It was customary that all three of us would fight over the television on who would watch their favorite cartoon. Every single day there was a battle between wanting to watch *Captain Planet, Bobby's World* and *Talespin*. My best guess for my brother letting me go this day was more than likely, he grew tired of me crying when I wouldn't get my way. The end result would always either be making Mommy send us to our rooms since we couldn't work out the problem or having Daddy make him turn to what I wanted to watch anyway. When a commercial came on I decided to tell Jere about the altercation between me and Kevin at school.

"Hey, Jere?"

"Yo!"

"You remember Kevin, the ugly boy who you call a fat, snot nosed punk?"

"Yeah, what about him?" Jere had a serious look on his face waiting for my response. He despised Kevin just as much as I did. If only Jere could've been my age for a day, Kevin would've been a done deal in no time and he would never bother me again.

"He keeps picking on me and won't leave me alone." Jere huffed and shook his head. I could tell that little buster, Kevin done got on his last nerve, messing with me and he wished that one day Kevin could be the fat cow that would jump over the moon and disappear.

"It's aw'ight little, Sis, I'll get my friend Curtis' little brother to beat him up tomorrow since Tim's in trouble. Other than that, just stay away from him."

"Okay."

At dinner I was able to show off my paper with the sticker to my parents. My mother didn't say much, but a dry ass *"Very good"* comment as she always said after I accomplished something and hung it on the refrigerator with a magnet. My father was ecstatic and rewarded me with five dollars to add to my piggy bank. I went to bed that night a happy camper and anxious to get to school the next morning. I wanted to see to it that Kevin got served his ass whupping and finally leave me be, so I could have a peaceful year of school.

***

Disappointed as ever, the next day Jere's friend's little brother didn't show up at school because he was sick, so the only thing that could be done was for Jere and his boys to chase Kevin around the yard. They emptied out his book bag onto the ground and then threw it on top of a roof. The school janitor had to go up to the roof and get it for him. He tried to rat on my brother and his friends, but the only witnesses around were me and a few other classmates. Because Kevin was such a badass and nobody liked him, we all acted like we didn't see a thing. It might've been funny as hell to watch him cry and get tortured, but the worst of it all was I had to pay an even bigger price for it later on.

A new girl was introduced in our class; she was transferred from another class and was seated next to me at the desk that used to be Kevin's. *"Hi,"* she said. I shyly smiled at her and turned my attention back to the teacher. Every other classroom I went to beside homeroom, Kevin bothered me recklessly. He did everything from squirting Elmer's clue onto my clothing, to throwing broken crayons at me, and pulling my hair. I think the part that hurt me most was when he tore my favorite *little mermaid* folder into shreds. Whenever I would fight back with Kevin I would get a warning from the teacher that she would call my parents. Lord knows that was the last thing I needed after having just been rewarded on good measures.

The icing on the cake was when at the end of school, I was the last one to gather my things into my book bag. The class and my teacher had already left without me and I went into the closet to retrieve my coat. I left the second sliding door open, so that I wouldn't get locked in. I noticed there was one more coat inside, but I didn't think anything of it. I never heard anyone enter the classroom when I turned around to exit the cubby hole and was violently pushed back in by someone and they closed the door. I screamed in a panic, it was dark and I was scared. I banged and kicked on the door for what had to be at least five minutes. I remembered it being very hot inside and I was soaked with sweat. I started crying hysterically and the door opened, I rushed out frantic and Kevin was standing there laughing boisterously at me.

"Shenelle, you a *scaredy-cat*," he said.

"Shut up, Stupid!" I tried to run away from him out of the classroom. He blocked my path, pushed me to the floor and started tugging at my uniform skirt. I screamed, telling him to stop. I was fighting him off and then before I knew it the new girl was tussling with him.

"Stop it, Kevin! Before I tell Ms. Thompson on you!"

"Girl, mind your biz'ness I was just playing with her."

"Well she don't want you playing with her, now leave her alone!"

Kevin pushed her. "Make me, ugly!" The girl kicked Kevin right in his nuts; he cried out in pain and hit the floor grabbing his crotch.

"Are you okay, Shenelle?" she asked, I nodded.

Ms. Thompson walked into the classroom. "Oh my Goodness, what is going on here?" Kevin was still on the floor crying and my face was drenched from my own tears. I was too bewildered to speak, so the girl spoke for me. "Kevin was bothering Shenelle and hitting her, so I kicked him." Ms. Thompson cradled my face with her hands. "Shenelle, are you alright, honey?"

"Yes, Kevin locked me in the closet," I sobbed and Ms. Thompson was appalled.

"He did? Kevin why would you do something like that? That's not nice!" Kevin continued to cry in agony and she shook her head at his condition.

"You girls get your things and go on home now. I'll take care of Kevin, and Ms. Perkins? Next time let someone know if anything like this ever happens again, okay. No more kicking you understand?" The girl replied, "Yes."

Ms. Thompson took Kevin by his arm, hauling him down to the Principals office while he was doubled over holding onto his crotch. The girl took off the bathroom pass from around her neck and put it back in place next to the hall of fame bulletin board. She got her coat from the closet.

"Come on, Shenelle." She draped her arm around my neck to comfort me. We walked down the stairs into the yard where my brothers were waiting for me. Before we parted ways the girl introduced herself. "My name is Alicia. You want to be best friends?" I smiled at her offer because I never really had a best friend.

"Okay."

"I'll call you She-She for short, see you tomorrow!" She hugged me goodbye and then ran off to her parents. That was exactly how my best friend Alicia and I first became friends, best friends to the end.

Chapter 3

Four years from our first encounter Alicia and I were inseparable. We were like the twins from the classic sitcom *Sister, Sister*, and did everything together. Sometimes we even styled our hair the same way and wore the same color outfits so we could look more alike. My other friend Tiffany was part of the club until we got to the fourth grade. She was put in another class and eventually veered off with a new set of friends. From first grade up to the fifth, I went through some random situations at school, like getting antagonized by catty girls and arrogant boys. But overall, life at school was still better than it was at home. I'm not going to lie though, ever since that whole closet stunt with Kevin, I went from being the happy go lucky girl to a nervous lost soul.

The only person I really wanted to be around was Alicia. I had other *so-called* friends, but just like how kids could be, they would have their mood swings. One day they wanted to be your friend, and then the next day they would turn on you like you were never even a factor. Alicia was the only one who I deemed to be true to me. It didn't take me long to realize I was a troubled child because somehow, I was always prone to becoming a victim to someone's anxiety problems or boredom. So in saying that, the bullshit never failed.

Alicia was absent from school one day and I chatted with some of the other girls from my class, but I couldn't seem to connect with them so I pretty much kept to myself for the remainder day until school was over. I was walking home when a boy named Jamal who was in my class came up to me.

"What's up, Shenelle!"

"Hi, Jamal."

"You're going to Crystal's birthday party on Saturday?"

"No."

"Why not?"

"Because I don't wanna go, Crystal is not my friend." He raised his eyebrows.

"Oh, but I've seen you talk to her."

I looked at him like he was stupid. "Not everybody I talk to is my friend, Jamal. I mean Crystal is okay, but I don't be around her like that and I wasn't even invited."

"Well, she invited Alicia," he mumbled. I stopped in my tracks.

"She invited who?" I knew what I heard, but I wanted to make sure I was hearing things clearly. He didn't want to answer. He had that look on his face like he said something he shouldn't have. It wasn't that I was mad or anything; it was just that I knew Alicia and Crystal didn't like each other. As a matter of fact, they hated each other. The situation was, Crystal had a huge crush on this boy named Aaron and she did whatever she could to get his attention. At first he overlooked her, but then he gave in and they became boyfriend and girlfriend. All that quickly changed though once he laid eyes on Alicia and then right out the window Crystal went. Aaron and Alicia started claiming each other as boyfriend and girlfriend, which caused a rivalry between Alicia and Crystal. As far as I knew, the beef still wasn't over.

"When did Crystal invite Alicia?" I asked. Jamal shrugged his shoulders.

"I don't know, last week I think." All of this didn't sound right, but I decided to keep my mouth closed and thought I'd call Alicia and talk to her about it when I got home. Before I turned the corner, going towards my house I told Jamal to go on about his way. I didn't want to be caught seen with a boy by my parents. He looked like he wasn't trying to move at first and I was determined to stand there until he did. Then what threw me for a loop was when he grabbed the back of my head and pecked me on the lips. I quickly pushed him off.

"Jamal, what are you doing?" I nervously looked around, hoping nobody saw us, especially not anyone from the church. Jamal put his head down in embarrassment.

"I always wanted to do that, Shenelle; ever since we were in Kindergarten." He never looked back up at me when he turned and walked away.

I had picked up on how Jamal acted whenever he was around me since kindergarten. Jamal was the kind of little boy you could tell really liked you because he didn't make it a secret. He wanted to always sit next to me on the bus while we went on school trips and during lunchtime, he wanted to share his Now&Laters with me. Whenever he saw me, he always had a lot to say. We used to be close and talked about everything from what costume we were going to wear for Halloween to which power ranger was our favorite one. Granted, Jamal was and had always been as cute as he could be with his creole self and unknown to him; I've had a crush on him as big as the one he had on me. He was exactly the type of boy I would go after, but the problem was, he was the puppy love companion of Crystal's best friend Dominique. With that being said, I think you would guess exactly what happened next.

***

I went to school the next day with Alicia and when we got in class, half the students were staring at us. Alicia knew about the kiss from Jamal and she found it to be glorious, but I was cautious. I also found out Jamal fibbed about Alicia being invited to Crystal's party and said it just so he could follow me. I had a bad feeling about that kiss and as it would be, my instinct was right on the money. Dominique, who was in my class, kept rolling her eyes at me and giving me the ill grill, while Crystal did the same thing to Alicia. They were exchanging nasty remarks about us among their little gang, but Alicia and I ignored them. Jamal on the other hand, he stayed low key, like he knew something I didn't know and was barely able to look me in my face.

During gym class was when it all went down, Dominique walked up to me with her road dog Crystal while I was sitting on the bleachers next to Alicia and asked aggressively like she thought she could intimidate somebody. "Shenelle, did you kiss Jamal?!"

I replied back in the same manner, "No, Jamal kissed me!" Alicia was sitting there quiet with fire burning in her eyes like she was waiting for one of them to get cute.

"Yeah well, Brandon told me that he saw you and him walking home together and you kissed him." My nostrils flared. Brandon was this little chump who acted like he was tough when he was around boys, but seemed to want to hang more around girls. He was the only boy in the school that had a big mouth like a sissy and told everything on everybody. I searched the gym looking for Jamal who was sitting all the way on the other side of the bleachers with his buddies and a look that read *Busted"* was written all over his face. I slit my eyes in anger at him.

"Dominique, Jamal tried to walk me home but I told him to..." Alicia cut in mad loud with all the ghettoness in her, "Shenelle, don't explain nothing to these two stupid girls. She knows that Jamal was the one who kissed you first. Just like that big doofy bimbo over there knows that Aaron dumped her to get with me!" Everybody who heard Alicia's remark roared in laughter and Crystal glared angrily at her.

"What you said?"

"You heard me, I ain't stutter!" Alicia spat.

Crystal wasn't the smallest chick in school, but I wouldn't call her fat either. She was just very developed for an eleven year old, and was one of the few girls who wore a push-up bra while the rest of us had nubs that were still in training. Dominique was the total opposite, short and scrawny and now funny thing was all of the guts she had to step to me were gone. My guess as it appeared from her body language was because she was scared out her ass of Alicia. Crystal did a coward move and snatched Alicia by her hair while she was sitting down and started punching her on her head. I punched Crystal in the face and then Dominique who had guts again started fighting with me, it became the quartet riot of the century up in the gym. It took damn near ten school safety guards to break us apart and all four of us were dragged into the principal's office. I was proud to say that both Crystal and Dominique got their asses whupped by us, but the down play of it all was Alicia and I got suspended. Those two just got sent home which wasn't fair since they were the ones who started it. I was going to have to hear it from my parents when I got home and I wasn't looking forward to it at all.

My father picked me up from the principal's office demanding an explanation. Growing up, my father had been adamant about me and my brothers doing well in school. The fighting thing he did not tolerate unless it was a self-defense case. Any other nonsense was flat out unacceptable. When I spoke my piece, he understood the dilemma, but still wasn't with it because he felt I could've walked away. Not to mention I totally left out the kiss part which is what started the mess from Jump Street. As my punishment, TV and phone privileges were cut off and I couldn't go outside for two weeks. For my mother it just wasn't enough, I had to get a verbal beat down from her and she tried to escalate it to a physical beat down, but my father put her to a halt before she could get that far and boy was I glad.

Once the suspension was up, my mother made it her business to further complicate things by showing her ass. She came to my school and sat in my classroom for two hours straight. She didn't even want me to look at her, just for me to do my work and pretend she wasn't there. For me that was humanly impossible because having her there was very uncomfortable. To say it was necessary for her to do such a thing would be bullshit to the extreme. It wasn't like I fought every day and was a trouble maker at school, but what the average person didn't know, my mother was a sadistic sicko. It was just her style to do the unnecessary to humiliate people and make them feel like shit. Alicia gave me that apologetic look while the other classmates snickered and made fun of me, but I sucked it up. Actually it was because of my mother and her nonsense I never wanted to fight in the first place. There had been many occasions at school where I was close to beating the living shit out of someone, but all I could think about was part two to the drama and what I would have to deal with when I got home. Other than that, I probably would've been a candidate for the America's most wanted list years ago.

My two week punishment was annoying. My mom and my brother Timothy were having a good ole time making me feel it. Timothy would tease me because I had to stay cooped up in the house while he and Jere was outside having fun. He would make sure the coast was clear though, so he wouldn't get put in the same boat as me. My mother all of a sudden wanted to do all this extra nice stuff with the boys that didn't include me, and dished out treats she knew I loved, but couldn't have because it was a restriction she added to my punishment. It was hectic, but I made my time comfortable by reading and doing cross-word puzzles; whatever that was effective to get my mind off their antics.

The two weeks went by fast and to be able to go outside again was a great feeling. The weekends were the only times I was able to take a mini vacation from my home and go over to Alicia's house to spend the night. My dad and brother Jere weren't home to drive me over to her house and my mother didn't feel like driving, so I had to walk. It was cool since Alicia lived six blocks away. On my way there I noticed a group of teenagers standing by a corner store. I didn't want to pass them because I knew they were probably on the grounds of trouble, so I crossed the street and walked on the other side of the block.

"Eh, Shawty!" I heard one of them say. I ignored them and kept walking. I heard another guy say, "Yo, ma!" I continued to go about my business and didn't pay attention to them, but then I saw them from the corner of my eye walking towards me. My heart started racing and I thought, *oh boy, here we go!* I could feel the heat of the devil's breath getting warmer as they got closer. I didn't want to run just yet and cause them to chase after me. I wasn't that far from Alicia's house, but I wasn't so close either. They made their way to me and circled my path. I stopped and stood there frozen when the first guy who called out to me stood in front of me.

"You ain't heard me calling you, girl?"

"No," I nervously replied.

"This little, stupid, broad is lying! She heard us, yo!" The second guy said. The first guy looked at me licking his lips. "You got a fat ass for a young jawn, anyone ever told you that?" I didn't answer his ignorant question.

"Excuse me," I said as I tried to squeeze my way in between them, but the guy pushed me back.

"Whoa shawty, where are you going? You ain't answer my question." My breathing became heavy and I went from being nervous to scared shitless.

"What's in your bag?" One of the other guys said and snatched my book bag from around my arms. He went through it throwing all of my clothes that were stuffed in it on the ground. He took out the ten dollars my mother gave me before I left and pushed me against the fence. It was a little late in the afternoon so it was getting dark, but it wasn't dark enough for me not to see my brother Timothy walking down the block across the street, looking dead at me. What made my heart skip a beat was when he turned his head and on to the next corner then disappeared out of my sight. I couldn't believe he would just leave me there to possibly get eaten alive by a bunch of preying dogs. I *really* couldn't believe that he wouldn't come to my aide and defend me or to even fight with me at the least if needed. The foul treatment of my brother brought tears to my eyes.

As I began to cry, the guy who took my money from my book bag started bantering with the rest of his crew. "Awwww boo-hoooo, the baby is crying y'all."

By that time it was even darker outside and I knew my mother was probably calling Alicia's house checking to see if I'd made it there safe. The guy forcefully grabbed me by my neck; when I was an infant learning how to pronounce words properly, my parents taught me to pray before every meal and before I went to bed. Plenty of times, I saw my mother on her knees and head bowed in the middle of the day. I remember asking her why she was praying if she wasn't at church. She explained to me that sometimes it was good to talk to God and that he was always available no matter where we are, so I said a silent prayer for the guys not to hurt me.

As much as I used to tell myself I wanted to die in order to get away from the shambles at home, I realized at that moment I really didn't want to die. I wanted to graduate from high School and college. I wanted to get married and have children, be able to spoil my grandchildren when I got old. Before anything major could happen, I heard God's angel shouting, "Eh yo, Mike! What the hell are you doing, man?!" My face lit up when I saw my brother Jere hop out of our parents' car he was driving and violently push the guy against the same fence he pushed me.

"Yo Jay, chill! You good, son!" The first guy said.

"Naw son, this is my little sister! What are y'all doing to her, why is she crying?!" Jere yelled in the guy's face with his fists clenched ready to beat his face in. The guy and the rest of them looked mad petrified.

"Yo, my bad, Jay! I ain't know she was your sister, son!"

Jere glared at him. "Y'all get the fuck outta here!"

I watched as they all walked off. I didn't care to mention the money that was stolen. I was just glad that God answered my prayer and impressed because I never knew my brother Jere had that much heart to him. I always knew Jere was tough, but I didn't think he had the respect to let five boys his age or so walk away with their heads hung low. My brother was that dude, and I was happy I was his sister.

"You aw'ight, lil Sis?" Jere asked. I continued to cry, stammering over my words explaining to him how Timothy saw those guys harass me and left me there all alone. It seemed like my brother Timothy's actions shocked me more and more. Jere told me he saw Timothy walking towards our house. Timothy had the nerve to stop to say hello to Jere, but he never mentioned the situation I was in. It was nothing but the grace of God that Jere happened to see me in passing. If I ever hated my brother Timothy before I hated him twice times more now.

"Shen, don't worry I' ma handle Tim when I get home. He knew better than to leave you hanging like that. Stop crying aw'ight, dry your eyes."

Jere helped me pick up my clothes from the ground and gave me a ride to Alicia's house. He promised me that he wouldn't tell our parents what happened. Since he shook those dudes off he didn't need to. He knew if my parents ever found out what happened with me they would hit the roof. My father would end up going to jail for killing someone and my mother seriously wouldn't let me see daylight or moonlight from nowhere ever again, except through the skylight. Jere covered for me that night and told my parents I got to Alicia's late because I was with him. He got told off of course being he didn't call and let anyone know anything, but Jere didn't care about that. As long as I was good he was good. That's how my big brother was when it came to me. He wouldn't only get in trouble for me; he proved himself on that day he would also risk his life for me if he had to.

***

My father and brothers were out and it was just me and my mother home. I wanted to discuss with her some of the issues I was having outside of home. My parents never knew about any of the things I had gone through. I kept my problems from them to avoid being transferred to another school and from living freely. My mother and I hardly ever had a heart-to-heart girl talk. That was mainly because I never wanted to tell her anything, knowing it would get thrown back in my face whenever she got angry, but I felt I needed her advice, so I took a chance. I went downstairs to the basement where my mother was doing laundry.

"Mom, can I talk to you about something?" She rolled her eyes.

"What?" Her gesture alone made me want to change my mind about talking to her, but I went ahead with it anyway.

"I wanted to talk to you about school and stuff."

"Alright, I'm listening." She kept her back to me as she was loading the dryer.

"I feel like I'm always getting picked on by people and I don't like it," My mother stopped what she was doing and looked at me.

"What do you mean picked on?" The tone in her voice and how she said it gave me a little confidence to want to tell her more. One thing for sure about my mother was she didn't play when it came to her children. She was like a vicious lioness ready pounce on someone in a heartbeat if they messed with me or my brothers. I wasn't going to tell her about the first grade closet incident because somebody would've gotten their ass kicked for not saying something when it first happened, and that person more than likely would've been me. To tell her about the latest incident where Jere showed up to my rescue was definitely out of the question, so I gave her a mild fabrication of the story that recently happened at school for an instance.

"Well, this girl at school doesn't like me because she thinks I'm trying to steal her boyfriend…"

"Boyfriend? Wouldn't she be a little too young to be worrying about some boyfriend?" My mother interrupted.

"Yes." My mother shook her head and pushed the start button on the dryer. "Go on."

"So, she asked me if I kissed her boyfriend and…"

"I know you didn't kiss no boy!" She rudely interrupted again.

"No, Mom," I said half truthfully.

"But she thought I did."

"And why would she think that?"

"Listening to someone who didn't know what they were talking about." I was regretting this conversation already. I could feel it was about to go in a direction I didn't want it to.

"So, is that why y'all were fighting like y'all ain't got any damn sense at school?"

I knew my mother wanted to say something negative about Alicia. She never really liked Alicia because she felt she was a bad influence on me. My mother would kill me with her opinions at times, especially when it came to Alicia. To my mother, it was as if I was this dumb string-puppet that Alicia or anybody could make do whatever they wanted. Any time I would hear my mother tell me what she thought she knew, inside my head I laughed because she would be so off base with her assumptions it was funny.

In all actuality, it was *I* who dared to do the crazy stuff… okay sometimes, because Alicia's ass was daring too. Either way, I always took the bat for my girl. Alicia might've been a hot head, but I knew deep down she was a good person. Alicia had personal issues, like everyone else in the world. My mother didn't like nobody anyway; she didn't even like herself. Going along with the original topic, I quickly replied, "Yup! Girls always seem to want to start something with me even when I'm not doing anything to them."

My mother pursed her lips. "Yeah well you know what, Shenelle? That's what happens when you try to steal the attention of someone who belongs to another female." She turned her back to me and continued where she left off from the laundry.

When my mother said that, I didn't know what to think. I wasn't even sure what it really meant. Sometimes conversing with my mother, if it didn't turn into an argument it always ended the same way, a lost cause. I hated when she made cynical, indirect comments, another reason why I never talked to her about anything. The only thing my mother could do when she wanted to find out things about me was read my diary I kept hidden in my closet, invading my privacy. Whatever information my mother found, other than negative derogatory remarks about her, was never the real deal and only a blueprint of what I really experienced.

It bothered me that I couldn't talk to my mother when I should've been able to, but then I realized not talking to her was actually better for my health. I left the basement and went back to my room. I really couldn't stand my mother sometimes and many times I even wished she and my father weren't together, so I could live with him and be away from her. But who would've thought that those deadweight feelings of mine were the foreshadowing of what was to come in reality.

Chapter 4

The following year was when my mother's true colors really started to show and every day it got worse and worse. It all started when one day I came home from school and I heard my parents going at it in a heated argument. They were so heavily into their dispute that they didn't hear me come in. I sat my book bag down in my room and crept by their bedroom door that was ajar.

"I cannot take this shit anymore, John! All you ever do is spoil that bratty daughter of yours. If you're not always working extra-long hours, you come home and first thing you do is run and smother her. What about me, your wife? Why can't *I* ever get hug or a kiss from you every once and a while? Why don't you ever bring me something nice when you come home? *I* am the person you married the last time I checked!" To hear the hostility in my mother's voice and how she talked so negatively about me made my heart sink. I didn't know she felt that way when it came to me. I thought she loved me; after all I was her daughter too. I stood by the door waiting to see if my father would speak up and defend me.

"Iris, please you are being childish, and what do you mean *my* daughter because the last time I checked Shenelle is *our* daughter. I swear if you're not at that church you walk around the house all day nagging and ignoring that girl like she doesn't even exist. You've been doing it since she was able to walk. I know because I've been watching you. All you do is baby up the boys and it sickens me. This is exactly why I do not want to come home most of the time, because you act so damn stupid!"

"I never told you this, but I really didn't want to have another child, John. I was fine with the two sons we already had. You knew we weren't able to afford another child, but YOU wanted a daughter and I went along with it because I wanted you to be happy. Now you have to work two jobs in order to take care all of us. You're barely home and that shit sickens me!" My heart was racing, the more the conversation went on, the sadder I got. To be a child and hear your own mother, the woman who gave you life talk so coldly about you, the feeling is unbelievable. I mean, I could understand my mother being mad because my father had to constantly work to support us, but it seemed like she was placing the blame on me. As if it was my fault he wasn't at home as much as he was supposed to. The last time I checked I didn't ask to come into the world.

"Well Iris, if you want to sit there and rant and rave about how much I love our daughter, then you go right ahead, sweetie. At least she doesn't complain and appreciates when she sees me. As far as I'm concerned, I'm just being a loving father to Shenelle and I treat all three of my children the same. I have no favorites, but apparently you do. You favor the boys over Shenelle. I believe something is really wrong with you, and suggest you get some help!" What I heard my mother say next would be something I vowed I would never forget for as long as I lived.

"I hate that little fucking girl and I'm starting to hate you too..." I heard my father angrily cut her off.

"What the hell did you just say?! *You what?*" My father's voice sounded scary and my mother knew she had slipped up because all of a sudden she was a mute. If I didn't know any better I would've thought my father was going to smack fiery hell out of her and I hoped that he would. I jumped when I felt a hand on my shoulder and it was my brother Jere.

"Shenelle, what are you doing by Mom and Dad's door?" he whispered. The pain in my heart wouldn't allow me to respond to him, so I just brushed by him and ran to my room locking my door and cried.

I thought about packing whatever little bit of clothes I could fit in my book bag and running away, but I had no place to go and going to Alicia's wasn't an option. All her parents would've done was call my parents and the jig would've been up, so I just kept myself locked inside my room for the remainder of the night. I was so upset that I didn't bother to eat the fried chicken, yellow rice and broccoli that was prepared for dinner, especially since my mother was the one who cooked it. I've heard of a saying *"mothers raise their daughters, but love their sons"* and this very day was confirmation to me that it was the truth.

From that day since the argument between my parents, I avoided my mother the best way I could. Sometimes I would walk through the door greet my father and not even look in her direction. Not that it made any difference because just as I ignored my mother she ignored me even more than she did before. Every day was just about the same regiment. I would go in my room and lock my door. I would only come out for dinner, to use the bathroom or speak to Daddy. Whenever my mother needed me to do something she spoke to me. No matter whether I wanted to do what she asked or not, I was the child and she was the parent, so to avoid hearing her mouth I had no other choice, but to oblige.

***

One Saturday afternoon I was lying across my bed listening to my Walkman, something that I often did to tune myself out from my miseries. My brother Jere walked into my room. "What's up, little Sis," he said as he took a seat on the edge of my bed. I removed my headphones from my ears, canceling my flow to the lyrics sung by SWV.

"What's up?"

"I don't know. You tell me." My brother was five years older than I and very mature for his age. Whenever he would sense something was wrong with me, he would stop by my domain and we would have a one on one brother and sister talk. Since he and I were so close, I didn't mind it at all.

"I don't know what you're talking about, Jere." He sucked his teeth knowing I was playing dumb.

"Shenelle, come on! Don't try and play like you and Ma ain't talking to each other. What's the deal with you and her?" I understood the concern with my brother, but the last thing I wanted to discuss was the tension between me and my mother.

"Jere, why don't you go talk to Ma and find out what's the deal because I really don't feel like talking about her right now." Jere just stared at me and shook his head.

"Shenelle, if I wanted to talk to Ma I would've, now I' ma ask you again, what's going on with y'all two? I mean every day I come in the house, you're isolated in your room not saying anything to nobody and you and Ma just walk past each other like y'all don't even see one another. I'm not going to front; I'm not digging that." I tossed my Sony Walkman at my side, sat up straight and looked him dead in his eyes.

"Jere listen, Ma does not like me and from what I heard, she hates me and wishes I was never born." Once I said that, Jere was revolted. If I thought hearing my mother personally say those words made my ears bleed, the expression on my brother's face said that it did just the same for him and worse.

"How you figure that?" he asked.

"Do you remember about a week ago when you caught me eavesdropping at Mom and Dad's door when they were arguing?" I didn't give him a chance to answer and continued.

"Well they were arguing about me, apparently Ma is jealous that Daddy gives me more attention than he gives her and for that she hates me. Then she said she never really wanted to have me and that she only did it to make Daddy happy, so it looks like you were all wrong big bro. Mom never wanted a daughter only Daddy did." I could tell by the sadness in Jere's face that this whole conversation was starting to get uncomfortable for him and going by the sound of his voice made it even clearer.

"Sis, I don't think that Ma really meant what she said, you already know how she is. Ma says things all the time that's hurtful, but she don't be meaning it like that, so if I were you I wouldn't even take it all that personal." I laughed at my brother's statement as tears of anger escaped from my eyes and I quickly wiped them away with the back of my hand.

"Jere, I know you're just saying all of this to make me feel better, but let's not pretend like the nasty things Mommy says to any of us, especially me, that she doesn't mean them. You and I both know she really does mean them. It's just what it is, big bro; Ma does not like me and I do not care because I feel the same way about her." Jere's nose flared in displeasure and he stood up. "Come here, bighead," he said softly. I stood up, he hugged me and I hugged him back.

"Sis, you gone be aw'ight you're a Patterson, you got tough skin like the rest of us. You ain't the only one that catches Ma's tongue lashing. I go through it with her sometimes, you already know Tim be catching it and Dad does too. So just do what we do and don't pay Moms no mind, just keep living your life. One day you're going to be doing big things and Ma is going to regret she said those messed up things about you and she's going to be proud, believe that. So you cool?" I falsely answered, "I'm cool!" Jere made a funny face to cheer me up.

"You sure, you good?"

I giggled. "Yes, I'm good."

"Aw'ight, love you, Sis. Keep your head up."

"Love you too, big bro, and thanks." Jere threw up the peace sign as he was walking out the door. The love that I had for my brother Jere was unconditional; before there was an Alicia, he was my first best friend. I have to admit that for as long as I was living at my parents' house, it was my big brother Jeremiah who kept me sane.

Early the next morning when I got up, everybody was out of the house except for my father. The timing was perfect because it gave me the opportunity to speak to him privately. I took a quick shower and got dressed in a black and yellow long sleeved FUBU shirt, denim overalls and a pair of black Reeboks. I finalized my look by running a comb through my permed hair and side swept my bangs over my eye like the singer Aaliyah. I put on my gold hoops and went downstairs. My father was sitting in his recliner in the living room with his feet stretched out watching the morning news.

"Good morning, Daddy!" It took him nearly a whole minute just to glance at me from the TV.

"Good morning, baby girl. I didn't even know you were here. I thought you were at church with your mother."

According to mother, Sundays were reserved strictly for church and it was a rule that everyone in the house must go. As I got older, I didn't always commit to going and neither did anyone else. After constantly fighting with everyone to try and make us stick to the program, my mother couldn't win and eventually gave up and went to church almost every Sunday alone. Sometimes I would accompany her so she would feel better or if she made me go, but really as far as I was concerned, no matter how often I went to church and how often I prayed, it still didn't cure all the hell that possessed our house.

I stood by the staircase looking at my father, trying to feel out his mood before I said anything. Because my father spent most of his time working, he barely watched TV. When he would watch TV, if he wasn't catching the *Knicks* game or an episode of *The X-Files*, the news was always his predominant choice. Normally my father didn't like to be interrupted while watching the news. When he was done, he always seemed to be ticked off about something bad that had happened and wouldn't want to talk to anybody afterwards.

"Are you alright?" my father asked, breaking his gaze from the news once he saw that I hadn't moved from the staircase.

"Yes, but I do want to talk to you." He removed his hands from behind his head and turned the Television off.

"What's up, Princess? What's on your mind?" I felt awkward at first because I knew I shouldn't talk with my dad against my mother when I should've been speaking directly to her, but I needed to talk to someone about how I was feeling and it was quite obvious that she wasn't the one. I just divulged it all.

"Dad, I don't like Mom!"

My father curled his lips. "Shenelle, I'm not dumb and blind; I've noticed."

"Am I wrong to be feeling this way? I mean I know she's my mother and all."

"Shenelle, I'm not going to sit here and say that I'm pleased with how you are feeling about your mother. She brought you into the world and you should honor her, but I do understand you are a female and most girls have a tendency of bumping heads with their mothers, so yes, how you're feeling is natural." I used that point to bring up their argument I eavesdropped on a few weeks prior.

"Dad, I overheard the argument you had with Mom and I heard everything she said about me." My father closed his eyes and shook his head as though he wished he never had that argument with her.

"Baby girl, please do not read into that whole situation. You know how your mother is. She loves you very much regardless to what flies out of her mouth; she really didn't mean what she said. If anything, she only said that to piss me off. It didn't have anything to do with you personally." As much as I would've liked to believe what my father was saying, I knew he was lying to preserve my feelings. Because I was the type of person who sometimes didn't know how to leave well enough alone, I went in for the kill.

"So, if that's the case then why does she avoid me? She only speaks to me when she needs me for something, other than that, she doesn't say more than two words to me." It was rare that it ever went up to three words. I could count on my fingers how many times my mother said the words *"I love you"* to me, that I could remember. The shameful thing was I still had a free hand. My father got up from his chair and slipped on his black Clarks by the front door. He snatched his car keys from the metal hook.

"Shenelle, once again do not read into your mother's nonsense. She's only doing it to get my attention, end of the discussion. Now come on and take a ride with me so we could get something to eat and then I'm going to drop you off at Alicia's house." I grabbed my jacket and walked out with him.

During the ride over to Alicia's house, I thought about our discussion. I started to wonder if it really was true that my mother was treating me badly, all because she wanted to get more of my father's attention. With that in mind, I discreetly looked over at my father from the corner of my eye and stared at him. Clearly my father was off the charts a handsome man. At forty two, he could've easily passed as a young thirty year old. He had a head full of wavy hair that was closely cropped with no bald spots or gray hair in sight; neither did he have any fine lines or creases on his cocoa brown face. His six foot frame was still sturdy and youthful and he had great posture, most likely one of the benefits of him serving in the military.

My father was a veteran for the marines; the military was where he met and fell in love with my mother. She worked as a cashier at Roy Rogers at the base where he was stationed. Four years later came the marriage, house and kids; all of what I would have considered the good life. Looking at my father, I could see why my mother would trip on any other female having the luxury of his attention, even if it was, his daughter. I kind of felt bad for my father to have someone like my mother as his wife. My mother, who was the same age as Daddy was strikingly beautiful on the physical tip and also appeared youthful, but her dark side took over her shine tremendously. My father was always known to be laidback and fun to be around while my mother was more conservative and stiff-necked. To any person standing on the outside of a glass house containing those two, it would be obvious that they were unequally yoked. My father pulled up in front of Alicia's house.

"Alright sweetness, here we are." He handed me five dollars from his wallet. "Do not spend it all at once okay and I want you home by seven no later. Got me?"

"Got you!"

"I'll let your mom know you're here, give me my sugar." I reached over and lightly kissed my father on the cheek. When I got out of the car, I saw a small pink and white teddy bear underneath the driver's seat. I wondered where it came from; it wasn't mine because all of my teddy bears had been put away in a chest after I turned eight. Before I shut the door, I let my curiosity set in and went with the questions.

"Daddy, where are you going anyway? You're going back home?" My father chuckled. "Girl, would you mind your own business and go on. I already called Alicia's parents and let them know I was bringing you over. They should be waiting for you and you're being very rude right now by wasting time questioning me, now scram!"

"Okay Daddy, forgive me. See you later!" He waited until I was in the door then drove off. I wasn't a hundred percent sure of it at that time, but it had begun to add up for me. The coming home late, not conversing with her, not wanting to go anywhere with her and do romantic things. My father barely even wanted to sit at the dinner table and eat with us if she was there. If my mother was mad at me of all people for having the best of my father's attention, then she was just plain delusional because from the looks of it, I wasn't the one she should've been worried about.

***

Later that night, I was able to negotiate with my father over the phone in letting me spend the night at Alicia's. I agreed I would leave with her for school in the morning and get there on time. I heard my mother in the background trying to get him to make me come home which was expected. It seemed whenever I could get a little taste of freedom away from her, she would try her best to interfere. Lucky for me, my father had the last say in everything. He swung by to drop off some clothes along with my books and gave me till seven 0'clock to be home the next day, which was my curfew time only on weekends.

I knew my father doing this solid for me was to allow me some space to get my mind off the conversation we had. This is why I loved my father so much more than my mother and also why I depended on him for any and everything. After joining Alicia and the rest of her family for dinner, she and I took our showers and were secluded in her room. I sat on the floor and watched *Malcolm and Eddie* as she cornrowed the front sector of my hair into a crown after doing my nails and feet.

"So what's up with you, girl?" Alicia asked.

"Nothing," I somberly replied.

"Are you sure about that?"

"Yeah, why you ask?"

"Because, you were dumb quiet most of the day. Are you okay?" I was aware that I wasn't acting the way I normally would when I hung out with Alicia. I was so under wraps with the issue concerning my mother that it put me down in the dumps and I was distant with Alicia for most of the night.

"I'm alright." I tied a scarf around my head and climbed onto the bottom bunk with her until I was ready to go to sleep. Since I already seemed antisocial, I broached a subject to heighten the mood. "Hey, show me the dance you were talking about on the phone yesterday."

"Oh, yeah!" she said getting all hyped up. Besides me and Alicia just hanging out and acting silly together, we would often do things to bring out our creativity like make up dances. She jumped up turning off the TV and turned on her boom box.

"Girl, you don't know! I've been practicing this dance all week and it's dope. Watch!" She fast forwarded past various tracks on a mixed tape and stopped when she got to a song by LL Cool J and Total. She started doing the running man and then moved her body in the pepper seed. I watched her as I bounced to the beat of the music and studied every move she made. I hadn't been watching Alicia for that long when my mind started to trail off from her dancing. I never knew why I did it, but I always seemed to drift off into space and become bogged down with random thoughts. I'd been doing this for some time and I wasn't sure what actually triggered it. Once Alicia noticed I wasn't paying attention to her, she stomped her feet calling my name in a whiny voice, "She-She!"

"Huh," I said breaking out of my zone.

"You're not looking at me. You're supposed to be watching so you could be able to do this when we go to parties." Alicia and I loved to get into dance battles when we went to cookouts and parties with our friends and family. The last party we went to was a birthday bash for one of the girls on the block named Kionna. Alicia and I got into a dance contest against Kionna and her cousins and we killed it, winning free movie tickets and a voucher for McDonalds.

"I'm sorry, Leecy, go ahead," I said feeling a little guilt-ridden for my lack of concentration. Alicia huffed and rewinded the tape back to the beginning; she restarted the dance and began wiggling her legs doing the butterfly and then did the cabbage patch. It seemed no matter how much I tried to keep my focus on Alicia, my mind kept wandering off and thinking back to my problems at home. In a matter of seconds, the music was turned down, almost to silence and Alicia joined me back on her bed.

"Shenelle, what the heck is wrong with you? I know you're not okay because you keep daydreaming, so tell me. What's the dealio?" As tired as I was talking about the situation, Alicia was my homie so there wasn't anything I could hold back from her. When I was done filling her in on everything, the same face Jere had when I first told him was now masking hers and all she could utter out of her mouth was, "Whoa!" and I said, "Yeah, I know."

"Dagg She-She, that's crazy and here I thought I had it bad with my annoying, trifling behind sisters. But your own mom, that's wild!" I couldn't say anything; I just sat there upset about the whole thing. Alicia threw her Brandy style, box braids in a stocking cap and went to peak outside of her room, making sure no one was around her door and got back in the bed. "So, do you think your dad is cheating on your mom?"

I shrugged my shoulders. "How would I know? I'm not his keeper." Suddenly out of nowhere, Alicia's door flew open and her sister walked in.

"What ya'll little heifers doing? Ain't ya'll supposed to be in bed? Ya'll got school tomorrow." Like me, Alicia was the baby in her family and her two older sisters liked to play mother to her and tried to boss her around, but Alicia was tough and was not having it.

"Ayesha, would you get out of my room and leave us alone. Shenelle and I are having a private conversation."

"I don't care what ya'll doing; I just know that ya'll asses need to be in bed, before I tell Mommy, and then Shenelle is going to end up sleeping downstairs in the living room, in the dark." I could see in Alicia's face that she was getting heated and if I didn't intervene soon enough, a fight was going to go down and all three of us were going to end up in trouble.

"Ayesha, we gonna go to bed in a minute, just let me finish talking to her, okay?" I pleaded hoping she would leave the room, but she just stood there like she was Momma Rose or someone with her hands on her hips.

"Aw'ight, go ahead and finish then. You got five minutes." Alicia sucked her teeth at the nerve of Ayesha giving us orders.

"We don't need your company! Get to stepp'n, bye!"

"No, I 'ma stand here until ya'll finish." Alicia hopped out of the bed and got in Ayesha's face.

"GET OUT! See that's why Shenelle's brother will never get with you, because you so ugly and dumb!"

Alicia was also always good for getting underneath peoples skin with words, because when she said that Ayesha's eyes turned cold. She had the biggest crush on my brother Jeremiah and wanted him for as long as Alicia and I had been friends. What Alicia said about her being ugly wasn't true for one bit though. Ayesha was eye candy for the guys her age, even the older men and she knew it too. At age seventeen, she was a caramel beauty with shoulder length hair and a Jessica Rabbit shape. Physically she was exactly what my brother would've liked, but she never stood a chance because, just like my mother, her attitude killed it. Ayesha mushed Alicia in her face.

"Shut the hell up!" Alicia pushed her back and I jumped in between them before it could get any further.

"Stop ya'll!" Then Alicia screamed loud enough to give the dead the tremors. "GET OUT! *MAAAA!!!!!*"

Alicia's mother stormed into the room in her flannel pajamas. Her short cut hair was freshly gelled into finger waves. "Look, you two need to cut it out! It is ten 0' clock at night and too late for all of this bickering. Ayesha, go to your room and ya'll two get in the bed right now!"

"Stupid!" Ayesha blurted out as she was walking out the door.

"Go to bed, Ayesha! Goodnight! You girls go to sleep now, no more talking. Ya'll have to get up for school in the morning; I don't want to have to call Shenelle's parents and have them come and pick her up. Goodnight!"

"Goodnight!" we both said in unison.

Soon as Alicia's mother closed the door and walked away, Alicia whispered from the bottom bunk, "My bad about that, She-She. I can't stand Ayesha! She gets on my nerves."

I whispered back from the top bunk, "It's okay Leecy, we'll talk on the way to school, let's just go to sleep. Goodnight!"

"Night!"

I laid there and listened to TLC from the radio until I drifted off to sleep. Poor Alicia, not only did she have to deal with Ayesha's stupidity, but she also had her eldest sister, Asia, who would taunt her at times too. I may have been all bent out of shape about the situation with my mother; I can imagine how Alicia was feeling about her issues with her sisters. The only times Alicia actually got along with her sisters were Friday nights when we were all gathered in front of the TV, eating jiffy pop and watching *"TGIF"*. Once all of that mess was settled between Alicia and her sister was when it finally occurred to me, if I thought I was the only one in this world going through some major family issues, I was dead wrong.

***

Alicia and I got to school earlier than we had planned and ended up waiting outside for the doors to be opened. We met up with a couple of friends from our class and were chatting with them, when I spotted, this cutie with curly hair standing with a group of boys. He was so fine. His creamy skin was like a spoonful of butterscotch pudding. I didn't want to stare too hard, but I couldn't keep my eyes off him. I guess he felt my eyes burning a hole through his soul because he diverted his eyes directly toward me and locked them with mine. He smiled and I quickly turned my head. I grabbed Alicia's arm and gestured to where Mr. Butterscotch was standing.

"Leecy, who is that boy standing over there? I've never seen him before." Alicia took a sneak peek over at him.

"You're talking about the boy in the blue *Pelle-Pelle* suit? That's Caesar. He's new, but he's been here for about two months now, girl. Where you been at? You mad late. All the girls were sweating him when he first came. He's cute as hell, right?"

"Yeah, he is cute," I giddily replied. I watched him as he pushed another kid out of his way, trying to stop him from almost stepping on his fresh pair of Jordan's. Not only was the boy cute, he was also tough, just how I liked them. The front door to the school opened and we started walking in. This time Caesar was the one doing the staring and I felt my stomach catch butterflies as he maneuvered his way through the small crowd over to me.

"Your name's Shenelle?" he asked and my mind was blown away, I gave him a funny look.

"How the hell do you know my name?"

"When I caught you grilling me I asked my boy and he told me." I tried to hold back my blush.

"Nobody was grilling you!" I denied. He rolled his eyes and smiled.

"Yeah aw'ight Shawty, whatever you say, but anyway, my name is…" I cut him off and said in my sexiest grown voice.

"I know who you are, Caesar." He threw his head back in shock.

"Oh word, I ain't know it was like that, shawty. You already know my name and everything. That's type funny because you know my government, but you expect me to believe that you weren't grilling me. What else do you know about me?" he flirted.

"Nothing, that's all I know, besides the fact you're mad cute." Now it was his time to blush.

"You dumb cute too, girl. So, you want me to walk you to your class?"

"I don't care; if you want to." Busy talking to Caesar, I lost Alicia. She ventured off with the rest of the crew flat-leaving me. Caesar walked me to my class and when we stopped by the door, he came right on out with it.

"Shenelle, you want to be my girl?" I thought about my parents and how they probably would react to me having a boyfriend at twelve years old, especially my mom since she was so paranoid of the sky high teen pregnancy rate. My father, I didn't even want to bust my brains thinking about how he would feel. In the end, I will only get to live life once.

"Aw'ight, cool!" I finally said. I noticed the gold initial ring that he had on his index finger and came up with an idea.

"Can I wear your ring and you wear mine?" He looked at his ring as though he'd forgotten he even had it on. Before he twisted it off, he stared at me like he didn't trust I would take good care of it. He didn't have to worry about a thing though, because I was very careful when it came to jewelry and as long as I had him, I would always have his ring. He gave me his initial ring in exchange for my name ring and I put it on my ring finger. It was a little big, but nothing a little scotch tape around the rim couldn't fix. After we swapped rings what came next caught me way off guard; he pulled me to a corner of the hall and stuck his tongue in my mouth. We kissed like how grown folks did on TV.

"So, I'll see you at lunch period?" he asked and I nodded my head in response, too awestruck to speak. We weren't in the same homeroom, so I watched as he walked off, still pleasantly surprised at what we did.

All I could think about throughout the day was that kiss from Caesar. It was the first kiss I had shared passionately with a boy, and my nose was so wide open each nostril could've been a resting spot for a family of cavemen. I recounted the whole experience to Alicia by writing notes back and forth during Spanish class. I couldn't even wait till lunch time to tell her, mostly because I knew I would be sitting with Caesar and not with her. I straight up told her ahead of time that us sitting together wasn't going to happen. Of course, she was all good with it, or at least that's what it seemed. Alicia was never the type of friend who acted jealous and cock blocked. She and I were sisters. We had a pact that couldn't be broken by males, no matter who they were or who they thought they were. She would get hers and I would get mines and neither one of us would try and get in front of that.

Chapter 5

As time passed, Caesar and I got along pretty well. Every day he walked me home, well halfway home. He would drop me off two blocks from my house, so my parents would never see him. Despite me keeping Caesar a secret from my parents, it still never really stopped us from being together the way we wanted to. He came to both my thirteenth and fourteenth birthday parties as Alicia's cousin instead of my boyfriend. We would talk to each other every night on three-way through Alicia's landline while she kept the phone down, and we spent most of our time at the recreational clubhouse where all the kids went after school. The only person who knew the flipside to our little game was my brother Jere. He was cool with Caesar. He kept our secret low key just as we did, as long as Caesar didn't get out of line.

Caesar lived with his grandparents and one Saturday in the summer, I snuck over to his house. I was supposed to be getting a book from the library; that was the lie I told my parents. I met his grandmother for the first time. She seemed to like me and was heedless of our mischievous plan to get inside the basement. The basement in Caesar's house was sort of off limits because it was where his grandfather spent his quiet time when he was home. Caesar wanted to take me down there and *"show"* me his new PlayStation game system. The biggest mistake Caesar's grandmother might've ever made in her life, was trust he and I in the basement alone. It was down there where Caesar broke into the golden gates of my womanhood. He was my first.

My parents didn't find out about our puppy love connection until we were sixteen. I'd like to say that it partially had to do with me doing a great job covering up hickeys and hiding love notes. By that time the tension between me and my mother had died down a lot because I wasn't in the house as much, but the spousal issues between she and my father continued. It was during Easter vacation when things between Caesar and I began to fade away. I practically had my whole future with him mapped out in my mind, but his mind began to go in a total different direction. For some reason he started changing, becoming distant out of the blue. We were walking home one night from the movies when I decided to interrogate him.

"Caesar, what is on your biscuit?"

"What do you mean?" He barely looked at me and watched the ground as he walked.

"I mean what the hell is your problem and why have you been acting so funny with me lately?" He wouldn't respond and kept his eyes lowered to the ground. We stopped in front of my house and I stood by the gate waiting for an answer. Caesar blew out a breath of air and looked into my eyes. "Shenelle listen, you know I love you, right?"

I smacked my lips. That was a line I swore up and down I hated because whenever a person started off with that phrase, it usually meant they were about to drop a bombshell on you. I liked to get right to the point; I didn't care for the crocodile tears.

"Caesar, just tell me what you're gonna tell me and get this over with." I folded my arms across my chest and glared at him. He wouldn't look me in my face for nothing and his words were hardly capable of being heard.

"Shenelle, we can't be together anymore." I felt the lump forming in my throat and I swallowed hard.

"We can't or you don't want us to?" I was getting hostile because I couldn't believe he was breaking up with me. He nervously brushed his hand against his corn-braided hair and looked at me with sorrow in his face that was unmistakable. "I don't want us to."

I bit my bottom lip and looked away from him, listening as he talked. "It ain't got nothing to do with you, Shenelle, cause you've always been my boo. It's me; I just ain't feeling the whole sticking to one girl thing like that anymore. I just wanna chill and do me. I mean, you never know what could happen, maybe later on…" I put my hand up for him to stop talking. I was fighting back the tears.

"Caesar, please just don't say anymore! You don't want us to be together, then cool! Consider it done! Give me back my ring!" He took off my gold name ring from his pinky finger. He had to switch it from his forefinger because it got too small over the years. We had been wearing each other's rings since the sixth grade. I snatched my ring from him and twisted off the one he'd given me and slammed it in his hand. I started towards my house. He tried to grab me and I hauled ass away from him.

"Shenelle, come on man. Don't be like that. I still want us to be friends." That was another line I hated, because I knew it was just a loophole for the other person to be able to woo you over and screw you from time to time. Really to me, it was more of an insult than it was a nice gesture.

"I don't wanna be friends with your ass!" Caesar's face looked hurt by that comment, but I didn't give a damn because as far as I was concerned, I was the one getting hurt.

"Shenelle, I can't even get one last hug from you at least? It's not over between us, boo. I just don't wanna be wifed up."

I snapped at him with my neck rolling in motion. "That's where you're wrong, Caesar, because it is over between us. I don't want anything else to do with you. Now you better get your ass the hell away from my house before I go and get Jere to escort you!" With that said, I quickly walked to my door. I wasn't one to cry and let out all my emotions in front of a guy. I had too much pride. I figured, why give a guy that satisfaction after he already dumped me. I heard Caesar yell out, "You mad foul, Shenelle!" I ignored him slamming the door behind me. I ran upstairs to my room and called Alicia balling my eyes out to her about the whole thing.

Alicia broke the news to me that she heard some girls discussing in the locker room, Caesar was breaking up with me because he was hooking up with this chick from my Chemistry class named Shaquana. He'd been secretly messing around with her while he was with me. *Don't want to be wifed up, my ass!* At first I was mad as hell at Alicia for not putting me on about that sooner. She explained that since I was so into Caesar, she didn't want to tell me because I would've felt she was just being a player hater and I wouldn't have believed her anyway. Funny thing was, no matter how much I may have trusted Alicia, she was probably right. She said she threatened Caesar to tell me before she did and I could believe that.

I was surprised I hadn't heard about all this myself since everywhere I went it seemed the walls could talk. When I hung up the phone from Alicia, I was devastated. I really thought Caesar was my future husband and we would live in this big house with a bunch of kids after we graduated from college. Since that became a non-factor, I threw away everything he had ever given me, so I wouldn't be reminded of him. I thought of ways to hurting Caesar back, but instead I did what I always did best and avoided him all through the rest of high school.

Caesar constantly tried to get me to talk to him after our break up. He would call my house or chirp my walkie-talkie in the middle of the night, and try to stop me in the school hallway between periods. Still, I never budged and eventually, he backed off. Any time I would come across Shaquana in class, she would laugh at me with her little clique of girlfriends. I referred to them as the "flock of birds" because they were all known to be relationship violators. Every time I saw that chick with her friends, I wanted to smack the piss out of her and them.

One of the things my mother taught me was to never fight over a guy, unless he was your husband. That was one of the many rules I made sure I followed, since the time Alicia and I beat up those two girls in the fifth grade over a boy. After Caesar, I went on a few dates with boys or rather I say another round of self-absorbed assholes. I wasn't interested in starting a new relationship, so I dedicated most of my time focusing on school and hanging with my friends. This was the first time I ever had my heart broken and it didn't stop there.

***

I was at Alicia's house practicing a dance we made up together. We were bouncing and shaking our behinds like it was nobody's business to rapper, Juvenile's hit song "Back that thang up". The whole time I was dancing I felt lightheaded and nauseated. Towards the end of the song we turned the music off and I sat down on the floor resting my head in my lap.

"She-She, you aw'ight? You wasn't dancing much. Usually you'd be all into the music, what's the matter?"

"Nothing, I'm alright, I just feel a little queasy. It must be something I ate." Alicia gave me an awkward eye.

"Sis, when was the last time you had your period?" It hadn't been that long since Caesar and I broke up and I did notice I hadn't gotten my period for a few weeks. I was trying to convince myself that my menstrual cycle was just on one of its switch-up moments. Not minding the fact my breasts had been tingling and magically gone up two cup sizes and I'd been peeing like a senior citizen on water pills.

"Shenelle, do you think you're pregnant? I've noticed your belly has gotten a little pudgy." Alicia teasingly pinched a half inch of my stomach. After she said that, I realized I also hadn't been able to button up any of my jeans and been wearing sweats for the time being.

"I don't know. I might be,"

"What do you mean you might be? You need to be sure, girl. What if you are pregnant, Shenelle? Would you keep it?"

"Hell no! For what, so my parents can kill me? As a matter of fact, scratch that! My mother probably would make me have it just so she could enjoy watching me suffer. Plus I am not trying to have a baby with that grimy ass Caesar anyway." Alicia reached over and poked two of her fingers hard onto my abdomen.

"OWW!" I screamed and my first reflex was to punch her dead in her face, but I checked myself.

"Um yeah! Hold that thought!" I watched Alicia jump up from sitting down next to me. She ran up the stairs and right back down. She threw a box at me of an EPT pregnancy test.

"There, go pee!" I looked at her confused.

"Alicia, you keep pregnancy tests stacked in your room?" She turned her nose up and giggled.

"No girl, what do I look like a chicken-head? You already know me and *depo* is like this," Alicia crossed her middle finger over her forefinger to emphasize her statement. A lot of my friends were hip to the new *baby-blocker* vaccine, Depo-Provera. Alicia made sure she was up in a clinic every three months for an injection. I didn't do pills, shots, or none of that stuff, because I feared it to be too dangerous. I stuck strictly to the rubber gloves.

"I got that from Asia's room. That hoe stays getting pregnant. Now hurry the hell up and go pee, I'm tired of waiting." I got up from the floor and just that quick, remnants of pepperoni pizza and Sunkist soda I had eaten earlier spewed from my mouth all over the place and onto Alicia.

"SHENELLE, OH MY GOSH... EWWW!!!!!!" she screamed all melodramatic. I ran to the bathroom and five minutes later came back with a positive pregnancy test.

Three days after I took the test, Alicia and I played hooky from school and this older girl she met while getting her nails done, went with us to the abortion clinic. It was free as long as I had someone over the age of eighteen with me. When I got there, I looked around at all of the young girls and women from ages fourteen to thirty sitting in the waiting room and every last one of them had the same nervous look on their faces as I did. I found out I was three months into the pregnancy and it took two and a half hours for me to get the procedure done. There were more than five girls ahead of me, so unfortunately I had to wait. Then I had to listen to a *"why you shouldn't have an abortion"* speech from a counselor, and I was forced to watch a terrorizing gory video of a woman actually having an abortion. Once it was my turn to go into the cold isolated room, I desperately wanted to change my mind and thought the whole thing would've been easier if I'd just jumped out of a window. I really didn't want to terminate a life that didn't ask to be created, but I had to do what I had to do.

After the abortion, I left the clinic feeling depressed. I felt like a coldhearted murderer, but I didn't need any more problems in my world regarding my parents. I had to think about how I would have been able to face them only to show them, how foolish and irresponsible I was. It was bad enough that I was even having sex without them knowing. Hell! Maybe my mother knew since she always assumed I was fast as a cheetah whose tail was on fire anyway. The little inkling that made me think she might've figured it out was when one day, out of the blue, she asked me why my butt looked like it had gotten bigger overnight. Either way, I was completely sure neither she nor my father would have been happy to learn I became sexually active at fourteen. I wanted to show my mom and dad that their baby girl wasn't going to be a disappointing statistic. Where there is pain it's always going to be that moment in life when certain things that may seem too difficult to do, just need to be done whether we want them to or not.

Chapter 6

I was seventeen years old when my parents' marital problems had really gotten out of control. The cat was finally out of the bag. My mother found out my father was cheating with another woman. Apparently, my father had been seeing this woman for more than five years and was living a double life. How my mother found out about my dad's dirt would forever be a mystery to me. I was sitting in the den reading a book when I heard my parents screaming and cussing at each other. I could hear crashing and breaking, thuds against the drywall from my mother throwing things. There was so much ruckus going on that even my cd player, on its highest volume, wasn't loud enough to drown them out. I didn't want to witness anymore of their chaos, so I used the back door to escape.

I called Alicia to make sure she was home and told her I was on my way over. She must've heard the distress in my voice because she kept questioning me, but I didn't want to explain anything over the phone. As I walked to her house, I kept seeing this vision of my father not being present for the remainder of my life. It was breaking my heart because my father meant the world to me and I might have to be stuck dealing with the pressure of my mother's suffering. When I got to Alicia's, she was standing on her porch waiting for me.

"Sis, what's wrong?" I broke down in tears and she embraced me. I could hear the panic in her voice as she kept repeating the same question over and over.

"She-She, what happened? Why are you crying?" After a few minutes, I gently pulled myself out of her hold. She handed me some tissue. I collected myself and explained the commotion going on between my parents. She shook her head at the details of the story.

"I'm so sorry, She-She." Alicia stared at me empathetically. For a split second, I was envious her parents' marriage was still going strong, while my parents' was tumbling down.

"You know, Shenelle, not saying this to be funny, but did you really believe that your father wasn't cheating on your mother all this time?"

"Hell no I didn't! My father was barely ever at home during the week since I was like ten years old. I mean he has always been a hardworking man, don't get it twisted. But I know he didn't have to work that damn much. Whenever he was home, he seemed to stay away from her and just focused on me and my brothers. The main thing I'm really worried about is my father not being around in my life as much anymore and if he isn't, I really don't know how I'm going to handle it, Leecy." Alicia's forehead creased.

"What makes you think he wouldn't around? The beef between your mom and him have nothing to do with you, so I don't understand why you would think that he'd stop talking to you or your brothers." I became slightly aggravated.

"Alicia, did you not just hear me explain that my father has a relationship with another woman. He might slip away, and I can see it happening. My brothers and I are grown now, so he's no longer obligated to us like he was when we were kids." Alicia knew there was a possibility that I could've been right. We had friends who went through that predicament, but for my mental state she was trying very hard to say something to make me think the opposite.

"She-She, that is not true at all. No matter how old we get, our parents are still our parents even when they're not together. God forbid, if your father was to leave, I don't think you wouldn't hear from him anymore. You have his cell number, so I'm pretty sure that you would be able to call him whenever you need him. Come on, you know your father is crazy about you, Shenelle. I could tell by the way he treats you, so don't even trip." I was listening to Alicia as new tears were falling. She probably could've been right, but there was something inside me telling me she also could be wrong. I was hoping like all hell that she was right.

"Then my mother… oh my god, she's gonna be driving me crazy with her emotions. I could see it now, Leecy. She's going to be picking fights with me and stressing me the hell out. She already got me doing extra chores and shit. You know she's scared to death of Timmy, so she's not even going to try and fuck with him." I plopped down on Alicia's bed and buried my face in my hands.

Speaking of my brother Timothy, he damn near became a menace to society and an even bigger terror to the family. At nineteen years old, Timothy had already done a year in jail for getting busted with an illegal weapon. He had two small children with two different women and was part of a gang known as *"The Bloods"*. Ever since my brother was a little boy, he was a wild child and he never respected my parents, at least not the way the average son should've. Besides that, my brother Timothy was a smart kid and a pretty boy as people would say because of his honeycomb complexion and silky hair. He was also very talented at basketball and he had big dreams of making it in the NBA, but seemingly out of nowhere, he just changed. He turned into a nightmare and whatever triggered the devil inside of him, the world would never know.

"Sis, you know you're always welcomed here if you ever was forced to leave. My mother has told you that before when all that bullshit with you and your mom started years ago."

The night my father dropped me off to sleep over at Alicia's house when I was twelve, Alicia's mother overheard me talking about my parents' argument. She came in the room and spoke with me about it. At first she was against me discussing my personal family issues; she didn't care how close Alicia and I was. In her eyes we were still children and needed to stay in our place and not to be discussing grown folks business. Overall she was concerned. She said that if it ever came down to it and I needed a place to stay; her house was always considered my second home. It was perfect, because I always considered Alicia's parents as my second mom and dad and they will be forever.

"I know Leecy, but really I can't ever see that happening. You know that my mother won't let me go but so far away from her. She hardly likes it when I spend the night out." I was fully aware that although my mother so called hated me and wished I was never born, in all actuality she needed me around because my brothers couldn't do anything for her. My brother Jere was normally the one who would help her out with whatever she needed, but he was away at college. As for Tim, he seemed to have that one characteristic from my father and that was avoiding my mother, so I was basically all she had to depend on. Alicia stared into space. I knew she was putting ideas together in her head, something she was very good at doing.

"Well, you have another six months before you turn eighteen. By then we'll be getting ready to graduate from high school and you would be considered a legal adult. So if you were to move out, your mother couldn't do anything about it, but just be angry at you probably for an eternity." I smirked at Alicia's last statement because sometimes I could've sworn that this chick was meant to be a prophet.

"So girl, the option is wide open for you if you ever think about moving out of your mom's next year. You can move here and live here until the fall then we'll leave for college together, how does that sound?" I let Alicia's idea process in my mind. Earlier that year we both got accepted to Virginia State University and when I first got my acceptance letter in the mail, I almost fainted. I was so happy I was going to be far away from home and even happier when I learned that Alicia was going to be right with me. I smiled and nodded my head in agreement.

"Aw'ight, I could dig it."

"Good, now come here and give me a hug chick." I gave Alicia a hug, and then headed home. When I got home, just like I figured, my father along with all of his things was gone.

***

Months passed since my father was out of the house and my mother was a raging she- devil. She wasn't going to church anymore like she used to, she started chain smoking cigarettes and drinking liquor excessively. For the period my father wasn't around, I'd only spoken to him three times. He apologized about everything that went on over the years and promised that as soon as he got settled, I could visit him whenever I wanted. I hardly was able to reach him after that. Whenever I would call him, more than a few times it went straight to voicemail. I felt kind of bad my mother was hurting, but then on the other hand I didn't because I felt it was her fault he left in the first place. My mother was so distraught over my dad leaving she didn't even keep up with her domestic duties anymore. The house would be filthy, the laundry wouldn't get done and she even stopped cooking. Of course, the person who she left the responsibility to do all of the house work was me and it was like I had no life of my own.

My mother and I fought almost every day, arguing over how I should live my life. It was like she wanted me to revolve all around her and be her lapdog. I couldn't even hang out in peace majority of the time without her calling my cellphone, expecting me to be home early and run errands for her. My curfew time, which was originally 11:00pm, had been knocked down to 9pm, so I could have dinner prepared by ten. Through all of that, I had to contribute to bills out of my little paycheck from Burger King. I often prayed and pleaded with God that he would mend my mother's broken heart, send her a man or something. The more time passed, the more my mother was gradually moving to her wits end and she was dragging me down that road with her.

I came home from hanging out with Alicia and some friends one weekend. It was a little after midnight and my mother hadn't called me. That was shocking considering it was way past my given curfew. The house was quiet and the lights were out; I knew my mother was inside because I heard the radio playing. I went upstairs to her room and opened the door. It was dark, but the music was up high enough to keep a person from falling asleep. I turned the volume down, flicked on the light and found my mother laying on the bed on her back in a deep slumber. Her eyes looked swollen like she had been crying all day long. Sitting on her nightstand was a bottle of Hennessy that was more than halfway empty and an open pack of *Unisom* with four pills missing. I got nervous, hoping she didn't overdose and I violently shook her.

"Ma! Mommy, wake up!" She did nothing but stir, moaning some. I kept shaking her.

"MOM!!!" I was relieved when she answered me. "What? Don't you see I'm sleeping girl! Leave me alone!" She turned over on her side facing her back towards me. I picked up the blanket that was on the floor to cover her and a piece of paper fell from it. I quietly picked up the paper and read it. It was a letter from the Supreme Court stating that my father was filing for a divorce. It dawned on me then why the classic song "Always and forever" by Heatwave was playing from her stereo. It was the song my parents danced to on their wedding day.

I looked at the state my mother was in and figured she obviously read the letter, got depressed and tried to drink and sleep her pain away. I swallowed hard at the reality of my family falling apart. Regardless of what I had to go through dealing with my mother, I still loved her and hated to see her like that. I put the letter back inside its envelope and sat it on the nightstand. I kissed my mother on the cheek, turned off the light and went to my room. I silently cried as I lay in my white metal, princess style bed. I thought about all of the other children who were blessed to have their families happily together, wondering why it couldn't be the same for me. The agitation made me grab the bottle of Hennessey I'd taken from my mother's room and I quaffed it down. It was something to numb my pain while I lay awake. I waited for the liquor to set in until my brain reached its peak and went to rest.

***

Spring started and graduation was going to be rolling around in no time. Alicia and I were at JC Penney getting fitted for our prom dresses. We were both excited and couldn't wait for the day to arrive. "Leecy, how do you think this looks?" I asked as I stood in front of her in a strapless, Satin Lavender gown with a beaded midriff.

"You look fly, She-She. I likey!" Alicia said and I smiled, feeling good. Alicia opted on a silk, lace front, silver dress that stopped right above the knee with a silver hand bag and silver three inch, open toed sandals.

"Girl, we're going to be killing it at the prom," I sang.

"I know right, I'm dying to see the look on Rondell's face when he picks me up."

"Girl, you already know he's going to be sick when he sees you looking all cute."

Rondell was Alicia's boo and was the son of one of her mother's close friends. They had been kicking it with each other for two years and were crazy about one another. When I first met Rondell, I did not like him. I thought he was a cocky ass, high yellow player, because whenever I was around him and Alicia, all he talked about was how every girl wanted to holler at him. I personally thought Alicia was too good for him. I could tell she hated that Rondell was conceited, but she always played it off like it was no big deal. I understood why Alicia fronted, because I knew exactly how foolish a female could be when she is in love. Eventually as I saw Alicia and Rondell together and how she constantly bragged about what he he'd done or bought for her, I had a change of heart. He was making my home girl happy and whatever floated her boat steadied mine.

"So what's up with you and Caesar, Shenelle? You're gonna let him take you to the prom or what?" I looked at Alicia wondering why she would be crazy enough to even ask me that.

"Um, hell to the no, screw Caesar!" I never got over how Caesar dissed me, but I did gain serenity. A year after Caesar broke up with me for that chicken head Shaquana, she ended up messing around on him with some other dude, got pregnant and then deaded him. Afterwards he tried to crawl his way back to me and I shot his ass down every single time. Including the time he had the nerve to ask me to the prom.

"I have someone else in mind who I want to take me."

"For real, who?" I became googly eyed thinking about the person.

"You know Tone, the guy who always cuts his fifth period class to hang in our gym class with Davon and them? He asked me a few days ago and I might go with him." Five guys other than Caesar had asked to take me to the prom. I never accepted any of their requests, but then I never actually turned them down either. Each one of them was cuties and it was kind of hard for me to decide which one I wanted to go to the prom with. I narrowed it down to the tallest one, who my attention really rested upon and that was fine ass Anthony who everybody knew as *Tone*, even his name was sexy. Alicia's face made a look like she was disgusted.

"Why must you always go for the bad boy, Shenelle? You could do much better than him." I frowned because I know she was not talking about who deserves who, knowing how *her* boyfriend was.

"Alicia, just because he snuffed up some boy yesterday doesn't make him a bad boy. Maybe he just doesn't take nobody's shit like we don't." I thought reminding her of us would help wind her down from bashing duke.

"Um, you do know *why* he snuffed up that boy, right?" I rolled my eyes. I knew about how my crush beat up a ninth grader because his clothes signified his gang colors, but that was not my issue and had nothing to do with the prom. "And may I also add that he's a stupid, super senior with a baby… Need I say more?" she reproved. I was already finished getting dressed and put the prom dress back on the hanger, getting annoyed at Alicia's remarks.

"Leecy, all of that is beside the point and I'm just about having fun. I could care less about everything else, it's not like I'm trying to marry the boy, dayumm!"

"Aw'ight, but I still think you'd be better off going with Caesar. He's way cuter anyway!" I ignored her because my mind was already made up. "Shenelle," Soon as Alicia said my name I rolled my eyes again, because I knew the conversation was far from over and she was going to bombard me with words. But that was how she was, so as usual; I let her do her preaching.

"What, Alicia!" I said in a bothered tone.

"Girl, I don't get you sometimes. Why do you keep holding on to what Caesar did to you? That shit is mad old. I mean I know you felt played and all, but it's in the past now. Forget that mess and just take him back because he obviously still has feelings for you." Now I was really starting to get aggravated. No matter how many hints I would give Alicia that I didn't want to talk about Caesar, she always kept going on and on, and I really didn't want to scream on her. I gave the lady behind the register my money for the dress, turned around walking up close to Alicia's face and made sure that my words were stern and clear.

"Alicia, I know what happened between me and Caesar is old, but I don't care. I don't want anything to do with him and I won't ever want anything to do with him, so would you please stop bugging me about this dude and lay low!" Alicia gave me that look as if she wanted to knock my teeth down my throat. It was very rare that she and I would get into beef, but for sure we had our disagreements and because we were both hotheaded, it got real. Alicia angrily inched closer to my face. We were so neck and neck that if one of us would've sneezed we'd bumped heads. With the same attitude in her voice I gave her, she said, "You know what, Shenelle? Whatever! If you want to stay stuck living in a cold old ass world, then go ahead. But you will see just how far you'll go, and need I inform you, it won't be that far!" Alicia walked off ahead of me. Whenever I would think back on this day, I would wonder if what she said was a curse.

***

It was the day of the prom and I just got home from getting my hair and nails done. It wasn't time to leave yet, but I couldn't wait and wanted to see how my dress would look along with my Lavender designed nails and Shirley Temple curls. I stood in front of my vanity mirror and turned from side to side. I looked good and was loving the way my dress hugged my shapely frame. While I was standing there admiring myself, my mother came busting into my room.

"Girl, why do you have your dress on like you going somewhere? It ain't time to leave yet. And I hope you know that you're not going anywhere until this house is clean." I quickly turned my head to my mother.

"What?"

"You heard me! You are not leaving this house until everything is clean. That means every dish better be washed and every floor better be mopped and vacuumed do you understand me?" My mother had to be either drunk or high, especially since she graduated from being a nicotine chain smoking, alcoholic, to a full blown pothead. I think saying she was a junkie would more like fit the bill. Her habits had gotten so out of hand she even sold some of her possessions to get the money to support it. I'm talking fur coats, jewelry and other heirlooms that were passed down to her. The house was repulsive and there was no possible way I could've had it cleaned by the time prom started.

"Ma, the prom starts in two hours, how do you expect me to clean the house in that span of time?"

"I don't know! I just know if you don't do what I tell you to do, then prom night is over for you. So I suggest you find a way!" On that note she slammed the door and I stood there dumbfounded.

Sometimes I didn't know who my mother thought she was raising. My name wasn't no damn Cinderella last time I checked. I sat down on my bed with my dress still on, heated like a muva. I didn't move for about a half an hour. I was so stuck in a daze that I didn't even feel the pain of me picking at my skin and drawing blood. Self-infliction had become a major habit over the years and something I had no control over. What broke me out of my zone was my cellphone ringing. I picked it up and saw it was Alicia calling. Before I could answer it, my mother came back into the room and took my cellphone away. I cursed her under my breath, and then went ballistic.

I took my dress off, went to my dresser and pulled out a pair of scissors. I cut the dress up into shreds, tossing them all over my room. Once I was done, I stood in the middle of the room in my underwear and stared at the mess I'd made. Pieces of my dress and the beads that were a part of it were cascaded everywhere. I was panting and shaking, my curls were sweated out and tears were streaming. I lied in my bed and put the covers over my face. I didn't want to see or talk to anyone for the rest of the night. It was just like my mother to ruin things for me whenever she knew she could. I definitely had more than my fair share of being bullied and picked on, but I have to say that my mother was by far the biggest bully I've ever met in my life. I started to believe the broad was just jealous because I was living my life and she apparently didn't have one, now that my father was out of the picture. I didn't realize that I'd fallen asleep when my mother came snatching the covers off me.

"Girl, get your ass up and clean this house! Why the hell did you cut up that dress? You must've lost your mind! And I guess you're not going to the prom because it started at seven and it is now nine thirty. You still have to clean up, so put some clothes on and let's go!" She stood at my doorway while I got dressed in silence. I walked by her and went downstairs. I grimaced at all the clutter and filth throughout the living room and kitchen. The dishes was piled high and roaches were just cruising, having the time of their lives, like I should've been doing at the prom. The house was so disgusting that I didn't know where to start from, so I just started by picking up clothing, *her* clothing from off the bottom of the steps. She watched me the whole time as I was cleaning the living room and directed me on what to do. Once I was done with the living room, I took on my next task in the kitchen.

"And I want you to find something in the refrigerator to cook after you're done cleaning. You might as well make dinner since you're not going anywhere." That was it for me! My mother might have birthed and raised me, but sometimes she did ask for a little too much. I slammed one of the plates I was washing down in the sink causing it to shatter and dirty sudsy water splashed all over me. "Why must you mess everything up for me? I don't get it! What do you have against me, Ma?!"

"What do I have against you? You're getting smart?" My mother punched me in my eye and I winced but took it like a G. She swung and hit me again and again. "Come on, fight me! You're grown right? Be a woman and fight me!"

She shoved me to provoke me, but I wasn't going to do anything. I was willing to let her beat me down, hopefully killing me, so it would add on to all of the other screwed up things that she'd done and live with it for the rest of her miserable life. She yelled as she waved her finger in my face. "I don't have shit against you and don't be slamming any damn dishes! You don't pay any bills in this house!" Somebody must've forgotten I was contributing towards the mortgage! I never liked arguing with my mother because once it started, it never ended.

"Ma, you don't pay any bills in here, Daddy's alimony and child support does. You don't work, all you do is lay-up and force me to do everything and I know it's because you hate me. You always hated me ever since I arrived on this earth!" My mother stood there astonished at my words. As much as I've tried to avoid any conflict with her, this day was different. Pressure busts pipes. I was tired of being treated the way that I was and I had to get everything off my chest.

"I know it's true because I heard you say it six years ago. For some reason you had this twisted idea that I was stealing Daddy's attention from you, but you were too blind to see that *he* didn't want to give his attention to you." Some daughters would've been scared to speak the truth to their mother, but this was a do or die situation for me and I didn't care what the result could've been. My tongue was in pain from biting it for so long and I couldn't take it anymore. My mother slowly walked up to me with death in her eyes.

"What did you just say to me?" I took a deep breath and my heart was pounding vigorously, but I wasn't going to let it stop me. I angrily told my mother all about herself.

"Ma, it is what it is... Daddy is gone and it's because of you! You weren't making him happy and you don't make any of us happy! You seem to believe that you do, but you don't! All you've ever did was bring us down mentally and emotionally! I hate you! I always have and I always will hate you! You are an angry, miserable, old woman and I am tired of you taking it out on me! You're a bad mother and God should never have given you children!" The next thing I knew, my mother was on top of me, choking me like she wanted to distort my vocal cords. I was trying hard to pry her hands from my throat, but she would squeeze tighter. After a while, I gave up and laid there waiting to see the light, so I could be with God and away from that devil. I felt my body begin to lose its energy until I heard an echo of someone's voice.

"Ma... Ma!!! What the fuck is you doing?" When my mother's hands were released from around my neck, I coughed violently and once I regained a settled composure, I noticed my brother Timothy holding her. I tried to get up off the floor, but was too weak.

"Get this little, ungrateful heifer out of my house before I kill her ass! And you're right, Shenelle. I do fucking hate you! You are a stupid, spoiled bitch and you ain't my offspring! You're the devil's offspring! I wish I had followed my first gut and aborted you!" My mother stormed out of the kitchen still screaming obscenities and for the first time ever, my brother Tim was nice to me. He knelt down beside me while I still struggled to catch my breath.

"Shenelle, you aw'ight, yo?" he asked softly. I nodded my head, grabbing his extended hand and he helped me up. I didn't know if Timothy was being so nice because he knew my mother was crazy and felt sorry for the position I was in or because he had some chick who was soon to be the next victim to his dirty, little game, standing there with her mouth dropped to the floor and eyes bulging out of her head. Whatever the case was, I just knew I was getting out of that house without rethinking it.

I rushed up the stairs, pulled out my suitcase and started throwing toiletries and clothes in it. It was a quarter to eleven and my mother drank herself to sleep again. I had Timothy get my phone from her room and saw several missed calls from Alicia and one missed call from my prom date. I called Alicia back and briefly explained everything to her. She said she came by the house twice before prom started, but no one answered the door. I didn't care to call my prom date back, assuming he had already hooked up with some other shorty, probably not even thinking about me. I called a cab and was lugging my suitcase down the stairs when my brother Tim questioned me.

"Yo Shenelle, where are you going at this time of night?" I didn't have the time to stay around and chat, so I just told him I was moving out and would get the rest of my things later. He helped me out the door with my way overstuffed suitcase and was generous enough to pay for my cab.

"Be easy, Sis," he said. I threw him the peace sign from the window and sped off.

Chapter 7

"Did you really cut up your dress, She-She?" Alicia asked sitting on the top of the toilet seat, watching me blow dry my hair. I replied, "Yup, I damn sure did!" Alicia shook her head. "Damn girl, I'd at least waited till tomorrow and returned that shit and got my money back. You paid seventy five dollars for that dress. You's a silly hoe, you know that don't you?" she chuckled.

"Of course I do," I admitted and had to break a smile. What Alicia said was type true and I could've really used the money, but in the heat of the moment, I didn't think about it. I was just relieved I was out of my mother's house even if I did have to go back there one last time. My first thought was to leave everything there and make do with what I had, but then I really would've been playing myself. It wasn't like I had dough like that to buy a whole new wardrobe. I examined my face in the mirror; I looked like a hooker who'd been ran through and thrashed. I had a black eye, a busted lip and purple bruises on my neck from my mother's fingerprints.

When I got in Alicia's door, her parents and sisters hovered around me in hysterics with a thousand questions. Alicia had to cover me with her jacket and help get me to her room. I was like an infamous celebrity being bombarded by news reporters. The shower I took was the best shower ever. It felt like I was washing all of my problems away. To get off the subject of the fight between me and *Mommie Dearest*, I asked Alicia about the prom.

"I didn't go, chick! If you weren't going, I wasn't going. What good would it had been for me to be there if I couldn't party with my best friend?" I looked at Alicia and we both smiled. I had no words. My home girl was just too adorable sometimes. I felt kind of bad though, because she had her hair styled all pretty in a curly updo and a prom dress, all for nothing. I bumped my hair with a curling iron, wrapped it in a doobie and applied some cocoa butter to my eye and neck. I yawned. "Sis, I love you, but I'm gonna hit the sack. I know you wanna stay up and talk, but girl I can't. I'm done for the night."

"No doubt! I'm about to go to sleep too, but Mommy wanted to speak to me, so I 'ma go see what she wants. She probably wanna know the 411 on what happened to you and don't sweat it, I won't tell her too much." We hugged each other goodnight. I laid down on the roll out cot from her trundle that had been upgraded from the bunk beds we used to sleep on when we were little girls. Alicia was heading out her door when she stopped.

"Oh, and unlike your crazy ass, I'm taking my dress back to the store to get my money back. Goodnight!" She laughed and I grabbed one of her pillows from her bed and threw it at her.

"Shut up!"

I didn't leave Alicia's house the next day until the evening. I called my house from a private number to make sure nobody was home. When I didn't get an answer, I knew my mother was probably at family's house or somewhere, playing the victim and ridiculing me. I took that opening to get the rest of my things. Alicia's dad drove me to the house. I let myself in and went right to business. I understood why my father left the way he did, he was tired of my mother's crap and officially I was too. I hurriedly cleared out the remains in my drawers and closet, stuffing all of my garments in three big, laundry bags. I carried them one by one to the front door. I didn't even stop for a breath of air until I was done. Alicia and her dad helped me load the bags into the trunk of the car. Before we left, I told Alicia to give me a moment while I went back inside for something.

I opened the door and dropped my set of keys on the coffee table. I stood there for a while, taking a moment to reminisce about all the good times I had living in my parents' house. All I could hear was my mother's big mouth, screaming and spewing hurtful insults. It was right then the picture became clear to me that the bad outweighed the good. Knowing I would never step foot into that house again, I walked to the door. I turned the knob, taking one last look at the hellhole I once called home. I shook my head in disbelief and walked out.

***

My mother made her measly, little attempts to contact me once she saw I wasn't trying to go back home, but I wouldn't talk to her if my life depended on it. There was no way in hell I was going to let her try to sweet talk me into moving back in, only to deal with more of her drama and crazy emotions again. I was determined I would survive, stress-free without her. I stayed at Alicia's as planned, but jumping from one ditch right into another, it didn't last long. The fights between Alicia and her sisters had gotten outrageous. Alicia's sister Asia was evicted from her apartment in the projects and she, her four kids and lowlife babies' daddy were living there too.

Asia's boyfriend was a squatter ass dog and on many occasions tried to flirt with Alicia and me, but we would immediately put him in his place. He even went as far as putting his hands on Alicia, sexually violating her. She walked past him in the hallway one day and the mofo was bold enough to grab her butt. Alicia told her mother and father and they spoke to Asia about it. Asia flipped out, disputing that her man would ever do such a thing. She really believed Alicia was lying because she was jealous of her. Truthfully, Asia's dude was no prize. He was a busted, dusty bum with no job or home training and way below Alicia's type. I spoke up for Alicia and told them about Asia's boyfriend's sexual attempts with me, and her parents threw that ass out. They threatened him that they would call the cops if he was to ever try to come to the house again. The ordeal caused Asia to become hostile and she attacked Alicia. Their parents and I had to break it up.

From that day on, both Asia and Ayesha teamed up and turned against me and Alicia. I didn't understand why Ayesha was mad at us because she had nothing to do with the equation. But then I figured, going by the way she was acting, she had to be screwing Asia's boyfriend on the low. Those two were nasty to us every chance they got and made living in that house impossible. The final straw was when Alicia discovered Asia was stealing money from her.

Of course Asia denied it, but Alicia already knew she stole from her. The day Alicia was barking at everybody about her money being missing, Asia's ten year old daughter inadvertently tattled and said Asia took some money out of Alicia's room to get her hair done. The confrontation between Alicia and Asia escalated into an ugly physical altercation. Alicia's parents weren't home, so instead of Ayesha helping me to pull them apart, she joined Asia.

They both tried to beat Alicia to a bloody pulp, and after quickly calling the cops, I jumped in and fought them with her. I didn't care if they were her family; I wasn't going to let my girl fight or take a beat down alone. The situation ended up becoming a terrible scene in the streets. Alicia's sisters were arrested and she was taken to the hospital to get treated for a bite from one of them on her face. When Alicia's parents came home and witnessed all the upheaval, they were baffled and on the verge of moving out of the neighborhood to spare them any further embarrassment.

That same night while I was waiting for Alicia in the emergency room, I called my brother Jere and told him the story. He picked us up from the hospital and allowed us to stay with him and his family. He offered for us to stay until it was time to head to college. Although Lataya, Jere's wife was mad cool and also insisted we stay, I declined. I didn't want to invade their space, so Alicia and I stayed only for a few days until we found a room to rent. Jere paid the two months' lease and security for us. That turned out good for me and Alicia because the months rolled by fast. We spent all our days celebrating our last moments of the city. We were partying, getting it in and when the time came, we were getting out.

***

At the end of June, I graduated from Adlai Stevenson High School. I received a full scholarship, thanks to hard earned grades. Shockingly, my father was there along with my aunts, uncles, grandparents, and my brother Jere to see me graduate. I cried when I saw my father. He knew about everything that had happened between me and my mother. He assured me I was going to be fine because I would be far away and all my problems at home were the past. After the ceremonial dinner, my father surprised me by taking me to a car dealership. I was in total bliss when he told me to pick out any car I wanted. I chose a small, four door, 2002 plum purple Mazda sedan with black interior; it was gorgeous, and the new car smell was breathtaking. My father paid for it in full and even more to my surprise gave me a bank card to an account in my name. It held ten thousand dollars. When I heard those digits, I wanted to dance on top of every car in the lot.

"Thank you so much, Daddy." I jumped into my father's arms giving him a great big hug.

"You're welcome, baby girl. You earned it. Do you remember what I always told you?" he asked with austerity in his voice, which was to be expected coming from a militant father.

"Yes Dad, I won't spend all of my money at once." My father winked his eye in approval. I wanted to scold him on why he had been so distant and didn't call to check up on me but decided against it. I was just grateful he came through when I needed him the most and with way more surprises than I ever imagined.

"Dad, really, thanks for coming and not because you had to, but because you were willing to." My father gave me another hug.

"The pleasure is all mine, Shenelle, I wouldn't miss your graduation for the world. You have my new number. I want you to call me as soon as you arrive on campus and call Jeremiah too, okay? Be good and I love you!" I felt the tears getting ready to pour.

"I love you too, Dad," I said as I gave him one last hug before we went our separate ways. I held onto my father tight because something in my heart told me that although this was a beautiful moment, I would never hear from him again. I watched as he got in his car; he waved as he drove off and I waved back. When I arrived on campus, I called my father, letting him know I was there safely. Any time I called him after that, his voicemail picked up and then the number eventually became disconnected. Up until this day, I never saw or heard from my father again.

Chapter 8

(2002)

Virginia State University was immaculate! The air was crisp, and the trees and bright green grass were mesmerizing; a far cry from the bird shit, infested trees and dead polluted grass in New York City. You saw rabbits hopping around as if they were welcoming you to their town. I considered my move to Virginia as a gift given to me. I hated I had to watch my feet to make sure rats wouldn't run across them while I was living in the Bronx.

I loved my new room, it wasn't the biggest, but it was nice and the beds were comfy. I shared the room with some other girl. At first, I was disappointed because I really wanted to be in the same room with Alicia, but because most of the rooms were already reserved, she and I both had to settle on different rooms with other people. She was only four rooms down from me, so I never really missed her. I was unpacking my luggage and putting everything into place when someone knocked at my door. I told whoever it was to come in and Alicia waltzed in the room with a Charms blow-pop sticking out of her ponytail. "What's cracking, hoe? You're still unpacking your stuff? I'd thought you'd be done by now." She was walking over to my bed and tripped over one of ole girl's shoes.

"Gotdamn! This chick doesn't have any home training. She mad dirty with her shit cluttered and scattered all over the place. Eww!" I laughed at Alicia. Home girl was type sloppy; her whole side of the room was nasty. She had clothes jumbled up from the top of her bed onto the floor. Chinese take-out containers were underneath the bed and there was an old two-liter Pepsi bottle next to her nightstand that looked like somebody pissed in it. I shook my head at the filth and hoped to god she wasn't some hermaphrodite, nutty, freak.

"How are the girls in your room?" I asked.

"They aw'ight! They're not dirty or nothing. I only met one of them, some white girl. Her name is Hannah and she seems cool so far. How about you, you met this chick yet?"

"Naw, we didn't meet yet?"

Alicia scoped out her area. "I see she's a mad Usher fan and that's a plus because you love Usher. I could see ya'll now jamming all night to that new song he got out and overplaying his album," she said referring to all the posters the girl had on her wall of Usher. I shrugged because I didn't know about all she was talking; I had to meet the girl first.

"Maybe, depending on what kind of person she is." As soon as I said that, the door opened and a girl walked in.

"Oh what's popping? You must be Shenelle. I'm Natari." The girl looked over at Alicia, giving her an unwelcomed gaze. "Um, who are you? You don't belong in this room," she said.

Alicia snapped her neck back at her remark. "Excuse you!" I cut in before she got started on the girl. "She's with me. Is there a problem with her being in here?" Natari didn't look at me and began clearing off her bed.

"Did I say that?" Before I could respond Alicia cut back in. "No you didn't say that, but you acted like it, so again what is the problem?" I gave Alicia that look for her not to start. Natari menacingly glared at Alicia like she wanted to rip her a new asshole and stated to me, "Yo, check your girl and tell her to calm the hell down!"

Alicia jumped up from off my bed in a fury. "*Check me?* Trick, I'm about to check you in a minute!"

"So pop off then!" Natari started towards her and Alicia reached to her back jean pocket where she always kept her razor blade.

I quickly got in front of Alicia and talked to her in a sincere tone so that she got my drift. "Leecy chill, we don't need to be getting into no bullshit. We came all this way to get away from the bullshit, so be easy aw'ight!" Alicia hardly paid me any attention and just kept grilling the girl, so I redirected my point towards her. "Natari listen, we just got here and we're not trying to start any problems. If it really bothers you that she's in here, then I'll make her leave."

"Good, then make her leave!" Natari said all snotty like. I pleaded with my eyes to Alicia for her to just go in peace.

She sucked her teeth. "Whatever! Sis, come get me when you finish." She took one last scathing look at Natari, rolled her eyes and mumbled the word, *Bitch!* Then left the room. I blew out air of relief that no drama went down. I was so tired of dealing with drama and didn't want to end up getting thrown off campus because of Alicia, and then I would've had to kick her ass for it. I finished arranging my last little bit of things and hung up my posters of the rapper Chingy on the wall. Natari decided to break the silence.

"So, that's your sister?"

"Something like that, she's my best friend. Why?"

"Just asking, ya'll two look alike." I sat down on my bed to relax. I looked over at her side and noticed that she fixed it up. I spotted the big Puerto Rican flag she had hanging on the wall and above it was a sign that said *"Throgs Neck"*

"So I see you from the Bronx, that's wassup!"

"Yeah man, but I've been living down here with my grandmother for the past four years though. You from the boogie down too?"

"Yup! The Bronx is what it is all day, every day!"

"Cool... cool, what part are you from?"

"Castle Hill,"

"Oh word, I got mad peeps over there." Natari got up and walked to the mini refrigerator that was next to her dresser. I did a quick once over on her, not that I swung that way or anything, but just to take in her full profile. Natari, beyond the hood rat attitude, was a pretty girl. She was tall, I'd give her about five foot nine in height, an inch taller than me and the way her body was built, she could've easily quit school if she wanted to and got a gig to be America's next top model. Her golden brown skin was flawless, and you could see by her waist length hair that she had in a ponytail and silky, baby edges where her Latin roots in her stood out.

"Do you speak Spanish?" I asked. She took out two cans of orange Fanta, tossed one to me and warmed up a pop tart in the microwave.

"Hell no! I was raised with a black momma, girl. I don't speak that shit!" I smirked. She stared at me as if she also was trying to take in my profile.

"You're going to really like it here. It's mad fun. Of course you know, they got their whack ass rules, but don't nobody be following them like that and yo, let me tell you now. Some of these VA chicks are crazy and you a freshman too, so they might try to fuck around with you. You good money though, I'm not going to let them run over you, but that friend of yours with her attitude, she act like she boss or something. She needs to chill with that because she's on our territory, so if you're her friend, you might want to let her know to calm that down."

Natari seemed real cool and all. But what she didn't know was, regardless how crazy she and those other chicks were, the road that Alicia and I came from and all the shit we've been through. They wouldn't have known crazy until they saw us in action, Bronx style.

"Man listen, Alicia is real free spirited and she's not the type to let anyone get in the way of that, no matter who they are. Overall she is a good person; you'll like her once you get to know her." Natari pursed her lips. "Aw'ight we'll see, but so far I like you though; you seem mad cool." She smiled and I gave her one back. Natari looked over at her alarm clock that was next to a picture framed of some light skinned dude.

"Come on, it's five 0' clock. Let's go to the cafeteria for supper." I slipped my feet into some black Chinese slippers and went to get Alicia. She tried to rant and rave about not wanting to be around Natari, but after arguing with her for five minutes, I finally got her to come with us. I could've seen it already that it was going to be a helluva four years of college.

All three of us sat at a big round table after we got our food. Alicia and I didn't waste any time gobbling down our meals. We hadn't eaten much during the seven hour drive from the city. We were so anxious to get away from home that we thought our hero sandwiches and a big bag of Cheetos were going to be enough to get us by.

"So tell me, what's the deal with you two? What made ya'll want to come down here?" Alicia and I looked at each other, a bit confused by Natari's question.

"What do you mean? We filled out applications and we got accepted, so we're here," I replied.

"Duhh!!!" Alicia sarcastically bellowed, I looked at Alicia and mouthed for her to stop, Natari ignored her.

"I'm just asking because I heard what you said earlier about how ya'll left to get away from the bullshit, so I just wanted to know what the situation was. If you don't mind me asking." Natari darted her eyes in Alicia's direction. Alicia looked at me and then back at Natari.

"What's your situation for coming here?"

"Whoever said that I had one?" Natari shot back. Alicia got quiet and stared at her. I knew she felt stupid, but I didn't even bother to intervene. I was too through with those two and their cattiness, so I just kept on eating my food and let them carry on. Natari was the one who chose to nip it and be the bigger person.

"Alright look, I'll start it off! As I already explained to Shenelle, I'm from the Bronx like you guys and my situation was I hooked up with the wrong dude. He was into the whole gang banging and selling drugs and shit. I've been dealing with him ever since I was thirteen and he was sixteen. You know how when you fall in love you get all caught up and start doing any and everything for a dude to make him happy?" Alicia and I nodded our heads in response. We both understood that all too well.

"Well, I joined the *"Crips"* to represent him. One day he made me cut this girl right in front of her child to get initiated and after that, I started getting into fights like almost every day. He had me robbing people, and then eventually I ended up doing six months in Juvie. I was his ride-to-die chick and he never even thought to visit me while I was up in there; all just to please his ass." Natari paused for a minute and looked down at her food. It was easy to tell by her sad expression that reliving the hurtful experience was hard for her, as it would be for anyone in that situation, but she found it within herself to continue.

"When I got out, I found out that this mofo done got one of my home girls pregnant. I beat her ass and went right back in to Juvie and did another six months. While I was in there, the girl's family started antagonizing my family and making threats. My mother was so fed up with all the bullshit that as soon as I got released at sixteen, she sent me down here to live with my grandmother. My grandma, she doesn't play, so I had no choice but to get my act together. I got my GED and then I came here." Alicia and I were staring at her speechless. I may have been through some hard times, but after hearing Natari's story I couldn't compare to her.

"So, what about ya'll? What's ya'll story?" Alicia and I looked at each other again and said in unison, "Family issues!" Natari smirked. "Of course, what else would it be, right?" We all laughed.

Alicia and I gave her a quick rundown of our history and she wasn't surprised by both of our stories, even though she was an only child that lived with a single mother. It wasn't hard for her to understand our issues of dealing with siblings, negligence, favoritism, and especially mother and daughter rivals. Natari was really a sweetheart underneath her tough skin. Alicia and I clicked with her like a Lego. Each day our friendship grew stronger and became nothing short of unbreakable.

My first few weeks at college was cool and rough at the same time. The classes were quite of a challenge and required a lot more studying than high school ever did. I already was put on to that, courtesy of my brother Jere. The homework was ridiculous and I found myself carrying five textbooks every day which was nerve wrecking. It was all good though because, the majority of the time I was having fun with the girls, touring. Natari was right about one thing; them VA girls were very confrontational. It seemed like once I got comfortable, the drama would begin. In my Biography class, I noticed all of the awkward and demeaning stares from this little group of girls who sat on one side of the room. At first I used to grill back at them, but once I saw it was developing into a routine, I stopped minding them. From the glares, came the snickering and gibberish talking. I fought hard to ignore it all; reminding myself I didn't need the bullshit.

Alicia and I were walking around one day when a few of the girls walked passed us and one of them mumbled under her breath, *New York, bitches!* I had to calm Alicia down to keep her from punching one of the girls in their face. She also was having her discrepancies with some of the girls in the school and was getting tired of it. One day she had to leave her class early and pulled me from out of my mine to vent. For us to think we were getting away from nonsense when we left New York, all we did was run into new nonsense in Virginia. I was walking from one of my classes onto the next when a girl stood in front of the doorway to block my path.

"Excuse me,"

The girl ignored me and wouldn't move. "You're not going to move out the way?" I snidely asked her. She loudly snapped her gum between her teeth and retorted, "Nope, and what are you going to do? Move me?" I just gazed at her.

I hated to fight; other than not wanting to hurt anybody and getting into trouble, I was a narcissist. I thought I was too cute to fight and didn't want to jack up my face, but I had to realize that in this world, pretty or not, you literally have to fight for respect. I removed my strap bag from around my neck and sat it on the floor, so it would be easy access when I answered the girl's question by flinging her ass out of my way. She stood up straight and watched to see what I was about to do when a voice came from behind and I was pushed to the side.

"Look, you need to get your ass in class and let her go in and do her work. She don't need no shit from you, Tanisha, so leave her alone before I'll have to kick your ass, again!" The other students guffawed.

"Oh please Natari, so now you want to be *mother-hen* to these young bitches since you keep flunking grades?" Natari shoved her and the professor got in between to stop things from escalating. "Ladies, that's enough! Get into class!"

Soon after that, we heard a bunch of ruckus coming from down the hall and students were running from their classes to see what was going on. Me and Natari ran down there and I had to bum rush people out of the way to catch the scene. All I could see were two girls on top of another girl rumbling with her, but I couldn't get a glimpse of her face. I looked around the crowd to see if I saw Alicia and couldn't find her.

"Nat, where's Leecy?"

"I don't know. She's probably in class." Something felt weird because it wasn't like Alicia to not catch up with us, especially during a big brawl. I pushed past some more people and saw that it was Alicia fighting with the girls. I rushed in between and tried to pull her out and Natari joined to help. The girl that I was about to get into it with a few minutes before decided to jump in my face and started fighting me. Natari ended up trying to pull both me and Alicia out of a fight with the help of other students. The more the fights kept going, the more the crowd grew.

The riot caused everyone who were surrounding us to topple to the floor. Some of the professors and campus guards were able to break us up. All six of us in total were sent to the Dean's office and were threatened with jail for our outrageous behavior. The only reason why Alicia and I got a *"get out of jail free"* card was because the girls we fought were known to cause problems with freshmen, but we did get a referral to the school's counselor for a penalty. Natari waited for us to be released from the office. She looked at us with our disheveled clothes and messed up hair and just shook her head. "I could see it now. It's going to be a long ass road for ya'll two heifers!"

***

It was mid-September and the weather was beautiful. There was a big annual celebration going on down in Alexandria. It was posted on the bulletin boards for months and half of the school was down there. The girls and I didn't have anything planned as we usually did, so we got in our cars and took the two hour drive down, joining everyone to see what all the hype was about. When we got there, it was crowded and the scenery was magnificent. There were different types of big balloons all over the place and the music was stimulating enough to make you want to climax. I was in awe as I toured around with the girls, looking at various paintings and sculptures, tasting all kinds of delectable food. I was enjoying myself so much; I was considering moving to this area after I graduated.

"She-She here, taste this," Alicia said, putting a strange looking piece of cake to my mouth, I tasted it and it was mouthwatering.

"Mmm, what is that?" The vendor said with a heavy country accent, "It's Jelly cake. Tastes good right?"

"Yeah it does." Natari came up next to me. "Yo, that shit right there is crack. I had like five pieces already."

Suddenly a loud noise boomed and we all looked on. Some of the guys from the *Alpha Phi Alpha* fraternity of our school started stepping and putting on a show. They looked incredible in their all black outfits and were doing their thing in the middle of the block. What really caught my attention was the dude that appeared to be the leader of the group. He was a cutie, tall and athletic, with the prettiest golden tan that went well with his chestnut brown eyes. Alicia, who was standing next to me, lightly elbowed me. I looked over at her and she seductively bit her bottom lip and raised her eyebrows as if to signal she too thought he was something delicious to eat. We both turned towards Natari who was standing on the opposite side of me and she was almost drooling. I draped my arm around her neck and whispered in her ear, "Wipe your mouth, Natari."

"Umph, I'd screw every one of them negroes all at once!" she purred. I giggled, but then stopped and studied her face, wondering if she was for real. After the show, the guys dispersed and another group took the lead. I didn't see that guy anymore, but I was sure I would come across him again on campus.

I took a break from the girls and went to the library to study for an upcoming algebra exam. I looked over my notes and was quickly getting bored. I was only using my notes as a refresher; in all reality I was damn near a genius at math and really didn't need to study at all. I packed my notes away and pulled out a book by author, Terry McMillan. I was so engrossed in my book that I didn't hear the group of guys that sat at the table across from me. When I looked up, there he was! The guy from the step show, sitting there with his crew and his eyes were fixed on me, I stared back and he smiled. I was so nervous I didn't know whether I should change tables or leave all together. I did the only thing that came to mind and got up to put back the Math book I had taken off the shelf. I walked around the library pretending I was looking for another book and glanced over to where the guy was sitting and he and his friends were gone. Even though I wouldn't have minded talking to him, I didn't have the balls to do it. I started back towards the table where my things were. When I turned the corner, standing face to face before me, was him!

"Hey, pretty lady!" he said. At first I didn't respond since he caught me off guard, but was able to utter, "Hey." He extended his hand.

"I'm Gary, what's your name?" I shook his hand.

"Shenelle."

"That's a pretty name," I gave him a half smile.

"Thanks." I trailed off to my table and he was right on my tail.

"So Shenelle, I want to get to know you. You want to go someplace to eat, so we could talk or would you rather stay here?" I had my back to him when I grinned in a Kool-Aid smile. He had the cutest southern accent. It had been a while since I was acquainted with a guy. I went on just a handful of dates after I broke up with my high school sweetheart, Caesar. I really wanted to get to know Gary, so I gathered my books into my strap bag and smiled at him.

"Sure, let's go!"

We went to a restaurant called "Jimmy's Grill" best known for barbecue food. I ordered a platter of barbecued Chicken and a ranch, cheddar, baked potato and he ordered the baby back ribs with sautéed Cajun shrimp and steak fries. "So, I could tell by your accent you're not originally from here. Where are you from?"

"New York!"

"Oh really! What part?" His eyes gleamed in approval. I noticed since living in Virginia that people outside of the city were intrigued whenever they found out a person was from the Big Apple. It would crack me up every time. Yes we had the luxury to shop from any ten grocery stores on one block and fast food joints, but little did they know; they weren't missing out on anything.

"I'm from the Bronx. What you know about that?"

"Not much, but I've heard of it and its craziness."

I chuckled. "Well the crazy part is definitely right. How long have you been living down here and are you from this area?"

"Yes Ma'am, born and raised right 'ere in Petersburg!" He took a quick swig of his soda.

"So you're a freshman, huh? What you think about being out here so far?" I blew out air in excitement.

"I love it here. I don't miss New York, not for one minute." He laughed.

"It's that bad, huh?"

"Umm hmm," He didn't talk anymore and just stared at me.

"What?"

"You are really beautiful. Have you ever thought of becoming a model, Shenelle?" I reminisced back to when I was younger. Family, friends and strangers would ask my parents about me modeling. My father's answer was always the same; he didn't want me involved in some worldly mess and I needed to stay focused in school. Even though I knew my big smile and high cheek bones could've won me an audition for the Pepsi commercial as a child, there was no way in hell I would've been able to stick to a celery and cracker eating diet. I shook my head to Gary's question.

"Nope, I like just being myself." He grinned at my confidence.

"I could surely agree with you on that, girl." We doggy bagged the remains of our meals. Since he paid for our food I decided to be generous and left ten dollars for the tip.

"You know you didn't have to do that, right?" I waved my hand off at his comment. "Yeah, but I didn't mind."

We dropped our bags off in his car and went for a walk, chatting and feeling each other out. It turned out that he was the head of the Phi Beta fraternity like I assumed and he was a junior, majoring in Teacher Education for Mathematics. I thought that was great, because that meant I possibly had someone who I could study with. Alicia and Natari hated math, but what I personally think they hated more was whenever we would quiz each other, I would blow them out of the water with my scores. No matter how many times I would ask them to team up with me to study, they would always shoot me down and I'd end up studying alone.

I made sure to keep all my answers to Gary's questions short and sweet. I didn't want to open up too much until I felt he was going to be somebody legit. He mentioned he saw how I was checking him out that day at the parade and I felt a twinge of embarrassment because I thought I'd given myself up too easily. I guess he saw the look on my face and decided to get personal. He expressed that he had asked one of the girls from the sorority team, who lived at my dorm to give me his number. I felt better instantly; happy to know he was interested in me. Gary was a pretty nice guy. He had a great personality and I was picturing myself with him, until the ignorant-male testosterone side of him kicked in. I noticed as we were walking, he kept licking his lips and peaking behind me.

"What do you keep looking behind me for?" I asked and he looked at me in a seductive manner.

"Nothing girl, it's just that you have a lot of junk in yo' trunk. You sure you're from New York because you got that Atlanta booty going on, and I'm fitting to sit a cup on it." I stopped walking, *oh, hell no he didn't!* He saying that brought out the Bronx in me.

"Listen, if you going to be a dog, then I really don't need to be talking to you!" The lustful expression on his face quickly changed to penitence. "Aw girl, I don't mean it like that. I just find you to be a sexy little momma that's all." I didn't say anything else to him and started walking faster ahead of him. I was frustrated; this dude done really killed the vibe as men always do, after the first fifteen minutes of a nice conversation. He grabbed my hand, stopping my pace.

"What is wrong, girl? Why you so uptight? You too pretty to be that way. You're not used to hearing compliments or something?" It wasn't that I was not used to hearing compliments because I was, but it just happened to be from all the wrong people and in senseless ways. I pulled my hand from his and crossed my arms against my chest.

"Gary, yes I am used to hearing compliments, but I'm just tired of hearing jackass compliments like the one you just gave me." He looked taken aback by my bold response and I knew I didn't have to say it that way, but that was who I was. I've always been a nice, mellow girl, but behind that I was also stern and I didn't plan on changing that for anyone. For all he could've known, it was a test. If he could accept me at my worst, then I wouldn't mind giving him my best.

"I hear you girl, I'm sorry. Please accept my apology." He leered. I looked into his pretty eyes, feeling myself getting drawn in and I realized then... I wanted him more than I thought.

"You good," I said casually and he chortled at my response.

"You really are something else Ms. Shenelle, but I like that. You're different." I didn't look at him when I replied; "I know I am." My whole life I was told I was different. At first I wasn't too sure what it really meant, so I would get offended, but eventually I grew to accept it because it made me unique and for those who didn't accept it, all well!

Just about every day after classes, I would meet up with Gary at the place we met, the library. We would study for about an hour and then get into conversations about some of the story books we've read and he would boast about his Marvel comic book collection. About math though, I had to give it up to the brother. He wasn't just good at it, he was skilled. I liked when we gave each other short quizzes at the end of our studies. It was always fun as we would playfully battle each other on our scores. The day of the exam I passed with the second highest grade. I was so thrilled and there was no one who I wanted to tell the good news to other than Gary. I ran straight to his dorm and told him about my grade. He humorously bowed down to me like I was his master. "Congratulations, girl! I already knew you would do it." I smiled at him.

"Yup, I'm glad you knew." He seductively sucked in his upper lip. I wrapped my arms around his neck and we engaged in a passionate kiss. I was really digging Gary and I hoped that our connection would grow into something worthwhile.

Chapter 9

I was in my bed taking a nap when I felt a pillow smack against my head. I woke up and saw Alicia standing over me. I looked at my alarm clock that was on the windowsill; it was after 4pm and I'd only been asleep for twenty minutes. "Leecy, what are you doing? Stop!" I said turning back over.

"Girl, wake up. I want you to come with me shopping. Get up!" I sucked my teeth, feeling groggy. "Alicia, I'm tired. Tell Natari to go with you." I was dog tired. I had broken night hanging out with Gary and got in mega late. Then had to turn around and get ready for classes, I wasn't in any mood to go anywhere. Alicia rolled her neck catching an attitude.

"Oh, so all of a sudden you too tired to hang with your girls now?"

"I know right! This hoe got herself a man now, so she done forgot about us. That's jacked up, Shenelle!" Natari interjected.

"I didn't forget about ya'll," I lashed.

Two months after Gary and I were dating, we made things official and started a relationship. From then on, I began spending excess time with him and less time with my girls. While Alicia and Natari went to see their families for thanksgiving break, I stayed behind and spent it with Gary and his family. Natari seemed all gravy with it, but Alicia was heated. She wanted me to be with her because she didn't want to have to deal with her obnoxious sisters alone. I understood her pain, but didn't see why I should set aside my plans to babysit her. After all, she was going to have her boo Rondell there with her and since I had someone as my boo, I wanted to be with him. I did feel a little bad that Alicia had to drive all the way back to the city by herself. I actually tried to convince her not to leave and to stay over with Natari and her grandmother since Gary's parents only lived a few blocks away from her, but she insisted on sticking to the tradition with her family and was anxious to get out there to see Rondell and I wasn't mad at her.

"Shenelle, seriously! You have been acting distant ever since you got with Gary and it's not right. Remember we have a pact. No man gets in between our friendship." When Alicia said that, I threw my covers back and hopped out of the bed.

"Alright look! Since you two want to whine and moan about me living my life, forget it! I'll call Gary up right now and break it off with him." I lifted up my pillow and grabbed my cellphone, dialing Gary's number. Alicia snatched the phone away from me.

"Shenelle, no! Why are you tripping? All we are saying is to not abandon us and start spending more time with us like you used to."

"Yeah Shenelle, that's all we're saying. Men come and go but we're going to always be your friends. Sisters before Misters, remember that?" Natari specified. I huffed and plopped down on my bed. I couldn't believe these chicks were riding my back. I swore if Alicia's boyfriend Rondell wasn't at another school and was on our campus, and Natari hadn't just broken up with her boyfriend; it would be a different story. I didn't want to be a sucker and give in just yet, so I reminded them about a part of the agreement they left out.

"Alicia, whatever happened to the other part of the pact? You get yours and I get mines and neither one of us are to try and stand in front of that! Do ya'll remember *that*?" Natari sucked her teeth and Alicia rolled her eyes and said sarcastically, "Yeah, we remember!"

"Alright then, so what are ya'll complaining for? I mean damn, I've only been with the man for five months. Can I catch a break, please?" They both just stood there staring at me, looking stupid. I went to my closet and pulled out a pair of *"Apple bottom"* Jeans, some undies and a shirt. I took out my towel and washcloth then stormed off to the bathroom to wash up.

I was still a little too drowsy to drive, so I rode with Alicia and Natari followed behind us in her car. They wanted to go on a spring shopping spree. I didn't need to buy anything. On my nineteenth birthday, Gary treated me to a romantic dinner and bought me more than enough clothes and a few pairs of shoes for the season. Natari and Alicia couldn't understand how I was able to get him to go that hard being I've only given him the booty twice, but what could I say? My New York stuff must've been magical.

I was bobbing my head and singing along with Alicia to Beyoncé's song, "Crazy in Love". We drove past the sticks and then through some neighborhood that looked like what had to be the ghetto part of VA. I've heard from relatives who lived in Virginia, you know, the *"other"* part of the family you only saw at reunions or funerals; they always said the hood wasn't much of a difference from the hood at any one of the five boroughs. Seeing from my own eyes it really didn't look that much different, maybe just an itty bit cleaner.

Our first stop was at *"Rainbow"* clothing store over in Richmond. For the first hour or so between *"Rainbow"* and *"Old Navy"*, I played the clothing critic role and helped them pick out what I thought were the best outfits for them. It started to get boring, so I called Gary and jonesed with him while the girls shopped away. I was in front of *"Nine West"* shoe store when I noticed some tall, crusty, scary looking, black guy with gold teeth staring at me. He looked like he was a broke ass bum, Richmond type. I told Gary and he instructed me to leave, so I went back into the *"Gap"* where the girls were. I started walking around, searching through the racks. Something told me to look behind me and there the man was again, grilling me, standing behind another rack pretending to be looking at clothing items.

"Boo, I think this guy is following me," I said to Gary. The guy started walking towards me and I was going to walk in the opposite direction, but I wanted to confront him. Before he got too close I yelled out, "Sir, why are you following me!" He was startled and looked at me as if I was crazy.

"Nothing sweetheart, I just wanted to see if I can talk to you."

"Talk to me about what?" Gary was on the other line asking what was going on, but I didn't respond to him. I waited for the guy to tell me what he wanted to talk to me about.

"Nothing important. I just wanted to know if you were single, I'd like to get to know you." Gary overheard what the man said and told me to tell him I was already taken.

"Um no. Sorry I already have a man," I walked away from him and he followed me again, grabbing my arm.

"Come on little lady, you can't knock it until you try it. I bet I can treat you better," I snatched my arm out of his hand.

"Get your damn hands off me and get the hell away from me!" I backed away from him and Gary was on the verge of hopping in his car to drive over my way, but I told him not to. I knew how to hold my own. The more I moved away from the man, the more he followed me. I saw one of the store clerks heading towards us, and then Natari and Alicia appeared.

"She-She, you aw'ight? What's going on?" Alicia asked.

"This man keeps following me."

"Aw, I'm not trying to scare the girl. I just wanted to talk to her," the man said innocently. Natari walked up close to him like she was about to pound his face in.

"You better leave her the fuck alone before I run a buck fifty on your ass!" I didn't see when she got it or where she got it from, but I spotted the switchblade she had in her right hand. Alicia quickly walked up next to her. "Natari, chill out! You don't need to be going to jail for this asshole. Sir, would you please get the hell on. My sister don't want to talk to you, she already has a man." The man wasn't trying to back down. He just stood there, staring angrily at Natari. The store clerk finally made his way over to us with his manager.

"Ladies, is there a problem here?" I explained the situation to him. They asked the man to leave and he started flipping off at the mouth to us. We cursed him out and snapped on his dingy clothes and the busted pair of sneakers he had on his feet. After the big scene at the store, the girls and I laughed at the whole ordeal, still talking a bunch of gibberish about that guy. I loved hanging with my girls. It was always live with them and I understood now when I wasn't around them why they felt like a big piece was missing. It was moments like these that showed me just how important I was to them and they were to me. When we got back to campus we ordered some Domino's pizza and partied all night in Alicia's dorm along with her roommate Hannah until we got tired.

***

Gary and I were sitting in his car hanging out. Things were going good between us and I could feel myself falling for him much quicker than I had planned to. He didn't appear to be like any of the knuckleheads that I came across back in the city, but then Momma didn't raise no fool and Poppa didn't school no dummy, so I didn't try to put anything past him.

"So, how was your week?"

"It was cool. I spent some time with the girls. I really missed hanging with them."

"But you haven't been away from them for that long."

"Yeah I know, but me and my girls, we're tight like glue, so we can't be separated from each other for too long." Gary smiled, knowing the meaning of friendship since he too rolled deep with his fraternity brothers.

"I understand that. It's good you and your friends are close. It's nothing like having friends who you can rely on."

"Yup! Those are my chicks for life," I grinned as I thought about my girls. They really were my true friends, but it was funny because, I'd been out with Gary for a few hours and neither one of them called to check on me as they usually did. They were probably just giving me my space after the way they were acting before.

"Since we're talking about friends, I would like for you to meet one of my close friends. He's on his way over." I looked at Gary in a weird way. It was after 10:30, so I didn't understand why I would be meeting any of his friends at that time of night. I thought I already knew all of his fraternity brothers and I also thought Gary had a lot more class than that.

"Who would that be? I thought I'd met all of your friends." He shook his head.

"You've never met this one. At least not through me, but don't worry, he's cool. You might like him." He grabbed my head and kissed me. Whenever I felt something strange was about to happen I would get this prickly feeling in my belly, I pulled away from him.

"Gary, who is this person that you want me to meet?"

"Don't worry about it, girl. Just kiss me," He pressed his lips with mine and put his hand up my shirt. He released one of my breasts and lightly bit down on it. My mind quickly converted from the mysterious friend Gary wanted to introduce me to and I started making out with him. He stopped and reclined the driver's seat, he tugged at his belt and exposed himself.

"You already know what to do," he said. I frowned at him, wondering who the hell he thought he was to be making demands on me like that.

"Excuse me?" He licked his lips and repeated himself.

"You already know what to do, Shenelle. Let's get it!" He grabbed the back of my neck and tried to force me down. I remembered experiencing a situation similar to this one and I violently snatched my head from his hand.

"Stop Gary! You know what?" I pulled the door handle to get out of the car, but it was locked. He had one of those child safety locks on and for the time I'd been with him, I never noticed it before. I immediately became nervous as I started to feel I had been set up. I was afraid, but I wasn't going to let him see it. "Gary, open this fucking door! Now!" I said in my most *"hood"* attitude, hoping to intimidate him back to reality.

"Or else what?" His face looked strange in a way I'd never seen before. My heart was beating violently against my chest. Next came was a knock at the passenger window. I turned around and the man who was following me when I was shopping with the girls was standing there. He waved, smiling mischievously at me.

"What the fuck! You knew this guy?" Gary also smiled a devious grin. "Yeah. I had him follow you. He's been following you since we've been together." I became confused and asked nervously, "For what?"

"Because I wanted to make sure you weren't fooling around on me, but see here's the thing. My friend here likes what he sees. I told him about all the goods you got going on and he wants to find out if it's true. I knew you wouldn't just willingly give it to him, so I arranged things." My mouth was hung open in shock. I couldn't believe what was happening. Gary seemed like a whole other person and not the same guy I was catching feelings for. He reached over and lightly pinched my cheek.

"Your friends aren't here to protect you, luv. So now what are going to do?" I hulked spit in his face.

"Fuck you! You stupid prick!"

He clenched his hands around my neck and was vigorously choking me. I punched and kicked him as hard and rough as I could. His friend opened the passenger door and dragged me out of the car across the ground. Gary held me down with his upper body and was trying to unbutton my jeans. He covered my mouth to muffle my screaming. I fought with them kicking the other guy in his face. I unrestrained myself from Gary's hold, kicked him in his chest and then took off running, running to exactly nowhere. I was riding in Gary's car instead of my own. Without a car in Virginia, it was impossible to go anywhere, so I was totally screwed. At night, it's so quiet you could hear crickets from miles away and miles away was how far I was from campus. I kept running and looked back to see the other guy chasing me. All I could do was run until I saw a house. It was dark, but I hoped and prayed that people were there and was just in bed asleep. I banged on the door.

"Help me! Somebody help me, please!" Nobody answered and I started crying, it seemed like everything I went through in my life was gradually repeating itself, no matter where I went to try to escape it. I couldn't understand it. I went in my pocket and retrieved my cellphone. I had just a little service signal and my battery life was down to one bar but steady enough to make a few calls. The first number I dialed was Alicia's. I was panting and shivering as the phone rang three times and I almost died when the automated voice picked up.

"I'm sorry… your service has been interrupted!" I screamed, kicking the door and then I really broke down,

asking God why this was happening to me. I heard a car drive by; the lights beamed and I heard Gary's voice from afar, "*Where she at?*"

I squeezed my eyes shut. I felt helpless. I knocked out one of the windows, and climbed into the house. I searched around for a phone; I found one sitting on an end table in the living room. I was relieved and had a little hope when I heard a dial tone. I called the police and stumbled over my words, quickly explaining the trouble I was in. The operator kept asking one hundred and one questions about where I was. I didn't know the exact location, I just knew that they needed to hurry up and rescue me before I was done for. I screamed when I heard a gunshot and the door was kicked open. I darted back to the broken window and sprang out. A piece of broken glass that was edged on the windowsill snagged across my leg breaking the skin and tearing my pants. I ran smack into Gary's friend, he laughed and grabbed me.

"Yo G, I got her man!" He punched me in the face and threw me to the ground. I wasn't one to give up a fight so easily when it came to my life, but I was on the verge. We tussled and I bit him on the ear, severing a chunk of his earlobe. Blood gushed and he shrieked, letting me go. I took off running again. I hadn't run that far from them when I saw a light. I sped up my pace then tripped on something and fell. Gary caught up to me. He turned me over and hit me with the butt of the gun; it felt like all of the arteries in my right eye exploded. He gun-butted me in the face again; I screamed in pain and tasted blood.

"Get on your fucking knees, bitch! And open your mouth!" I didn't oblige. His friend kicked me in my side and Gary pulled my hair, positioning my head off the ground. I could feel hair strands at the back of my neck ripping from its root. He put the gun at my temple. "I said open your mouth!"

His friend unbuckled his belt and started pulling his pants down. I felt the warm liquid of my urine flood the crotch of my pants and I cried. I still didn't part my lips, but I was giving up. I felt that my life was over as I saw flashes of my world come before me. Me hanging with my girls... the good times I shared with my family... the last encounter I had with my father... and my brother Jere. Tears fell drastically when I saw Jere's face. I knew if he'd been there that for sure those busters would've been handled and I would've been alright, but he wasn't and I felt alone. None of the people I loved was there to rescue me. They didn't even know what I was going through at that very moment. I used what I assumed was my last breath to say a silent prayer that if I died, I would go to heaven and have serenity for eternity. I felt a sting at my head and everything went black.

Chapter 10

I awoke and found myself neatly covered with a cotton sheet and woven blanket in a hospital bed. I looked around the room trying to gather my vision through one eye; my other eye was patched up. I didn't see anyone, but then I felt a hand touch my arm and Alicia's face appeared. "Shenelle, thank God you're awake." Her voice sounded as though she'd been asleep. She laid her head on my chest and silently cried.

"You scared me, Sis. You scared all of us." My face felt heavy and there was a lot of compression on my head. My jaw hurt as I moved my mouth and I felt stitches on my inflamed bottom lip. "What happened to me?"

Alicia wiped her eyes with her sleeve. "You were beaten up by that bitch ass boyfriend of yours and his crazy friend, but you're gonna be okay. He won't ever hurt you again." I saw flashbacks of the scene and the fear I felt that night shook me. I remembered everything.

"Did they rape me?"

"No, they were going to, but the cops showed up before they could get that far. They were caught red-handed and the cops arrested them. They had ecstasy pills on them too." I was on edge and was eager to hear more.

"How did the cops know where to find me?" Alicia kept wiping her teary eyes; she was so devastated at my condition, she barely kept it together as she spoke.

"Their unit traced your call back to the house you called from. By the time they got there you were already unconscious." I touched my head and felt the gauze that had been wrapped around it. "Don't touch it, Shenelle! You're good. You only have ten stitches on your forehead and your face is a little swollen and bruised, but you'll live and get back to your regular self soon." I liked how Alicia subtly tried to make my appearance not sound so horrible, but I could feel for myself that my face was far worse.

"Where's Natari?"

"She's at the police station. I told her to go down there to identify those guys and explain to the detectives who they were, while I stayed here with you. I tried calling you last night to check on you to see if you were alright, but your service was disconnected. I didn't think that far into it, so I didn't panic and just let you do your thing." Tears welled in her eyes again. "I'm so sorry, Sis. I didn't know," She cried and made me cry. I played in her hair to calm her.

"It's okay, Leecy. You couldn't have known. How did you even find out?"

"One of the nurses charged your cellphone and saw that I was the last person you called. We ran to you right away when they told us the news." Alicia grinned a little. "God looked out for you, girl, even the nurse acknowledged that. She said that you are blessed." She stroked my sore cheek. "I called Jeremiah; he jumped on the first flight down here and should be here soon." I sat up quickly, out of nervousness causing pain to spike through my body.

"You called Jere?" I buried my face in my hands. "Alicia, nooo!"

"Shenelle I had to, I didn't know how bad things were. I hardly knew if you were going to live or die. I had to let someone in your family know. At first I was going to call your mother, but I knew that you would definitely flip out. Jeremiah was my only option." I couldn't be mad at Alicia because she did the right thing. I was actually happy I was going to see my brother Jere. I just didn't want him to see my battered face; with that thought in mind, Natari walked in with Jere behind her. His face was distraught; right away my tears began to fall.

"Oh my god, Shenelle! You're alive baby, you're alive!" Natari hugged me tight as she cried. I hugged her back with my eyes glued to Jere's.

"Ladies, let me speak to Shenelle for a minute, please," Jere said. One by one the girls kissed me on the cheek, expressed their love for me and left my room. Jere sat down in the chair Alicia was sitting in. It was obvious he was pissed off and was trying to find the words to speak. He eyed all of my injuries, looking angrier.

"Shenelle, I'm only going to ask you one time. Who the fuck did this to you? I want their names, their addresses, I want everything." I wanted to cop a plea with Jere to leave the issue alone, but I knew it would be hard. Not he nor my entire family cared about what the law enforcement could do. When someone hurt a blood relative, we became blood-thirsty and that was the end of it. As soon as I was about to try to talk Jere out of making any retribution, he raised his voice.

"SHENELLE!!! Who did this you? You already know we have Fam down here. You should've called someone; you know Uncle Matthew and them would've killed those punks in a heartbeat!" I kept shaking my head no to Jere as he talked and wasn't even going to try and hear otherwise. I hadn't spoken to my father's brother and my cousins since I was a little girl. Picture me calling them all because I was in some drama.

"Jere, it doesn't make a difference now. The cops caught them; it's over for those guys. I thought Alicia told you everything."

"Alicia called me at one in the morning and said that something happened to you. She hadn't found out anything yet." I was contemplating if I should tell Jere that he was the last person I saw in my mind before I wound up in the hospital. I didn't know how it would've sounded or what he might've thought, but then I heard a little voice in my head say to tell him anyway.

"Jere, I wanna tell you something. Before I was knocked unconscious, your face was the last thing I saw. What do you think that means?"

Jere raised his eyebrows in surprise. He was quiet for a while; it looked like he was interrupted by his thoughts. Then he said, "You know, it's wild that you said that because right before Alicia called me, I was asleep and I was dreaming about you. My dream went from the time when mom and dad first brought you home, to when you were a toddler and then for some reason it went back to the day when you were eleven years old and I rolled up on you surrounded by those punks looking like they were about to do some slick shit to you. You remember that day, right?" I nodded my head and was wondering where he was going with the conversation.

"Well in the dream, all I could see was the scared look on your face and then out of nowhere, I could've sworn I heard you call my name as if you were in my house. I woke up and my phone was ringing; it was Alicia." He sighed and shook his head. "Shenelle, my cellphone was on silent. When I hung up from Alicia I was so bugged out that I checked to see if the sound was turned up. It wasn't and was still on silent. I don't know how the hell the phone was able to ring, but I didn't worry about it. I was just grateful someone was able to contact me." What I heard had me so stuck I don't think I even blinked my eyes as I listened to him speak.

"I prayed that you would be alright and I'm glad that you are. I love you, Sis, and I'm gonna always hold you down; you know this already. You're my baby sister and will be forever." Jere wiped his tears before they could fall and he hugged me. I couldn't even give him a proper hug back and could only imagine the expression I had on my face. It was apparent the nurse Alicia had spoken to was right, blessed was what I truly was and there was no doubt about it.

"While I'm down here, I'm gonna put you on my family plan with T-Mobile, so that way you can call me whenever." When Jere told me that I thought, *Good!* That

Sprint Company was worthless. "You ain't gotta worry about the bill, I'll keep it paid. You just make sure you stay away from these busters out here and focus on school. Ya heard?" He gave me that look, slightly lifting his chin, signaling for me to keep my head up. I dimly smiled.

"Got you!"

After a week spent in the hospital, I was able to go back to campus. My injuries were almost completely healed and I was nearly back to looking like myself again. Jere used my car while in town to drive me around. He stayed at a hotel for a few weeks in order to stand by me in court until the trial was over. The trial didn't last long since the cops who arrested Gary and his friend took the stand as witnesses. Also it turned out I wasn't the only girl they'd sexually assaulted. Once the word got around at school about what happened to me, a few other girls spoke up. One of them was a soror and stated she was drugged after a party one night and Gary, along with other guys from his fraternity gang raped her. She was so humiliated that she never told anyone until my story came out. The whole time while I testified about the dreadful experience, Gary looked pitiful and kept his head down.

The way his family felt, forget it! His mother damn near had a nervous breakdown and his father straight up walked out of the courtroom because he was so ashamed. It was just as emotional and nerve racking for me to have to relive the crisis and speak on it in front of people, but my brother Jere, Alicia and Natari gave me the courage to run it through. Both Gary and his friend, who I later found out was named Christopher Owens, were sentenced for eight to ten years without parole for sexual assault charges and possession of drugs. At the end of the day, I was able to walk out of the courthouse with the little bit of dignity that was left in me because justice was served. However, till this day I don't think I've ever forgiven them for what they did to me.

***

Once 2004 came in, I was like a walking time bomb; I didn't trust anybody. If I felt somebody looked at me wrong, I was ready for war. The humble, friendly, sweet girl I used to be was gone and my dark side had taken over. Almost everyone I loved and thought would love me in return had found their own little way to hurt and destroy me mentally and physically. I'd gotten to the point where I no longer wanted to be loved and wasn't even sure if I believed in love anymore. So to make sure that this word called *"love"* could never hurt me again, I kept my heart locked in an icebox. I was cold to everyone, that way no one could have the power to break me.

Ever since the assault and attempted rape incident, I'd been having nightmares of that horrific night and all the other bad things that had happened to me throughout the years. I couldn't sleep, my hair was falling out from stressing, and I was barely able to concentrate on my school work. My grade point average went from a 4.0 to a 2.5 and was decreasing as the semesters went by. I had to exert myself in the dependent study program in order to get my credits up and to keep my scholarship. Alicia insisted I go to counseling with the school's therapist, but I would go head to head with her about it as I often did with the teachers and everyone else.

The girls and I were in the library studying for our upcoming finals. I kept trying to focus on reading my textbook, but my mind would do its own thing and the pages would be reading me. "Sis, are you alright?" I heard Alicia say, but I was too stuck in a trance to answer her. "Shenelle!" she called a little louder. I broke myself from my daze and answered.

"Yes?"

"Are you okay?" She and Natari were staring at me, looking afraid and concerned.

"Yeah, why wouldn't I be?" I put my attention back on my textbook and started reading again.

"You're not okay; we could see it in your face," Natari said.

"I'm good, Nat. I just be in deep thought."

"What you be thinking about? You want to talk about it?" Alicia asked.

"No," I watched from the corner of my eye and listened on as Alicia and Natari whispered between each other. Because they were so close to me, they knew exactly what was rummaging through my brain and why I was coming off as such a big psycho.

"Ya'll do know I can hear ya'll, right?" I asked without looking at them.

"Shenelle, look at me!" I turned to Alicia. "What?"

"You're scaring us, girl. You need to talk to the counselor so you can get all of this negative stuff off your mind." There she went again with the damn psychotherapy talk.

"Alicia, please don't start that!"

"No! For real, Shenelle, I know what it is that's been making your ass cuckoo and I understand. I just don't want it to get to you too much, that's why I'm trying to get you to talk to a professional. You should at least do that, if you're not going to talk to us." I just stared at Alicia. I appreciated her concern, but she was bugging if she thought I was going to see a shrink. I wasn't that crazy.

"Shenelle, I hope the reason you don't want to get counseling isn't because you're embarrassed. You already know you're not the only one who's gonna be doing it. I'm still talking to a therapist and you should really see Dr. Taylor, she's good. I mean seriously, if it wasn't for her, I'd be in jail for committing murder right about now," said Natari.

If I believed I would appear crazy for talking to a therapist, truthfully I really shouldn't have because Natari's ass was off the hook. It was the dean who referred her to see a therapist; actually it was more like a command if she still wanted to attend school. First he suggested she take anger management and Natari failed that on the first day by almost getting into a fight with one of the girls in the group. I would be lying through my teeth if I said I hadn't seen a drastic change in her since she began having sessions with her therapist. The girls both stared at me, waiting for an answer. Alicia gave me a nod for me to look into it. I took some time to really think about it, and then I gave in.

"Alright, you bitches win! I'ma do it!" Alicia clapped all happy and Natari shouted, "Hallelujah!" I laughed.

"Yeah, whatever!" I didn't know what kind of miracle this therapist was going to work on me, but I hoped she would and quickly.

One Wednesday after classes, I went to meet with Dr. Taylor. I waited outside her office with these two girls and a guy. As I sat there, I observed all three of them. The girl I was sitting next to was spaced out and smiling as if she had some crazy game plan going on in her head. The other girl looked depressed, like she just lost her best friend and was about ready to hang it up at any moment, and the guy who appeared to be in the Goth club just looked straight up and down insane. From what it seemed, I wasn't the only one on campus going through hell in my life. Since I knew I was going to be waiting for a while, I did the next best thing and let my mind drift off into a world of random thoughts. Three hours later my name was called by a young Caucasian woman. I walked over to her and she introduced herself.

"Hello Ms. Patterson, my name is Dr. Taylor. It's very nice to meet you." I shook her hand while I kept a straight face, not bothering to reply to her greeting. I sat down in a cushion chair that was positioned in front of her and she took a seat behind her desk.

"So, Ms. Patterson. What made you come to my office today?" I quickly and dispassionately replied, "Problems."

"Well, what kind of problems?" I really didn't care to go down the list of everything that happened to me. I just knew that problems were what my life revolved around from the day I was brought to this earth.

"Ms. Patterson, I can't help you unless you tell me what's going on," Dr. Taylor calmly stated. Before I could let the words escape from my mouth about the sexual assault case and so on, my throat jammed up and I felt tears emerge. I jumped out of my seat and stormed out the door. I walked fast and was out of the building before Dr. Taylor could stop me. I got in my car and cried; I was all worked up over my issues and was on the verge of losing it. I needed more than a therapist to help me get over all that I went through, but the thing was I didn't know exactly what.

**

I felt bad for the way I acted in Dr. Taylor's office, so I used the card that Natari gave me and set up another appointment. I doubted if it would really change how I was feeling, but I went along with it, hoping something good would come out of it. When I got there, luckily I didn't have to wait. I walked into her office and greeted her in a more proper manner.

"Ms. Patterson, I'm glad you're here. Since we started off on a rough patch last week, let's try this again. What's going on? I didn't miss those tears in your eyes before you abruptly ran out, so something must be terribly wrong." I opened up to her and told her not exactly everything, but the things that particularly bothered me the most. I started with the story of my deranged, scorned mother, to my estranged father who chose the deadbeat road so he wouldn't have to deal with her. Then I talked about how I went from being involved with one asshole to being with the biggest asshole of all. I felt a little more comfortable with her when she didn't appear to look at me as the little lost black girl I knew I was. Although I could still feel that there was something else she was more concerned about.

"Ms. Patterson, I understand that you've gone through the worst of times, but have you ever thought of just letting it all go since it's rather old and in the past? Life may come in many shades, but it's up to you if you want to stay at the darkest area." I wanted to scream at the top of my lungs at her! If my problems were that easy for me to let go of, I wouldn't be sitting in her freaking office! I chose to be passive, yet a little sarcastic.

"Would it be that easy for you to let it all go if you were me?" Her face became somber and I gave her a cynical smile. I wasn't quite sure if she knew where I was going with my question, but I've always been nice at reading facial expressions and I think she did. For her to have her doctorate degree hanging on the wall right above her head to emphasize how educated she was. There was no way she could've been that far gone. She cleared her throat.

"Maybe you're right, Ms. Patterson. I guess it really isn't that easy to get over such traumatic experiences." I was beginning to think that she wouldn't be any help to me after all and I really didn't understand how she could've helped Natari.

"Dr. Taylor, I'm going to leave now. I have some studying to do." I noticed the rejected look on her face.

"Are you sure?"

"Yup!" I got up and walked to the door.

"Ms. Patterson,"

"Yes, Doc?" She looked at me with a caring facial expression.

"You know I may not have experienced what you went through and I could imagine the amount of pain it caused you, but that was then. Today is a different day, so why do you choose to remain so angry?" I looked at Dr. Taylor in her eyes and said, "Because when I was nice, in return I always got hurt." After that I was ghost.

For the rest of the year, I decided to keep having sessions with Dr. Taylor just so I could vent about other things. That became a total waste of time, because eventually she felt I had some major mental issues and suggested I take anti-depressants as a calming substance. I felt she had to be crazy if she thought I was going to take "brain" medication. I mean, I always knew that there was something wrong with me or if it wasn't me, for sure something was wrong. I ended up giving the pills a try just to see what it would do and how it would help relieve some of my stress. I was calm alright and that was because I was always strung the hell out. All the meds did was make me sleepy and feel queasy. I practically had to fight to stay up during class and I couldn't even study. As soon as my eyes would hit the paper, I would begin to doze off.

Everything was all bad! It started off with me not acting like myself when I was around my friends to literally not being myself. I dropped down from a size ten to a size eight in jeans and my grades were getting lower and lower. I got off those pills instantly and never wanted to see another therapist again. While I quickly gained my weight back, I kept myself busy by going to the gym. In the mornings before class, I would run laps on the track field, working off the stress and getting myself healthy. I was studying hard body and when I had some free time, I would read books of all genres. It all paid off nicely in the end too. My calves were more toned, my butt was firmer, and the abs in my mid-section was much more defined. I was praying a lot more for guidance and my prayers worked fast; my grades shot up way above average and I was looking to graduate from college on time. I was even feeling more confident about my problems as I came across many different urban novels about young women from the ghetto who reminded me of myself. Everything was going smoothly. I was finally at the place that I needed and wanted to be.

Chapter 11

"So Shenelle, are you coming with us?" Natari asked from sitting on the floor as I braided her hair. She and Alicia had been trying to convince me to go to this frat party all day and were talking about it for the past month. Since I'd been in a new peaceful place, I no longer found going to parties or events interesting. I wasn't even interested in meeting new people.

"I don't know, Natari. I really don't feel up to it."

"Girl, you never feel like having fun. Why would you not want to party? We're still mad young, single and sexy as hell. We ain't got no babies tying us down or no men trying to control our lives, so we might as well get it done and over with now." I shook my head at Natari's statement, although she was making a good point, I still wasn't with it. I felt I was in a better atmosphere when I was in my room reading a book about some fictional character's crazy life story and keeping my mind off my own. But to stop Natari from pressuring me I said, "I'll think about it." She smacked her lips.

"Please! Whatever, Shenelle. You know your bland boring ass ain't going nowhere." Because of her smart ass comment, I purposely braided Natari's hair tighter to where it pinched her scalp.

"OUCH!!! Trick, I told you not to braid my hair so tight like them Africans. I only want them so I could have crinkles when I get out the shower, damn!"

"Alright then, so stop getting smart!"

"Oh Shenelle, you just got to take things so personal do you?"

"Yeah and you know this, so I don't know why you keep trying me," I finished up the last braid on her head and walked towards the door. I felt Natari drape her arm gently around my neck, pulling me towards her.

"Girl, what is up with you? Why you acting like such a *Punta* with me? You know we're sisters and it ain't nothing, but love. So stop acting all white on me and Leesh. Man, even Hannah don't act like that." I removed Natari's arm from around me and giggled.

"What happened? I thought you didn't know Spanish, trick!" Natari grabbed her garments and towel from off her bed.

"Uh, correction booboo, I never said I didn't know Spanish. I said I didn't speak Spanish. Actually, to be exact, I said I don't speak that Shit!" She laughed and I joined her.

"Yeah, you're right. You did say exactly that."

"I know I did and find something to wear to the party tonight because you coming with us, point blank period!" Natari left the room before I could reply. I didn't know who she thought she was telling what to do because she knew I didn't play that and my mind was already set. I was not going to that frat party with them and that was point blank period.

***

The girls and I arrived at the party an hour after it started. As soon as we walked in heads turned; we all looked good and chicks hated on us hard. I was looking good in my black and white, elbow sleeve Coogi mini dress and a pair of white ankle band stilettos; I had my hair pulled up in a bun with a side swept bang. My huge gold, bamboo, heart shaped earrings were gleaming and my lip gloss was popping. Alicia wore a red, Baby Phat dress with red lace-up four inch sandals and her hair was in drop curls. She looked gorgeous. Natari, who seemed to make sure to always one-up us, got all hooched out. She had on black, cut off daisy duke jeans, a white, fishnet shirt showing off her black, diamond studded bustier bra. White fishnet stockings and six inch black knee high boots rounded out her outrageous outfit. I had to give my girl her props though; she looked hot to death and had those little preppy, white collar boys loosening their ties. The party was on and popping. The DJ was doing it up as he played all of the hottest hits by Keyshia Cole, G-Unit, Bobby Valentino and throwback jams from Shabba Ranks and Color Me Bad. Every song that played, the girls and I were singing, jumping and dancing to it and sweating our asses off.

I was really glad Alicia made me change my mind about going, but it was how she made me change my mind that was funny. She literally dragged me out of my room by my shirt, pushed me into the shower stall and turned the water on with my clothes still on and all. I was mad at her ass too and cursed her out terribly afterwards. She wasn't fazed one bit as she stood there with her arms folded across her chest, supervising me while I got dressed like a mother would do. Natari just laughed and I cursed her out too for letting Alicia do that to me. I didn't talk to Alicia the whole ride with her to the party, but just like how men would do after beefing with their boys, we all made up and were partying like rock stars together like it never happened.

After two bottles of Corona, and a couple of Jell-O shots, I was wasted and my head was spinning. I wasn't really torn up at the max, but I was nice and lit. I stood next to Alicia while she took a break from the little bit of dancing she did with other guys. She was trying to be a prude since her boyfriend Rondell proposed to her on Christmas the year before.

"Hey you, I see you were going hard tonight. *'Ms. I don't wanna party no more!'*" she teased and I blushed. I really did go hard. I danced with like ten different dudes and with a few girls too. I didn't care who I was jamming with; I was chilling and I deserved the moment.

"Where's hot ass Natari at?" I asked and she nodded her head towards my left. I looked and saw Natari grinding her behind to R. Kelly's song "Slow Wind" on one of the guys from the school's basketball team. They were all over each other so much they could've exchanged DNA through their sweat. I looked back at Alicia with a shocked gaze and she just rolled her eyes and shook her head. It was nothing unusual for Natari.

Alicia and I conversed for a while; we were pretty much danced out. We watched as the fraternity brothers and sorority sisters did their step dance routine. Their routine was hot; they really outdid themselves. I remember when I first entered college, I thought about joining a sorority, but I wasn't into the whole hazing each other and being confined to one clique. When the show was over, everybody was screaming and cheering some group of people. Alicia and I got up from our seats and ran over to the scene next to her roommate Hannah and Natari. These guys were dancing and grooving to the loud music. I bobbed my head and bounced my shoulders getting into the vibe. Everybody was going wild at this one guy who was dancing his ass off, his bionic dance moves and black flips were so cinematic and so captivating that it made Usher look tasteless. I took a glimpse of the guy's face in the light, and honey was he *Goooorgeous!* Girls were ready to fight each other trying to take turns dancing with him. I kept telling myself over and over in my head to not start as I felt my hormones getting ready to stir out of control. Having so many trust issues with men caused me to almost never want to date again, but I also had needs. A part of me missed the companionship and being affectionate with a man. On the other end, all I would think about was getting my heart hurt again and the place where I was at in my life, I didn't need any disruptions. I sighed and laid my head onto Alicia's shoulder and just watched as the guy went from one girl on to the next, rubbing his pelvis on them.

"That's Darryl," I turned towards Natari who whispered to me.

"What?"

"That guy over there you're watching, his name is Darryl McLain." I frowned my face feeling a little uneasy, hoping she only knew his name.

"How do you know?"

"He doesn't live too far from my grandmother and he goes to our school. I'm surprised you haven't seen him before, but then again you be in and out of your zone, so it figures." I ignored her smart comment this time and asked, "You cool with him?" I stared at her intently while holding my breath. She rolled her eyes in a circle.

"No, I haven't screwed him, Shenelle, if that's what you're asking. He's in my Music and Art class. He's a quiet boy. He don't be lovey doveying around with these chicks over here. At least not from what I see. He's like you. He just be about his business and don't bother with too many people." I looked over at him, still drilling a hole into the dance floor. My stomach jumped when his eyes locked with mine. He did a full body scan of me and his eyes glistened like I was the most beautiful creature he'd ever seen in this world. He smiled and grabbed my hand, pulling me into the crowd. I nervously pulled away from him and scampered my behind right back with the girls. He stared at me funny because I turned him down.

"She-She, why you ain't dance with him? He is fine!" Alicia excitedly shouted.

"I know right? She fronting, but it's okay; let her ass miss out! Shit, I'll dance with him for you, girl," Natari said. I snapped at her with an attitude for chastising me.

"Yeah I bet you would! Go ahead and dance with him then, I'm not gonna stop you!"

"Aw'ight bet! Here, hold my purse." I took her bag and watched as she strutted her way toward Darryl, breaking in between him and another girl. The girl looked like she wanted to smack Natari, but walked off and danced with another guy. Missy Elliot's song "Work It" blasted through the surround sound system and they both started gyrating their bodies on each other to the music. They were killing it and I felt a little twinge of jealousy at how she was grabbing all up on him. I kind of felt like she was doing it on purpose. I watched them all the way to the end of the song. When it got to the part where Missy sang *"Give you some-some-some of this cinnabun!"* Natari backed her ass up and wiggled onto his groin like he was a stripper pole and I was done.

I was so heated I wanted to leave and go back to my dorm. I asked Alicia to give me a ride to campus because I had a headache. Knowing me inside and out, she already knew it was a cop out and that I only wanted to leave because I was pissed off at Natari. She told me not to worry about her because there was no competition between she and I, but that was the least of my worries. I never allowed myself to fall into that category with my girls. In my eyes, we were all pretty in our own nature and sisters beyond the matter. Alicia wasn't ready to go yet and didn't want to just leave Natari hanging. I wished I had driven my own car, but I knew I was going to be drinking like a mad woman at the party so I didn't bother. I rode back with Alicia's roommate Hannah who wasn't much of a drinker, but a heavy smoker. The girl had nicotine fits and smoked so much you'd think she was on death row. When I got back to campus, I bought a bag of cheez-It crackers from the vending machine and just crashed in my room. My mind went back to the glimpse of Darryl's face. The club was mostly dark with red, blue and yellow beams flashing from a strobe light. From what I could remember, he was very attractive; dark skinned and different. I started to think that since I had no plans on ever becoming a nun, maybe I should just go for someone different and retire from light skinned men, since my luck with them went in vain.

***

I was on MySpace chatting with my brother Jere from my laptop when I heard a knock at my door. It was two in the morning and the whole branch was empty because everybody was either at the frat party or elsewhere. I couldn't see who would be knocking at that time of night and I knew it wasn't Natari because she had her key, so I didn't move. The person seemed to not want to give up. After three more knocks I got up and asked who it was and the silly individual answered, "Special delivery!" *Special delivery? What the hell!* I opened the door and froze when I recognized it was Darryl. He smiled, holding up a brand new bottle of Tylenol.

"A little birdie told me you might need this." I smiled and shook my head knowing that this set up was all by Alicia. I just stood there for a minute still shocked and taken aback by the smell of his Versace cologne. We looked into each other's eyes. The moment was awkward and neither one of us knew what to do or say. Darryl was the one who came up with the nerve to speak.

"Um, here. This is for you," He handed me the box of pills.

"Thank you!"

"You're welcome," I wanted to let him in, but that would've been going too far.

"So, does your head feel a little better?"

"Yes, I took something earlier," I lied right through my teeth, knowing damn well I faked the whole thing.

"Good," he smiled again. *Umph,* he was fi-uh-uh-uh-inne! He looked even more appealing up close than he did in the club. His brown, chinky eyes were exquisite with long thick eyelashes most girls would kill for. They were so dark and curly that if I'd been mentally challenged I would've thought he wore mascara. His teeth were perfect and white and I loved how they contrasted to his chocolaty skin when he smiled; it reminded me of an Oreo, my favorite cookie. Because of his chiseled features, Darryl was far past the true definition of gorgeous. The man was pretty, an exotic master piece from God.

"Well, now you have something extra just in case you need it later. You should really get some sleep." I bit my upper lip to hide my smile. Darryl's voice was sexy and it made him even sexier. Unbeknownst to him, he could've talked my ear off and I would've gracefully picked it up to listen to his sultry, baritone voice all night long.

"Thanks for delivering my package," I flirted, and he chuckled showing off his pearly whites.

"No problem, Ma. Goodnight!"

"Goodnight!" I closed the door and stood there with my back against it cheesing. Going by how Darryl spoke, I could tell there was no way in hell he was from Virginia. I knew he had to be a New Yorker and his swag made it more obvious. I flipped open the top of the box to take out the bottle of pills and I felt a tingle whiz through my body when I saw his number written in blue ink underneath it. It read *"Call me anytime."* my breath was stolen; I was so much in awe that I slid down the door to the floor. I done got the man's number without even trying. Instead of wanting to go out and look for my ideal guy, I asked God in prayer to send me a man that was sexy, sweet and respectful and I think this was his calling.

I didn't call Darryl right away, I wanted to give myself more time to worry about me before I worried about getting to know some guy, and I didn't want to seem vulnerable. It was spring break and the girls and I were spending our time off at Natari's grandmother's house. Natari was right about her grandmother; she was tough as nails, but when talking to her she was pretty cool and overall appeared loving. I chilled out in the guest room that I shared with Alicia and watched TV, while she and Natari went out shopping for bathing suits for the beach down at the Hampton Roads. I didn't go with them because they took too damn long to decide on what they wanted to buy, even when they were only going to purchase one or two things and it drove me out of my mind. I already had a bathing suit that I bought three years back. Since I was still able to fit into it, I didn't care to waste money buying another one. I still had a decent amount of cash left in the bank that my dad gave me and was trying to save it for after I graduated. Surprisingly twenty minutes later, Alicia walked in the room all enthused.

"Hey you, we're about to go down to the beach. Here I bought you something." She handed me a bag from Beverly Boutique clothing store. I went into the bag and was appalled when I pulled out two pieces of barely visible material.

"Alicia, what the hell is this?"

"What does it look like girl, it's a bikini. Try it on. I want to see what it looks like on you."

"Girl, you are crazy if you think I'm squeezing my big ass in this!" Alicia scrunched up her face in offense.

"Big?" Not only did Alicia and I resemble each other in the face, we also had the same body type. We both were voluptuously, curvy girls and were far from big. We weren't no thin pretzel sticks, but we weren't a cheeseburger away from being fat either. The difference between she and I was my high, peach shaped butt. It made my pant size a size bigger than hers and way too big to be rocking a size six bikini.

"Alicia, I was talking about my ass. I'm not wearing that bikini."

"Oh She-She, cut it! Your shape is bomb girl and you know that. You'll go down there and have them VA boys thinking you're Buffie, the body."

"Yeah and they'll think you're Esther Baxter."

"I know right!" We both laughed then Alicia suddenly stopped.

"What happened?" I asked and she smiled.

"I'm happy you're back, She-She. I missed you," I playfully patted her on her face.

"I've missed you too girl and don't worry, I'm back and I 'ma stay this way." She tightly hugged me. She went into another bag and pulled out another bathing suit.

"Here, I knew you wouldn't wear a bikini, so I bought you this," She handed me a sexy one piece gold bathing suit that was cut out on the sides and in the front enough to show off my cleavage and pierced belly button. It was way more erotic than the boring Speedo I had. Looking at it, I thought about my parents and how they would have thrown the swimsuit into a blazing flame before they would let me walk outside in something like that, not caring whether I was grown or not.

"Now this is what I'm talking about right here! Thanks, Leecy. What are you going to do with the bikini?"

"It's Natari's. I brought the bag up for her while she went to the store for her grandmother." I rolled my eyes.

"Oh, I should've known." I pulled out the other bathing suit that was in the bag. It was a cute hot pink bikini with diamond buds that lined the header top and the bottoms. Out of my five favorite colors, pink was one I liked most. I looked up at Alicia cheesing impishly.

"Uh-uh, girl. You can't have that!" She quickly snatched the bikini out of my hand before I could even get used to the touch. We playfully fought over it. I loved my bestie Alicia; sometimes I didn't know what I would do without her.

***

The beach was jammed packed and skin was out everywhere. I already thought the bathing suits the girls and I had on were slutty, but compared to other girls there, we were barely passable. We were able to find a comfortable, shaded area over by the bay. I laid my humongous towel down on the pretty white sand and stretched out across it. The sun was beaming, but because of the water, there was a nice breeze. Natari smothered her body in suntan lotion like she wanted to wrap herself around a rotisserie rod and roast.

"Shenelle, here put some on," she said handing me the lotion and I looked at her like she was retarded.

"Uh, how much blacker do you think I need to be?" The sun had already transformed my soft brown skin, giving it a burnt orange undertone. Instead of looking like the mocha queen I've always been, I looked like the second kin to Ernie from Sesame Street.

"Girl, don't you know, *the blacker the berry, the sweeter the juice*," she declared licking her lips in a seductive manner.

"Well trust me my juice is sweet enough, thank you." Natari waved her hand at me and put the lotion back in her beach tote. Alicia turned on the radio and Reggae blasted through it. She hopped up from her towel and started swaying her hips.

"Oww, this is my jam ya'll!" Natari and I were laughing at her and I even peeped a few fine brothers watching her. I looked at her left hand and noticed she wasn't wearing her engagement ring. "Alicia, you're over here shaking your tail-feather when you know you're someone's fiancée. Where your ring at?" She kept dancing.

"I got it! It's in my bag. I took it off, so I wouldn't lose it when I get in the water." I cooled it understanding her comeback. The last thing I needed was to hear her fiancé's mouth, asking why she took off her ring.

"Please, it ain't like he's here and he ain't the boss of her, so she can do whatever she wants," Natari added. I kept my mouth shut on that one because Natari didn't know Rondell. He was mad overprotective of Alicia and whether he was present or not, he probably had eyes everywhere through other people. Since the day we stepped foot on campus, he had been calling Alicia off the hook, trying to keep track on her. It had gotten so bad to the point where whenever Alicia was hanging out, she would keep her phone off. The guys who were scoping out Alicia made their way over to us. One of them asked Alicia if he could dance with her while the others tried to mack to me and Natari. Alicia and I turned them down; we looked at Natari as she lowered her sunglasses from her eyes and smiled.

"Naw, I'm cool," she said and the guys walked off. Natari, not quick to jump off with a dude and a handsome dude at that, something was up! We both looked at where her eyes were directed and my heart dropped to the pit of my stomach when I noticed she was eyeing Darryl. He was sitting on a beach chair ten feet away from us with some friends, shirtless and flawless. I rolled my eyes at Natari. She knew I secretly had the jones for him. She also knew all about how he came to our dorm that night to drop off the bottle of Tylenol with his number on it. She claimed she was happy for me. I caught the envious look that appeared on her face right after I told her, so I took her claim with a grain of salt.

I splashed around and frolicked in the clear blue water with the girls and a couple of guys who joined us for a few hours. Then we went and grabbed some Philly cheese steaks and frozen lemonade from the food bar and just relaxed. I looked around the beach searching for Darryl, but I couldn't find him. I figured he must've left, so I thought I would finally give him a call when I got back to campus.

"So She-She, when do you plan on calling that boy?" Alicia asked, raising her eyebrows and grinning. Before I could answer her, Natari put her two cents in. "Never because her scary ass is too shy!" I loved Natari and all, but sometimes she really got on my nerves when she felt the need to always answer for me when nobody asked her to.

"Damn, Natari! She wasn't talking to you! She was talking to me and I can speak for myself!"

"Excuse me? Who do you think you yelling at like that? Check yourself!" She snapped back at me.

"No, you check yourself and mind your business!" She and I started going back and forth.

"Alright you two! STOP!!!" Alicia yelled. We both got quiet and then I threw in the last word. "She needs to learn how to speak when she's spoken to!"

"Uh-oh ya'll, look who's coming this way," Alicia sang. We all looked and Darryl was striding towards us. *I thought he left!* I watched Natari from the corner of my eye. The whole time while we were sitting she had her towel wrapped around her torso, now all of a sudden she wanted to remove it and stretch out across it, profiling herself. I looked over at Alicia and she rolled her eyes, annoyed too at Natari's flaunts. Darryl walked up in front of us.

"Hey Mama, why haven't you called me?" he asked, sounding all sexy. Then of course, Natari had to open her mouth. "Because you ain't give your number. Why you ain't called me? I gave you mine," She flirted.

"Yeah sorry about that, shawty, I've been busy lately. Actually I was talking to Shenelle." Natari's face dropped. Alicia busted out laughing and even I had to cover my mouth and laugh. He played her ass lovely and I felt the victory, Alicia laughed until tears fell. Natari got up, not wanting to seduce Darryl anymore.

"You know what? Screw ya'll! I'm going back in the water. Leesh, you coming with me?" Alicia was still laughing. "Yeah I'm right behind you. Later, ya'll!"

Darryl waited until the girls were gone and he sat down on my towel next to me. I took a glimpse at his feet. A man could be a fine piece of art, but if he had ugly teeth, hands or feet, he didn't pass in my book. Darryl had the prettiest feet I've ever seen on a man. They didn't look crusty with ugly toenails like how some men's feet looked. His toenails were clean and they still looked masculine. I didn't notice he was staring at me the whole time when I looked up at him and he was smiling at me.

"So, I see you're a foot person, huh?" I chuckled because I knew I was caught.

"It's Aw'ight; I'm a foot man myself. You got pretty feet." I was happy I did my toes in a cute design before I left the house.

"Thanks."

"You're welcome. So why haven't you called me? I was waiting." Did he really just say that he was waiting for me to call him? I'm not going to front, it was flattering, but I wasn't going to be so quick to fall for it. Alicia explained the day after we went to the frat party; Darryl walked up to her and asked her why I left the club. She told him everything, and then not thinking twice about it, gave him the location to my dorm. For all she knew, he could've been another psychopathic killer out to finish what Gary started two years back. Because Darryl was so sweet, I didn't bark on her and let her rock, but I reminded her never to do that again.

"I have just been busy, Darryl; taking care of things and studying."

"I feel you. You graduate in another year right?"

"Yes and I can't wait! I worked very hard. When do you graduate?"

"The same time as you." He looked away at some girl who was screaming, being chased by a guy smacking her butt with his towel. Let me tell you, not only did Darryl have a very handsome face, his body was magnificent. His arms were solid and cut, his calves were big and firm, and the abs in his stomach were so ripped, I could've played a whole game of tic tac toe on it. Darryl was just blessed all around.

"Do you think your friends would mind if I stole you away for a while?" Darryl might've seemed nice, but I didn't know him to trust him like that yet. Also I was still recovering from the tragic experience the last time I spent alone with a guy I thought was nice. My friends were still in recovery as well and weren't about to let me go but so far from them. I said as nicely as I could, "No Darryl, not today. Maybe some other time. Right now I rather just chill and hang with the girls."

"Aw'ight, no doubt! Well you have my number; whenever you want to talk or chill some time, holler at me."

"Okay."

"See you around, Shenelle. I hope to see more of you soon." I watched him stand up and walk away. Darryl appeared to have a pleasant and sincere attitude in wanting to know me better. I hoped I didn't make him feel rejected and lose interest in wanting to know me at all.

I was up early the next morning which was surprising because the girls and I got in the house at daybreak. I turned over and checked on Alicia who was in the bed next to me and she was out cold snoring like a thunderstorm. I got out of the bed and cracked the door open to Natari's room to check on her and she too was sound asleep. I went into the bathroom washed my face and brushed my teeth. It was nine in the morning and there was nothing to do. I didn't want to turn the TV on and wake Alicia. I smelled the scent of bacon in the air, so I went downstairs to the kitchen. Natari's grandmother was standing at the counter, adding sugar to a pitcher of iced tea when I walked in.

"Good morning, Ms. Willis." She jumped as if I startled her.

"Oh, Good morning, baby! Go on have a seat and fix you a plate." She had everything; bacon, sausages, eggs, pancakes, fresh sliced fruits. All of the breakfast foods you could think of was laid out nicely on the table. I sat down and grabbed one of the biscuits that were designed into a tower on a china dish and spread some grape jam on it. It had been years since I sunk my teeth in a homemade biscuit. I remembered back in the day when I used to spend the night at my grandparents' house. At breakfast time, my grandmother did the same thing with her biscuits; she would layer about twenty of those bad boys into a tower. Me and my brothers would pretend we were playing Jinga with them and watch as they would all fall onto the table. Grandpa would scream at us and threaten to get his belt if we didn't stop playing with his food. I giggled out loud at the memory. Natari's grandmother turned around from stirring something on the stove.

"You alright over there, Chile? What you laughing at? What's so funny?" I told her about the biscuit story and she laughed too. "I guess that's something all us old school grandmothers do. Our Mommas used to do it when we were younger, so that's where we get it from," she said in her very recognizable country accent. "Your Momma didn't place her biscuits for ya'll in the morning?"

I frowned at the thought of my mother. I could recall my mother getting fancy at times when she cooked. It was more so just to impress my father and get his attention than anything else. My mother was old school, but not that much. I responded to Ms. Willis by nodding my head to avoid talking about my family. "You know you shouldn't nod your head when someone asks you a question. Only donkeys nod their heads. I'm sure your grandparents have told you that. Right?" Nodding my head was an old habit that I had when I really didn't want to talk.

"Yes, Ma'am," I respectfully answered.

"I had to tell Natari about that all the time when she was a little girl." At the tail end of Ms. Willis's statement, Natari walked in the kitchen with Alicia, yawning and stretching behind her.

"Grandma, what you down here running your mouth to Shenelle about? I heard my name, so I know you were talking about me." Ms. Willis stopped what she was doing and said sternly, waving her wooden spoon, "Now you listen here, little girl! Don't be questioning me in my own house. Do you understand me?!" Alicia and I looked at each other grinning, just like little kids would do whenever someone got in trouble. Natari clucked her tongue.

"Aw Grandma, stop it. I was just joking, gosh! I swear you, and Shenelle should set a date for bingo night and hang out some time since ya'll two like to take things so personal." I paused as I was about to stick a forkful of eggs into my mouth and snarled at her. Alicia choked up her orange juice in laughter.

"I see ere' body steady eating, but I didn't hear anybody say grace," Ms. Willis said. She joined us at the table, placing a napkin on her lap. "Now ya'll sit your forks down and lets pray and thank God for our food." She blessed the food and we all dug in. I really missed chowing down on a good, home cooked meal. The school's cafeteria food had their foot-in moments, but nothing could beat the hands of a home-based chef with an old soul.

***

I called Jere to check in with him and let him know I was
enjoying my vacation and promised him on my next one, I
would visit. The last time I'd seen Jere was during
Christmas break the year before. I had been telling him I
was coming back up there ever since, but never made it.
The weather was muggy and it was raining outside, so the
girls and I just stayed in the house and camped out in
Natari's bedroom. We were munching down some hot
cheese popcorn and watching, *The Forty Year Old Virgin*
when I thought about Darryl. I recalled Natari saying he
didn't live too far from her grandmother and I wondered
what he was doing in this weather. I was thinking about
giving him a ring and chatting with him for a bit, but then I
didn't want to hear Alicia or Natari's mouth about cutting
into their time. Natari especially! It seemed that whenever
Darryl's name was even mentioned, she would get
aggravated and start acting all uptight. I figured I should
break the ice and discuss the matter with her. She and
Alicia were in the middle of laughing at the movie when I
interrupted.

"Hey, Nat? Why do you get so annoyed whenever Alicia
and I talk about Darryl?" Just when I said his name,
Natari's jolly face disappeared. Alicia, who was probably
wondering the same thing, looked in Natari's direction
waiting for a reply. Natari flared her nose.

"Shenelle, why does it matter?"

"Natari, tell me the truth. Did you have something going
on with him?"

"Why?" she said again a little louder.

"Because I want to know; if you had something going on with him then I won't talk to him." I never liked dealing with anybody's sloppy seconds, especially when it was a friend. I always felt it was too close to home, like sleeping with your sister's ex-boyfriend. As many men as there are in this world, I couldn't allow myself to stoop that low.

"Why not? What are you trying to say?" I noticed how Alicia stayed quiet as we talked. Usually she would stop us before things got heated, but she saw herself how Natari acted when any discussion of Darryl came up. She probably wanted to know the answer just as badly as I did.

"I'm not trying to say anything. I just don't wanna feel like I'm stabbing you in the back, that's all." Natari's face became a little calmer. She looked like she was thinking about what to say, or what bogus lie to come up with. She waved her hand as if everything was no big deal.

"No Shenelle, I've never had anything with him, nothing at all. I just thought he was cute and wanted to see what was up with him. I been wanted to hook up with Darryl, but every time I've tried to holler at him, he never seemed to wanna holler back. He obviously wants you and it's cool; I could see ya'll being a good couple." I smiled at her comment; it sounded genuine coming from her and it really made me feel good about our friendship when she spoke well of me. Then she quickly killed it when she thought to mention otherwise. "Plus, I'm not really into darker guys. Light skin is more my thing." My smile faded and the one that was on Alicia's face did just the same. We both looked at her and shook our heads.

"What? I'm just saying!" It killed me how some women just couldn't help themselves when they would hate on the next woman for having something they wanted and couldn't have. But what the hell, that was women for you. We are emotional creatures and when we hate, we hate!

Chapter 12

Mother's Day was on its way. Some of the students got together and had this big bake sale on campus. Others had their section set up where they were selling gifts and cards. I walked around looking at teddy bears with the custom made VSU apparel and sniffed different plants and flowers. There was one vase that was full of tulips; they were my mother's favorite. As I stared at them, it took me back to one Mother's Day when my brothers and I saved up our allowance and gathered it together. We went to the flower shop after school and bought my mother a big bouquet of colorful tulips and surprised her with them. That was the one time I could remember my mother being very happy. Her face glimmered when she looked at me and she kissed me lovingly on the cheek. When she did that, I thought the world was coming to an end.

"Are you thinking about buying those for your mom?" I smiled when I recognized the sexy voice behind me, but I kept my back toward him when I made my response.

"Hi, Darryl."

"Hey. Are you alright?"

"Yeah, I'm fine."

"So why aren't you looking at me?" Before I turned to face him, I wanted to get something straight, because sexy as hell or not, I wasn't about to get into the same predicament twice.

"Darryl, are you following me?"

"Naw, I'm not following you. I'm here walking around and looking at things like everyone else." I could hear a little bit of offense in his voice. My soft side wanted to believe him, but my hard side wasn't going let it go that easy.

"Are you sure?" He chuckled at my sassy nature. "Yeah girl, I'm a hundred percent sure." I told the girl behind the register to ring up the vase and turned to Darryl. He smiled and my heart melted.

"Now that's the face I like to see. You're much more beautiful from the front than you are from behind, Ma." I couldn't suppress the smile even if I wanted to. He knew just what to say to make a bitter woman blush.

"How are you doing?"

"I'm fine."

"You still haven't called me. I guess you're one of those women who like to keep a man waiting."

"Maybe, is that a bad thing?"

"No, it's not a bad thing at all." Darryl said, sounding all sensual.

"*AH-HEM!*" The girl behind the register cleared her throat loudly to interrupt our conversation. I looked at her and she felt the need to get sarcastic. "Do you feel like paying?" I flashed her a cold glare, signaling for her to slow her roll. I went into my pocketbook to take out some money.

"Don't worry about it, Shenelle." Darryl dug in his pocket, taking out his wallet and passed a twenty dollar bill to her. For whatever reason the girl sucked her teeth, grimacing like she had a problem. I thought, *damn, what is up with girls these days!*

"Keep the change for your trouble, Miss." Darryl told her, and we both walked off. I stopped at another vendor table and picked up three cards and two Teddy bears, one for my brother Jere's wife Lataya and the other for Natari's grandmother. I planned on shipping the tulips off to Alicia's mother since she was more of a mother to me than my own.

"You really didn't need to do that, Darryl. I had money." He shrugged off my comment.

"I know you're self-sufficient, girl. I'm just a nice type of guy. Trust me though, I don't do that for everybody." I smirked at his charisma. "So, where are you heading to now?" he asked. I was hoping he wouldn't ask me to go anywhere with him. The nervousness about going out with guys hadn't yet subsided and I didn't want to have to turn him down, again!

"Back to my dorm."

"Yeah, you're not going to chill outside in this nice weather?" The climate outside was beautiful, the sun was shining, the air was clear and there was barely a breeze. Usually when the weather was like that I would go for a walk along the shore and view other areas of the town or I would buy some fruit, sit under a tree and read a book or the latest celebrity tabloid. However, to keep him from coming up with any suggestions, I replied, "No, I have some things to do. I just wanted to pick up these gifts and get them out the way."

"I hear that. I already picked up some stuff for my moms. I shipped it out to her early." He gestured his head towards the bag of teddy bears I had in my hand.

"You and your moms must be close. I see you bought a lot of stuff." I sighed but wanted to laugh. If he only knew the real deal about me and my mother. I bet he would have snatched back his comment, shoved it in his mouth and swallowed it. We stopped in front of my dormitory.

"Darryl, I'm gonna to go. Thank you for walking me." He looked at me thrown. "You sure you're aw'ight?"

"Yes, I am. Why do you keep asking?" Before he spoke, he stared into my eyes for a moment.

"Every time I see you, you always seem so bothered. It's either your head is down like you're sad or you got a sour look on your face." I've heard many people tell me those same things, but the crazy thing was I never realized it before now. "Shenelle look, normally I don't be sweating girls like this, but I'd really like to get to know you. I didn't give you my number for no reason. Please, call me!" I batted my eyes at his persistence.

"I will. See you later, Darryl." I didn't hear footsteps as I turned to open the door, so I knew he was still standing there. I didn't know what it was about me that Darryl was so willing to get acquainted with but I knew one thing, his determination compelled me to consider getting acquainted with him.

For the past two days my mind hadn't been able to trail far from the last words Darryl said to me. I decided to finally call him and he was ecstatic to hear from me. We talked for about an hour with mild flirtation. He threatened to never speak to me again if I didn't go out with him for dinner. It made me laugh because I found it to be silly and I finally agreed to go out with him. I took a nice hot shower, lathering my body four times with citrus scented body wash. I wanted to make sure I was squeaky clean, smelling like a fruit basket. When I was done, I wiped the fog off the bathroom mirror and stared at my hair. I was due for a touch up on my honey blonde highlights. I hadn't been to the beauty parlor since the vacation with the girls and had my hair in a ponytail. I didn't know what to do with it and wasn't trying to go out on a date looking like plain Jane. I ran a blow dryer through it and flat ironed it. My hair had grown a lot and was much healthier since I'd been keeping up to par with it. My hair length was always past my shoulders, but it had grown even longer and suited my face nicely.

I went through my closet, not sure if I should wear a pair of jeans with a nice blouse or a curve hugging dress. I had seven outfits laid out on my bed, contemplating on what to put on. I chose to go for the black skinny jeans and a blue and white, flower patterned, off the shoulder blouse. I wore my white gold, one carat diamond studs that I got from my parents for my not-so-sweet sixteenth birthday. I slipped my feet into some white wedged sandals and I was good to go. I was thirty minutes late meeting Darryl at seven, trying to do myself up for him, so he came knocking at my door. I sprayed myself one last time with Victoria's Secret body mist, checked to see if my auburn lipstick was still neat, then grabbed my purse and opened the door. There he stood, looking incredible in a red and white Phat Farm shirt, blue *True Religion* jeans and red and white, high top uptowns. His face was freshly shaped up, his waves were spinning and the earrings that shone form his ears finished off his look perfectly. We both smiled when we saw each other. He scanned my body the same way he did when our eyes first met.

"Wow! You seriously are gorgeous, Shenelle! You look beautiful," he said it with so much passion in his voice that I couldn't even thank him. All I could do was blush.

"Come on, let's be out!" Even though he was wonderful and all that good stuff, I decided against riding in Darryl's car. I still didn't feel secure enough, so I chose to be the one to do the driving. My mother once said a lady should never chauffeur a man around in her car. The man ought to be the one driving and chauffeuring a woman around. After my traumatic experience being stuck without any means of transportation for my survival benefit, I was good and that phrase became lame. I didn't bother to explain anything to Darryl about why I refused to ride in his car and he didn't argue or question me about it. That showed me he had a sense of civility and it made me like him even more.

I didn't really care for dining anywhere fancy, so Darryl and I agreed on a regular burger shack. We ordered our meals and sat at a table on the outside of the restaurant and talked. "So girl, other than you being physically beautiful and feisty," he chuckled. "What else is there to know about you?" I made sure to swallow every bit of my burger, so I wouldn't spit anything out as I spoke and turn him off.

"I don't know. I guess it only depends on what more you want to know about me. What do you want to know?" Darryl looked at me with a straight face.

"I want to know everything. I want to know who Shenelle is inside and out." This dude couldn't be for real! *He wanted to know me inside and out?* I never heard that one before, so I asked, "What do you mean?"

"I mean I checked you out when we were at the frat party. You seemed mad nervous when I asked you to dance." I raised an eyebrow and corrected him.

"Actually you never asked me; you more like pulled me onto the dance floor." He almost gagged on his soda as he chortled. "Yeah you're right. You got me. I didn't ask, but you from New York though. I thought you would be used to that sort of thing. You know when you go out clubbing with your girls and a dude is dancing, if he see's someone he likes, he would grab her hand and make her join him."

"Yeah, they would do that."

"Okay, so I didn't really pull you, I more like guided you and you rejected me." I smiled looking away feeling guilty.

I knew he had felt rejected that night. The expression that was on his face told me that. So far I'd rejected him twice from the time when we were at the beach. It made me think; if I hadn't agreed to go out with him for dinner, that'd been my third strike and I probably would've blown my chances with him.

"Darryl, what if I didn't go out with you tonight, would you have really stopped talking to me?" I tested him and he shook his head.

"Naw, I would've kept trying to pursue you. But I knew that reverse psychology would work, it always does." Damn, that was a good answer.

"Darryl, why haven't I seen you on campus? Don't you live there?"

"Hell naw, I got my own spot off campus. I ain't into sharing a room with no dudes, I'm good!" This guy had mad swag, just how I liked it.

"I feel you on that," I said. He looked at me in a peculiar way.

"Why you ask anyway?" I knew what I was about to tell Darryl might sound strange to him, but it was for my own purpose.

"Darryl, I'm not going to lie to you; for a minute I thought you were following me around." I assumed that once I told him how I felt, he would get offended and end our date early. Instead he kindly replied, "I know, but why would you think that? I ain't no loony tune." I just liked how he added a little sarcasm!

"I wasn't trying to say you were, Darryl. You just never know who's crazy nowadays; that's all."

"True story, but that ain't me." He smiled, and then his face turned serious.

"I still want to know about you, Shenelle. What's really good with you? The party wasn't the first time I saw you. I've seen you around campus, coming and going with your friends. I've always wanted to talk to you, but whenever I saw you alone you just seemed antisocial and depressed. I wondered what was on your mind at times. So now I want to know; why do you seem so panicky and distant all the time? What are you afraid of?" I huffed, I wasn't sure if I wanted to engage in that kind of conversation with him yet.

"Darryl…" I softly said, but he cut me off.

"Shenelle, I'm not going to judge you, if that's what you're worried about." Darryl then took my left arm and began to roll up my sleeve. I tried to pull my arm away, but his grasp tightened.

"What are you doing?" I asked nervously.

"Stop," he whispered. I cringed as the pattern of old gashes on my wrist and forearm were exposed. He softly brushed his thumb against them.

"What happened to you, Ma? Why did you do this to yourself?" I swallowed hard. I couldn't think of anything to say. I didn't expect him to see my flaws this early, but then I remembered it was the same arm he took hold of for me to dance with him that night at the frat party. He must have seen my scars then. What amazed me was how he was so concerned when he hardly knew me.

"Why do you care? What does it matter to you what I've gone through in my life?" He gazed at me for a second.

"Because, I'm your man and I need to know these things." For a minute I thought my ears were playing tricks on me. I needed a little more clarity.

"Say what?"

"I want you to be my girl, Shenelle. I know this is soon, but I feel we should be together and get to know each other more as we move along. I want you to be mine's. You don't want to be mine's?" I wanted to scream to him, *hellll yeah!* But was too afraid. I was afraid I would get hurt again and before I would let myself get lured back into that experience, I rather to stay alone.

"Darryl, I don't know. Right now I'm at a place in my life where I am stress free and I'm happy this way. I've been hurt multiple times in the past and I don't want to get hurt again." Darryl had a look on his face like he empathized with me and understood where I was coming from.

"Shenelle, I'm not like the rest of the other guys, I'm different. I don't want this because I want to hurt you. I want this because I want you along with that," He placed his fingertip at my heart, his eyes never leaving mine. "You're going to let me have you along with your heart?" I still couldn't come up with the right answer to give him and I didn't want to tell him no. The more I thought about giving Darryl my heart, the more my heart ached all over again from past hurts and it scared me. For nearly two years, I hadn't dated a soul and wasn't thinking about it. Alicia tried to convince me to go out again. She reminded me that every man wasn't the same, but how did I know that? From what I saw in my twenty one years, starting with my father, my brother Timothy, and to the guys I've dated, all of their tendencies were the same. Once Darryl saw I was having a hard time answering him, he came up with a suggestion.

"I'll tell you what, let me show you what kind of man I am and then you let me know when you're ready for this. We're going to take things slow. Cool?" I let out a breath of air, thankful he didn't pressure me. I really did want give Darryl a chance, but I didn't feel ready for another relationship and the proposition he gave was fair enough.

"Cool!"

"You ready to go?" I looked at my cellphone; it was ten 0' clock and I saw that Alicia had texted me to see if I was okay. I needed to get home, so I could brag about my date to the girls and be able to wake up for class in the morning.

"Yeah I'm ready." He threw some money down from his wallet onto the table and we rose up out.

When we got back to campus, Darryl walked me to the door of my dorm to make sure I got in safely like a true gentlemen. "So, did you have a nice time tonight?" he asked. "Yes I did. Thank you for everything." He displayed his million dollar smile.

"Anytime!" I stood in front of the door and we stared at each other. I wanted to kiss his full, luscious lips, but I didn't want to make the first move and send him the wrong signal. Darryl licked his lips, grasped the sides of my face and kissed me on the forehead. Feeling the soft texture of his lips against my skin made my hormones immediately began raging. I backed against the door, making a light thump.

"Are you okay?" Darryl whispered as he rested his forehead onto mine and I nodded my head. He stroked his fingers through my hair, tickling my scalp and it made me shiver. He was so close I could feel the intensity of his body heat which was a beautiful feeling, but not helping my hormones slow down at all. Just as I was about to say something to him, the door opened and I went stumbling back, almost busting my behind. He grabbed me at my waist, catching me just in time. He was caught me so fast that it felt like I was Lois Lane and he was Superman. I turned around facing both Alicia and Natari.

"Oh, Shenelle! Ya'll back!" Alicia said. She leered at me.

"Did you guys have fun?"

"Yes. We had a great time!" I replied. She looked at Darryl with a straight face.

"Darryl, you better not ever hurt my girl. This is my best friend, my sister, my twin, my life line and when she's hurt, I'm hurt." Darryl listened as Alicia tackled him with her speech and he didn't seem bothered by it. If anything, the look he had on his face said he understood.

"Not to talk crazy or anything like that, but if she gets hurt, you're going to have to deal with me!"

"The both of us! And I promise you it won't be pretty," Natari said.

"I'm all over it ladies, don't worry. Your girl is safe with me." He looked dead at me when he said that. Alicia and Natari replied in unison, "Good!"

I laughed. "Goodnight, Darryl. Thanks again for everything. I'll call you tomorrow." He too chuckled.

"Aw'ight, Goodnight." I saw him out the door and closed it. I looked back at my girls who had big Kool-Aid smiles on their faces. We all got excited, jumping around like little girls and I went straight to talking telling them about my night.

***

Things between Darryl and I started off as slow as needed and as Darryl promised. I didn't see him every day, but at least three times in the week. I spoke to him on the phone day in and day out and it was always fun. Sometimes we would flirt, at other times we would tell each other jokes and talk about casual stuff and whatnot. We found out we had a lot in common. One of his favorite colors was black, which was my number one favorite. We both were die hard Usher fans and music addicts. We had the same taste in food, liked the same movies, and shared the same political views. We were both raised as Christians and had some of the same opinions when it came to religion. He was also very romantic and was just too cute with his little ways. I caught a nasty cold and he spoiled me rotten by *special* delivering red roses to my dorm and bringing me soup, orange juice and all kinds of cold medicines. He even fed me soup and didn't seem to care that I looked like the possessed, green mouth girl from *"The Exorcist"*. Darryl was just unbelievable and different he certainly was.

After three months hanging together, I still hadn't told him my life story. He respected my pace and remained laid back, allowing me to take my time. We did basically everything together; we went to the library and studied together, had private picnics, date nights, went to festivals. Every time he would show off his smooth groove, dance moves at parties, I would be standing right there blessing him and he always acknowledged me. One time at a house party, after he'd made the girls go wild from his performance, all those heifers were in his face like they were expecting bare chest autographs and the whole nine. Brushing them off, he walked over to me and lifted me in the air, planting a long, passionate kiss for everyone to see. It was actually our very first kiss. I felt like a queen as the haters strolled away and the players cheered us on. Darryl was like my new best friend and everybody knew I was his girl, or so they thought since he and I hadn't really made it official yet. He had the biggest, most tender heart I thought a man could ever possess in this world.

Very soon I ended up unlocking my own heart, setting it free to him against my will of trying not to. I swore to myself I would never break his heart because he'd proven himself too good for that. In a very short time, Darryl showed me such a wonderful side of being in a real relationship and what it felt like to be appreciated. He made me feel special. Next thing, I found myself fighting with my emotions trying to convince myself I didn't love him yet, but I did care for him and was falling harder for him by the day. I held enough strength to never admit that to him, but did everything a good woman could do to show Darryl I appreciated his companionship just as much as he did mine.

Chapter 13

I was just getting out of the shower one evening when my phone rang. It was Darryl. He sounded all hyped, asking me to meet him outside. "Meet you outside, for what? Darryl, I just got in from the gym and already showered. Now I'd like to relax," I whined. "Come on, girl! Get dressed and come outside. I want you to go with me somewhere, so hurry up!" Before I could say anything else, the phone call ended. I took my sweet time getting dressed and headed out to see what this silly boy was up to. When I got outside, Darryl was leaning against a cherry red Lexus convertible. He looked sexilicious in a brown flight jacket, forest green wife beater, faded black jean shorts, and beef and broccoli Timberlands.

"Oh, so you think you fly now that you got a new whip?" I teased and he laughed. "Damn right and you going to be fly too," I looked at him confused.

"What do you mean?"

Darryl walked up to me and wrapped his muscular arms around my waist. "Look, I know that we haven't made things official yet, but you represent me and whatever I got represents you." I smiled and laid my head on his chest. He was really killing me softly with these Casanova lines of his. Darryl planted a big wet kiss on my forehead, his signature mark, and patted me on the butt.

"Now get in!" I got in the passenger side of the car and fastened my seatbelt. I was at a good state with Darryl where I trusted riding with him in his car. The car had that fresh smell I loved and the black interior with the I-Pod stereo set was beautiful. I ran my finger across the dashboard and not a speck of dust was lifted.

"Darryl, where did you get the money to buy this car and what did you do with the old one?" He looked at me like I had no business asking him that question.

"What are you worrying about it for?" I smiled at him biting my bottom lip deliberately taking a while to answer him.

"Because, I'm your woman and I need to know these things." Darryl's face lit up when I said that. He cheesed, flashing his perfect set of teeth.

"You're serious?"

"I've never been more serious in this lifetime," I replied seductively. Darryl licked his lips. "Come here, girl!" He lightly pulled my chin towards him and slipped his tongue in my mouth. We kissed passionately. I loved that his lips were so soft and I savored the moment. I was used to only receiving the pecks he'd given me on the forehead and cheek. It was the second time we'd kissed like that and my body quivered as bodily fluid seeped from every single pore my flesh owned. I've never felt that way with any male not even my first love and it felt like paradise. He pulled away and my body was frozen in place. I thought I was paralyzed. Darryl looked at me in a worried kind of way.

"You aw'ight?"

"Yeah, I'm good!" I sat back up straight playing everything off. He shook his head chuckling.

"Now, hold on to your seat, baby. I drive type fast!" I snickered to myself as we pulled off. He pressed play on his IPod and Usher's song "You make me wanna" blasted through the speakers. Darryl knew exactly what he was doing to me and where he had me. He knew it very well.

Darryl pulled into a driveway of a small town house up on High street and unlocked the doors. "Darryl, where are we?" He took a quick glance at me when he answered, "We're at my crib." He hopped out of the driver's side and walked over to my side, opening the door and he grabbed my hand.

"Aww, what a gentleman!" He playfully rolled his eyes.

"Yeah, yeah!" I followed him to the front door, he turned his key and we walked in. I looked around and it looked like a typical bachelor's pad. He had a black leather sectional recliner; a small coffee table with a bunch of video girl magazines stacked on top of it, a big screen TV with the surround sound system and a black, wooden square table with four matching chairs. The kitchen was a decent size and separated from the living room by an island lined with three high chairs. I admired how neat his place was. For a young guy, Darryl was very well organized and clean. I found it all very attractive.

"You got a nice spot here, Dee!"

"Thanks, but you ain't seen nothing yet. Come with me, but you gotta take off your shoes though." I took my K-Swiss sneakers off and walked into a room with him. Dude flicked on the light switch and the whole room turned red, I chortled at his decadent style.

"Oh okay, I guess Usher's new song "Red light" has really gotten to your head, huh?"

"Hell yeah, that song is fire!" The room was nice and big with a Mahogany, king size, platform bedroom set, a resting bench that obviously came with it and two night stands. He had a black leather recliner and of course another big screen TV. I loved how the plush carpet felt between my toes. He took me upstairs where there was a pool hall rec room. I playfully tapped his shoulder.

"Look at you, boy! Let me find out you a baller."

He laughed. "Naw, don't get it twisted. My parents paid for all this. I just foot the bills, Sweetness." My face dropped when he said that. "What?" he asked. It was funny that Darryl called me Sweetness, a name I hadn't heard in a while. That was the pet name my father used to call me, the very man who footed all the bills in our household. I shook off the memory.

"Nothing!" Darryl's forehead creased. He took my hand and pulled me closer to him, looking into my eyes.

"Naw, something is wrong. Was it something I said?"

"Nothing's wrong. It's just that you are really lucky to have both your parents by your side." He sighed, giving me a hug and kissing my forehead again.

"Don't get caught up on the hype, baby." He squeezed my hands kissing them too. "We're gonna talk, as soon as you get comfortable and settled in and don't worry, I won't call you "sweetness" no more!" He lightly pinched my chin and walked downstairs towards the kitchen. I raised my eyebrows in astonishment, *how the heck did he catch on to that?* Could it have been that the connection Darryl and I had was that deep already?

***

Music was playing from Darryl's stereo system in the living room as we sat and ate Chinese take-out. "So, I'm ready to hear your story, Shenelle. What's the deal?" He had this serious look on his face showing he was really interested in finding out about me. I procrastinated for so long telling Darryl my story, but as time passed, I came to realize he truly was a genuine man I felt I could reveal my secrets to. When I began to tell him my story, I became nervous as usual, so I tried to be slick and ease myself off that topic.

"Who is that girl in the picture with you and your parents?" I asked, gesturing my head towards the picture frame that was sitting in the corner of his entertainment center. I first noticed it when I surveyed his place. It was a photo of Darryl and a girl in their teenage years. The glimmer in her eyes was all too recognizable.

He smirked at my question and replied, "She's a friend of the family. Stop venturing off the subject. Why do you do that whenever the topic is about your life?"

"Darryl, I get nervous. I don't talk about my life to people," I shyly admitted. His response was profound.

"I'm not people. I'm me and you're talking to me right now. Where are your parents, Shenelle? Why don't you like talking about your family?"

He stared into my eyes and I stared back. It was the mere fact he didn't want to know my business just to judge me that encouraged me to tell my story. It seemed as though he actually cared and that made my nervousness lessen some, yet even still, I had to say to him before I told him anything, "Don't judge me!"

"Don't worry about it! I won't." I took a deep breath and let loose everything from A to Z leaving nothing out. As I talked, Darryl's face was inviting and it made me feel comfortable as I carried on. The more he wanted to know, the more I told him things, things even my parents didn't know. He knew about my ordeal with the sexual assault which wasn't surprising since everyone at school knew about it. The surprising part was when he claimed he didn't know the victim was me. Once I was done reading my life book out loud to Darryl, the look on his face was priceless. You would've thought I'd told him the campfire story from hell. He didn't say anything for a long time and I almost thought I'd made a mistake telling him the storm and rain of my horrid story.

"Do you look at me differently now?" Darryl shook his head and said kindly, "Everybody has a story, Shenelle, some are worse than others. You're not the only one." I smiled at his appeasing comment.

"So what about you? What's the hype I shouldn't get caught up on?"

"Well, you already know I'm a Harlem cat. My parents were married for ten years, and then got divorced. Both of them are remarried. My moms married this buster who I hated, but he eventually grew on me. They have a son together, my baby brother Dante. My Pops married a young Japanese chick. She's cool and seems to make him happy as far as I know. I have a pretty good relationship with my parents and step-parents." Darryl got along with not two parents but four parents, lucky him.

"I used to do a bunch of stupid shit when I was younger. I stayed getting into trouble, selling, and getting high, but I straightened up once I was sent to Juvenile detention. When I was released, I stopped bullshitting and got on my grind. I graduated from high school with good grades and then came here to VSU and that's my story. Now enough about the past. It's whack!" He picked up the dirty dishes to put them in the dish washer.

"Um, you left out two things."

"What's that?"

"You forgot to tell me what you did with your silver Honda and where you got the money to buy the Lexus." He bit his top lip to suppress his smile at my good memory.

"You're right! I did forget. I sold my old car to someone I know and my father put some money into my account, so I combined the dough and bought a new whip." Darryl got up from the sofa and went to the kitchen. He came back to the living room.

"Shenelle, do you like music by Pretty Ricky?"

"Of course!" He popped in a CD and the song "Grind With Me" began to play. I smirked, wondering what game he thought he was playing.

"What made you want to choose that song?" He shrugged. "No specific reason, I just like the lyrics. You can't knock me for that, can you?" I couldn't lie; it was a sexy song.

"Stand up, Shenelle." I stood up in front of him.

"What?"

"Let me see you dance."

"What you wanna see me dance for?" I said, twisting my face. I didn't expect that one.

"You saw me dance, so now I want to see you dance."

"Oh, boy!" I laughed.

"Shenelle, stop acting shy while you're around me. I told you, Ma. It's me, so do you and dance for your man." Just because I liked the way he said it, I started swaying my hips and moving my body to the rhythm of the music as I was staring at him. He put his finger up and I stopped dancing, looking at him funny again.

"One thing you're doing wrong is you keep watching me. Don't worry about me, just do you and bust a move. Focus on you not me." He restarted the song. I began dancing and getting into my groove as if I was in the room alone. I was so much in dance mode I hadn't even realized that Darryl wasn't watching me anymore. I felt his arm wrap around my waste from behind me and he gyrated with me.

"You got good rhythm, girl. See what happens when you do you and not worry about anybody else?" I smiled and turned facing him. I wrapped my arms around his neck. He kissed me slow and long and I danced my tongue with his. He stopped for a second only to lead me to the bedroom.

***

"Oooh, girl. Look at you! You are glowing!" Alicia said when I walked into her dorm room. She and Natari were stretched out comfy on her twin bed and Hannah was sitting at the computer desk. She broke her concentration from typing up a paper to look at me. "What nonsense are you talking about, Leecy?" I asked, squeezing in between her and Natari.

"Girl, don't even try to front like you ain't head sprung for Darryl, your sexy, chunk of chocolate boyfriend," Hannah said.

"She knows she's glowing. He be tearing it up and got her saying, *ooooweee!*" said Natari. We all laughed.

"Ya'll bugged out!" I looked over at the empty bed where Alicia's other roommate slept. She was a Spanish girl who

I only met one time and for whatever reason, she was always missing in action. If I happened to run across her, she was either running out early or walking in late and she would never say a word.

"Hey Leecy, where does your other roommate be at? She's hardly ever here." Hannah sucked her teeth and rolled her eyes as if she didn't really care for the girl and Alicia chimed, "Please, ain't nobody worrying about that chick! She obviously feels she's too good to hang with us. She's always on the go."

"Yeah, she doesn't talk to us, so we don't talk to her. She just be all about her boyfriend who's on the football team and nobody else," Hannah said. I glanced over at the girl's bulletin board that was by her bed. She had at least fifty pictures of her and her man all huddled up.

"And don't you even start that mess up again, Shenelle. You know how you can get, you get a man and next thing we know, we won't see you no more," Natari said.

"Mmmhmm, right!" Alicia hummed. I rolled my eyes to the back of my head beginning to feel agitated.

"Look, we already had this discussion before ladies, so cut it!"

"So Shenelle, let us know, how is he? You're not glowing for nothing," Hannah asked. I looked at them and all their eyes were glued on me. I frowned.

"How about *Nunya* cause I'm not getting into that."

Alicia smacked her lips. "What do you mean? We you're girls. Don't be acting brand new and hiding stuff from us!" As an adult, discussing about how I got down in bed with my significant other was something I didn't do. I always felt it was best for a woman to keep her friends' imagination clear from any sexual visions in regard to her man, because it disables them from getting any ideas.

"For real! Unless he's whack and you have no comment," said Natari. I hopped off the bed to remove myself from the girls' scolding, but made one last statement to tickle their fancy.

"Negative sweetie, like Hannah said. This glow ain't for nothing and that's all I' ma say!" I heard the girls go wild as I walked out the door and I laughed shaking my head.

Chapter 14

As I looked into her angry face, she was screaming horrible things at me. I would sit there quietly while the tears streamed. I didn't do anything. I was just in my room, minding my own business when she walked in bringing up crazy stuff because she couldn't keep her mind off the old baggage. The name calling, the hits and smacks to my face came repeatedly and she dared me to do something about it. I would be in bigger trouble if I fought back. During the whole time, I wanted to scream out and tell her she was going to die a sad lonely woman. The hate in my heart would sky rocket every time I saw her face and I wanted to get away from her. "Do you hear me talking to you, bitch?" she yelled. I didn't answer her, so she walked up to me, snatched me by my shirt and shook me vigorously and she kept shaking me... Until my eyes opened up and saw Darryl.

"Babe, are you alright? You kept twisting and turning," The light in the room was on and he had a worried look on his face. I sat up and felt my silk teddy sticking to my skin from perspiration. Before I met Darryl, I hadn't had recurring nightmares for a while. I thought after a year had gone by without them, I was free from them, but out of the blue they just came back. Darryl and I stared at each other. He wiped the sweat from my forehead and kissed it. Since we'd been together, I was staying at his place from time to time. There weren't many times I experienced a nightmare while I was with Darryl. The few times I did experience one, I was glad he was always knocked sleep. I didn't want him to see me tripping like that.

"What time is it?" I didn't even think to look at the cable box on top of the television when he looked over at it.

"It's two in the morning." I hadn't been asleep that long; it was a good thing it was the weekend and I didn't have classes in the morning. I went to the bathroom and when I looked into the mirror, my eyes were droopy and I was starting to develop bags underneath them. I threw some cold water on my face to bring down some of the tension from my nightmare. When I walked in the bedroom, Darryl was sitting on the edge of the bed.

"Do you feel better now?" I got back in the bed and lied down.

"Yes, it was just a nightmare, Darryl; nothing to worry about." He just looked at me, too concerned to drop the issue.

"Of course I'm worried, girl. You're not sleeping well." I liked when something was awkward with me, how it mattered to Darryl. In this world, it isn't easy to find a man who cared about his woman like that.

"I'll be okay," I said as I felt my eyes getting sleepy.

"You will?" he asked and I nodded for him to let it go. I knew Darryl wasn't feeling too good about my condition because it wasn't something he was used to seeing. Although I was sure he had an idea of where my nightmares stemmed from. He moved back to his side of the bed, leaned over and kissed me. "You are going to be alright." He turned off the lamp on my nightstand. He took my waist and pulled me closer to him. I nestled my head in his neck and fell back to sleep.

When I woke up Darryl wasn't in the bed, which was odd because it was the afternoon. Usually he would sleep in since he was off on weekends from his job at the Coca Cola factory. I got up and looked out the window to see if his car was in the driveway; it wasn't there. I took a quick shower and threw on some clothes to run around in. I called Darryl and got his voicemail, so I called Alicia. I figured since the boyfriend thought it was necessary to start the day without me I should continue my day without him. As soon as Alicia's sleepy voice picked up the phone, I heard Darryl's car pull into the driveway. I abruptly cancelled the call to Alicia, telling her to go back to sleep and that I would get with her later. I wanted to question Darryl when he walked through the door. I sat on the couch waiting for him and he came in with bags from a Café.

"Hey sexy, I'm surprised you're up." He sounded jolly like nothing was wrong. Even though I originally planned on hitting him with my interrogation process, I kept quiet. I didn't want to jump to assumptions and end up feeling stupid afterwards. He looked puzzled as he sat the bags down on the island and walked over to me. "What's wrong, babe?" I just looked at him.

For me to ask him where he had been after watching him bring in restaurant carry-out bags would be the ultimate dumb question of the day, but then I didn't understand why he would leave without letting me know.

"Why didn't you let me know you were leaving this morning? I was worried," I made sure my tone was unflappable, I didn't want to give the impression I was being demanding. He shrugged like I was worrying over nothing.

"I wasn't gonna wake you up just to let you know that I was stepping out. I only went to get us something to eat. I was coming right back." His answer sounded truthful, but then why was his phone off when I called? Instead of asking him that, I knocked out the thought and figured it was probably really nothing.

"Okay cool." I got up and walked over to the island where the bags were and started taking out the food. He stopped me by gently taking my wrists and turned me to him.

"What?"

"You don't believe me do you?" He looked at me with puppy dog eyes like he was in his feelings. I huffed and released myself from his hands.

"Darryl, I would tell you if I didn't believe you."

"I don't know that?" he replied. I smirked and said sarcastically, "Well sweetheart; that just goes to show you really don't know me as well as you think, now do you?" He stepped back as I brushed passed him, I didn't have an appetite anymore. His reaction made me wonder if the Café was all he went to.

"Shenelle, what is the problem?" He slightly raised his voice. Believe it or not, I was turned the hell on. I always loved a man who could stand his ground with his woman, still I didn't back down.

"I don't know, Darryl. What is the problem? I said that everything was cool, but you kept on going, so tell me. What are you hiding and stop playing mind games with me."

"Mind games?" He looked at me like I was tripping. I was getting aggravated; I hated Ring Around the Rosie arguments.

"Yes mind games! You know what Darryl, since you want to play dumb, I'm just going to come out and ask. Why was your phone off when I called you and where did you go besides the Café?" He rolled his eyes and chuckled which ticked me off even more because I didn't find anything amusing.

"Shenelle, I only went to the Café like I said and as for my phone, go in the room and you'll see it." He turned his back to me and headed towards the island. I walked into the room to see Darryl's cellphone hooked to the charger on top of his nightstand. I don't know how I could've missed it, but it wasn't like I was searching throughout the room looking for it either. I felt beyond stupid, but if he would've just left things alone it wouldn't have gone any further. I went back into the living room where Darryl was eating his food. I joined him at the table and fixed a plate.

"So, do you trust me now or would it take a little more time?"

"Darryl, would you please drop it. I never said that I didn't trust you." He smiled giving me butterflies and I began to blush.

"What do you want to do today, babe?" he asked.

"I don't know. We'll figure it out after we eat." We sat and ate quietly with nothing more to say.

***

Stoney Creek fun center was where we settled on; I was having a great time, feeling like I was back in my childhood. Darryl and I ran around playing laser tag like big kids and roller skating in the rink. Roller skating was one of the things I really missed doing. I was the bomb at it and still had some of my moves. I showed Darryl all of my wild moves and teased him because he could barely keep his balance. We took turns playing games at the arcade, tallying each other's scores, determining who the biggest loser was. We did a little rock wall climbing and shared a funnel cake. We were walking hand in hand through the park. I smiled as we walked passed a couple who looked happy with their young children trailing along.

"Do you want kids someday, Shenelle?" Darryl asked and my guess was he saw me smiling at the happy family.

"Yes of course. Who doesn't want children?"

"I don't, I hate kids!" My heart literally jumped and I stopped walking "You're kidding, right?" I said halfway frightened. He busted out laughing and said lightly squeezing my hand, "Yeah baby, I'm just messing with you. I would love to have kids one day and watch them run around, tearing up the house."

He laughed again. "Wow girl, you almost lost your head there." I laughed along with him. I almost lost my head was right, as gorgeous as Darryl was and the connection we had. It would've been a shame if we couldn't continue as an item because he didn't want something I wanted in the future. After all of the family issues I undergone, it was important I someday have a family of my own and create what I didn't always have, happiness. Darryl kissed the back of my hand.

"Don't worry, Mama. Maybe it'll happen with us when the time is right." That was all that could really be said. Whatever nature had in store would be revealed in due time.

It was dark when we got home. We had done a couple of other things after the arcade. We caught a movie, ate dinner at an Italian restaurant, and picked up some groceries for the house. I was the first one to get to the door. I was beat and wanted to wash off the day's activity and get comfortable. When I opened the door I saw an envelope on the floor that was apparently slid under. I picked up the sealed envelope and it had Mr. McLain written on it in cursive. I looked back at Darryl who was unloading the trunk. I held the front door open, waving the envelope in front of his face.

"You've got mail, *Mr. McLain*," I said jokingly taking the bags from him and gave him the note. I watched him rip it open while I was putting the groceries away. I tried to read the expression on his face to figure out what the letter might be about, but I got nothing. He smirked tearing the letter up into pieces and threw it in the trash can. I didn't know whether to find the whole thing strange or just look past it, but my curiosity compelled me to inquire.

"What was that about?" He turned away from me, focusing on putting the plastic bags from the groceries into the storage closet for reusing.

"Oh it was nothing babe, just one of my boys from around the way talking about some dance- off party he was throwing next weekend." *A dance- off party,* the Darryl I knew loved to party and damn sure loved to dance. I found it strange for him to brush something like that off.

"Why did you rip up the note? You don't want to go?" He barely made eye contact with me when he answered.

"Naw babe, I don't care about that party. I got the weekends reserved for you, remember?" There I went blushing again.

"Aw sweetie, you can go if you want to go. I won't be mad." He wrapped his arms around my waist and looked into my eyes.

"No Shenelle, seriously I don't want to go to the party I'm not worried about it. I got you now and that's all I care about." He kissed me passionately and took my breath away, but I was able to utter out, "Are you sure?" He nodded.

"Yes baby, I'm sure." His hands moved from the nape of my behind and he grabbed my solid cheeks. I left well enough alone, smiling alluringly at him and skipped off to the bathroom to run the bath water.

***

Sunday evening Darryl and I stayed home. We were stretched out comfortably on the bed, eating Ramen noodles and watching *Coming to America,* one of our favorite movies. "Babe, do you like seeing me dance?" I asked Darryl and he gave a naughty sneer. "You know I do, girl." I sat my bowl down.

"Alright, well I'm about to put on a show for you right now." We were at the part in the movie where the African dancers were performing. I got up and started dancing making a half ass demonstration of them. Darryl burst out in laughter.

"You are silly, Ma."

"Boy, you already know, but what? You didn't think I could do the dance?"

"Naw, you good!" He laughed and I playfully punched him on the shoulder.

"Shut up! Why don't you teach me then, Mr. *Dancing Machine*?" He blew air from his mouth.

"Chill, you going to need an African dancing machine for that," We laughed again.

"It's aw'ight though, sexy. I don't expect you to know how to do everything." I beamed up clinging to his every word.

"I know you don't. You don't expect me to be anybody, but me." He winked at me.

"Come over here, girl. Bring those pretty lips to me." I straddled his lap and obliged his demand without hesitation. To say that I was in love with Darryl would be too simple, our bond was strong. I loved our relationship; Darryl never judged me and loved me for who I was without trying to change me. Our relationship was more than just mutual affection; it was a friendship. Whenever he laughed, it was always with me and never at me and when we would have our fun together, it was grand. I laughed as Darryl started mimicking the voice of the king's assistant when prince Hakeem was meeting his selected bride.

"Oh no, Boo, stop singing and keep dancing." He chortled at my remark.

"That's one of my favorite parts of the movie," I moved from his lap and put my attention back to the film. I peeked over at Darryl and thought about telling him what I had been rehearsing in my mind for the past month. I wanted to tell him I loved him, but my pride wouldn't let me. I felt I was too good to tell a man I loved him first before he told me. I would think, what if I do tell him and he doesn't respond or his response wouldn't be what I expected. After two minutes of thinking it through, I decided not to tell him anything and rolled the ball into his court. I thought I should be easy and just let life run its course and in time if Darryl really did love me, it'll eventually be expressed.

Chapter 15

"Hey, She-She," Alicia said when I opened the door to my dorm. She didn't look too good and I sensed that something was wrong. She slowly walked to my bed and sat down and I nervously sat next to her, not knowing what to expect. I was hoping to God nothing bad had happened to her while I was at Darryl's over the weekend.

"Leecy, what's wrong?" She suddenly burst into tears and my heart nearly burst right behind it. She continued to cry and the water fall of my own tears fluxed too. For the length of time that Alicia and I had been friends, I've known her to be an emotional person, but between her and me, she was always the stronger one. Alicia knew how to steady her emotions way better than I did, so to see her cry, not only did it hurt me, it disturbed my peace to the core.

"I'm pregnant and I don't know what to do. My parents said if I messed up in school that I was on my own," she panicked and I felt for her.

It was common for parents to tell their children if they were to have a baby without establishing a proper life, their lives would fail and they would have to deal with the responsibilities on their own. Every parent has used that line in hopes of instilling fear in their children, so they won't make that mistake. While many young people have made that mistake anyway and their parents reneged on their rule, every situation was different... different people, different parents. In Alicia's case, she was pretty much the golden apple in her family. Because her sisters disappointed their parents in many ways, her parents depended on her to be the one to succeed and were always adamant she stay on the right path. I didn't have to ask Alicia whose child it was because I knew her fiancé Rondell was the father. For the past couple month's he had been driving down on weekends to visit her. Although Alicia was grown, it bothered me that she wasn't being careful; at VSU if a student got pregnant, she would have to be discharged from campus. That meant if Alicia was going to have to leave then I was going to leave with her. Not that I would have been alone on campus because I had Natari, so it wasn't that. Alicia and I came on this college journey as a duo and there was nothing in this world that could interfere with my commitment to her. I draped my arm around her neck.

"Leecy, don't worry. We only have eight more months before we graduate then we'll be out of here. Do you know how far along you are?"

"No, I only missed my period for a month, so I shouldn't be that far." I looked at the time on my cell phone to see if it was still early enough to try and catch the school's medical clinic.

"Look, it's not six 0'clock yet. Why don't we go to the medical center and see what they say." I took the initiative and drove her to the clinic, all the while silently praying that her situation wouldn't be a bad turning point for her when she told her parents.

Alicia was nine weeks into her pregnancy. She considered getting an abortion, but I told her since she was engaged to be married it wouldn't make any sense. I thought what purpose would it have served for her to have such a burden on her heart or her conscious when she was on her way out of school? When she called Rondell and told him the news; he was happy and ready to transfer from his school as soon as possible. Alicia's mother was disappointed and her father was angry, but their loving hearts caused them to want to work something out with her. They helped her make the arrangements to move into an apartment off campus, so she could still be able to stay in school. That played out well because she was still close to the campus and two blocks away from Darryl's townhouse, so for me to see her whenever I wanted to was no trouble. Rondell was transferred from John Jay College to VSU and moved in with her, so he could be with her around the clock until it was time for the baby to be born. They cancelled their plans of having a traditional wedding ceremony and got married at a courthouse.

Everything worked out perfectly with Alicia. I was happy my prayers were answered and things didn't turn sour for her and screw up her life. Things on campus concerning Natari were still the same and she thought it was necessary to call me and Alicia flat leavers. Since Alicia was wifed up, I was always with Darryl and Hannah had her sweet thang named Nicholas, it caused Natari to feel excluded. She was single and by herself most of the time. I told her she needed to cut all the bull crap though because I was still rooming with her three days out of the week, so she wasn't totally left out. But then God, being the great man he is did another great thing. Me, Alicia, Natari and Hannah were eating at a diner one day and this fine light skinned brother named Shawn walked up to her. They ended up getting together and Natari's lonesome days withered away. Life was becoming so sweet; I had a good man, good friends, and good grades. If anyone was to ask me, I had the whole package and I couldn't have asked for anything better.

***

Darryl and I was having a moon light picnic by the lake. We cuddled, while music was playing from his car. My head rested on his chest as we lay atop the blanket we spread across the grass. I watched as the ducks swirled around in the lake under the glimmer of the bright full moon. The scenery was extraordinary, like nothing I had ever experienced.

"It's so much better living out here than the big city, right?" Darryl asked.

"Yes, I could really see myself doing big things out here,"

"Yeah, what could you see yourself doing?" After all the time I spent with Darryl, I was able to express my dreams to him without acting bashful.

"Well, I would like to build a community based foundation for young girls who have gone through the same challenges in their lives like I have... family issues, sexual abuse, depression, all those type of things. I want to give them a home away from their home, where they could be able to break free from the closed in walls of their mistreatment without feeling judged." Darryl's eyes enlarged and he grinned.

"Word, that's wassup! I can see you making a move like that."

"For real!"

"Yeah, you can do whatever you want to do, Shenelle, but you going to have to stick your mind to it."

"You're right. Oh I forgot to tell you I got an *A* on my literary exam."

"Nice, keep up the good work, baby. You're doing your thing, I'm proud of you." It made me happy Darryl was proud of my triumphs. I wished my parents could be proud, but since I wasn't around them, it was good to know someone was.

"Would you like to hear the poem I wrote for an assignment?"

"Aw'ight," I went to the car and retrieved the poem from my bag and sat back down on the blanket. I looked at his face to see if he was ready and cleared my throat to recite my poem to him.

Have you ever cried at night and no one knew about it, or in public, drying your eyes as quickly as you can, trying your hardest to hide it.

I am carrying a ton of bricks on my shoulders while still trying to hold my head up high.

Deep down you are suffering with so much heartache and pain, but every day that passes you hinder it with a smile and your tears turn into joy.

Your voice is as mellow as it could be. Your heart and your mind is where it is supposed to be, but only if people could just see how hard it is to be you.

I am carrying a ton of bricks on my shoulders while still trying to hold my head up high.

Others say that it is impossible to be sad and show such happiness at the same time, but that isn't true. What you go through and how you deal with it they wouldn't have a clue.

Whatever pressures or circumstances you are under, you use your inner power not to show it, because you are too strong to let people know it. If anyone was to walk up to you and ask what is troubling you, you don't tell them your story and just reply,

I am carrying a ton of bricks on my shoulders while still trying to hold my head up high.

When I looked back up at Darryl, he was staring at me and I could tell my poem moved him. "Wow that was fire, Shenelle." I cheesed out of self-pride. "Why thank you!" The song by Alicia Keys that was playing switched to Usher, featuring lil Jon and Ludacris' song "Lovers and Friends". It was one of my favorite songs from Usher; it had a nice flow to it. Darryl stood up from the blanket, walked over to the car and turned the music up. He came over to me and extended his hand.

"Come, babe. Dance with me." I clasped my hand with his and got all excited inside. I loved spending romantic evenings with Darryl, when it was just the two of us and no one else. I loved doing everything with Darryl. We slow danced together; the headlights of his car were beaming, giving us a spotlight in the darkness. I laid my head onto the crease of his chest and hummed to the melody of the music.

"You got me feeling like I'm in the fifties with us dancing to slow music under the moonlight like this," I said wondering if I would've felt this good with Darryl back in that era.

"Good, then that means that my mission is working. Your mind needs a break from all the old baggage and be in tune with what's happening today, now Ssssh. Just keep moving in the groove with me, girl." I smiled. Darryl was right; my mind did need to be in tune with the present day. I was in better spirits when I was in the present and not stuck in the past. The only thing I needed to do was try to keep myself there without any help.

***

I didn't have any classes, so I chilled out at Darryl's until he came home from work. He and I had been seeing each other for six months and I earned the luxury of having a key to his place. Since I wasn't doing anything in particular, I figured he would be hungry when he stepped in, so I performed the deeds of a good woman and prepared dinner for him. I chopped up vegetables and mashed some potatoes to go with the pan seared chuck steak I had simmering in the oven. I even ran to the store and bought an Entenmann's apple pie to go along with the vanilla ice cream that was in the freezer for dessert. At four 0' clock everything was done and the aroma of the meal was throughout the house. I sat down and watched an evening sitcom waiting for Darryl to arrive any minute when my cellphone rang. I picked it up and saw that it was an unknown number. At first I wasn't going to answer it because I didn't answer private calls. Everybody I spoke to on the regular was stored in my contacts, but then I thought what if somebody was in trouble and couldn't use their own phone. I answered the call on the forth ring.

"Hello." The person didn't say anything, so I repeated again.

"Hello!" A female voice answered.

"Hello, is this Shenelle?"

"Yes, who's speaking?" She sucked her teeth and replied, "That's not important, but what I want to know is who you are to Darryl." Once she said his name, my body shuddered and I started to breathe heavily.

"Who is this?"

"This is Kim, Darryl's *legal* wife!" I felt my bones tremble with anxiety, but before I fully fell for the scam I bellowed, "You're lying to me chick, because Darryl is not even married!"

"Humph, that's what he wants you to believe, but you know what? I'm glad I stole your number from his cellphone when he was with me today sleeping in my hotel bed. I've been wondering why he's been acting so strange lately. He rushed out ten minutes ago, talking about he had things to do, but I guess he's really on his way back to you." All I could hear other than that woman's voice was my heart racing at one hundred and ninety beats per minute.

"Bust this though, girl, I hope you've had your fun with my husband because it's about to end real soon. Believe that!" The phone clicked off and I practically lost it. I stripped out of Darryl's t-shirt and my night shorts and ran to the bedroom, quickly throwing something on. I wanted to get out of that house before Darryl came in and I ended up committing murder. I frantically packed my clothes in my suitcase as tears fell drastically. I couldn't believe this dude! I specifically told Darryl that I didn't want to get hurt and he looked me right in the eye and told me a phony bullshit lie.

When I finished packing, I rolled my luggage to the front door and thought to do a few things before I go. I took the steak out of the oven and flung the pot against his wall putting a dent into it. I watched as the steak slid down the wall leaving a nasty greasy stain from the gravy. Then I put dish detergent with water in a cup and watered down the vegetables and mashed potatoes that were on the stove. I took the apple pie out of the box and threw that at the big screen TV and left the ice cream sitting in the sink with the water running. Hey, since the nucca was married, his wife should go all out and cook for him. I didn't even bother taking the keys off the key rack and got in my car leaving the door unlocked and ajar, hoping that some crack head from Richmond would raid his lying punk ass.

I drove my car five blocks away from Darryl's house and stopped to speed dial my brother Jere's number. When he answered on the second ring, I broke into tears explaining to him that I needed to leave Virginia right away. He was barely able to understand what I was saying and kept telling me to slow down, but it was hard for me to even catch my breath. Jere, after a while just told me to drive to the airport. I was glad he looked out and booked me a flight; I was so emotionally drained that it would've been impossible for me to be able to concentrate while driving back to the city by myself. I didn't even stop to say anything to my girls and just kept it moving. I needed to get out of VA fast before I lost my mind and did something I might've not regretted. My insides were burning with rage. I remembered at one point I thought all men were dogs and there couldn't be anyone who would be different. Now on to strike three, I had given Darryl the benefit of the doubt, believing he'd proven me wrong, but once again I was way off.

***

It was still daylight when my plane landed at LaGuardia airport. I rushed to baggage claim. I was anxious to see my brother Jere. When I got my suitcase, I spotted him sitting in the waiting area reading a newspaper. My brother looked so much like our father it wasn't even funny and it made me miss him. All the crap I was going through with men, it was a shame I didn't have my dad to run to for paternal comfort, but if God felt my brother Jere was a good stand in, then I was thankful for that. I gave Jere a big hug and he helped me carry my luggage to his car. I sat in the passenger seat of the car and was more at ease to be around family and away from phonies.

"So what's really good with you, Sis? What other corny ass loser did you get caught up with now?" I rolled my eyes at him. "Jere stop! Not right now."

"Naw, on the real though, you stay getting into bullshit with some dude. Have you ever looked into just staying single until you graduate and get your career going?" I didn't answer and just turned my head looking out the window. What my brother didn't know was that I stayed single before and just focused on me, but it seemed no matter how single I tried to be. I would meet someone, my heart would go astray and I ended up getting hurt.

"Yo Shenelle, I'm talking to you!" I looked back at Jere, giving him the impression that I wanted to hear his speech though my ears were closed.

"Why don't you just chill out for a while, get your life together and leave the men alone?"

"Jere, I don't go out and look for men, they find me first of all, and how could you ask such question when you've been with Taye since you were a freshman in college?"

Jere nodded his head receiving my point. "True story. You're right, but see the difference is, Taye hasn't shitted on me since I've been with her." I sucked my teeth and looked back out the window.

"Shenelle, all I'm saying is you're messing up dealing with these dudes. Look now you have to take time off from school because of some shit that went down between you and duke." Jere shook his head. "You need to chill yo, seriously. I know you a woman now and you may not want to hear this, but I'm just keeping it funky with you because I could see things getting worse if you don't do what you need to do for you and stop worrying about the next dude." Jere slowly stopped his car and I could tell by the sound of *Mister Softee's* ice cream truck that we were in my hometown. I sat and waited while he went into the grocery store.

It was fall season and the weather was a little humid. I watched as young people entertained each other. The girls sat on building stoops and walked in groups, talking about everything from their romantic relationships to the hottest clothing fad. The boys blocked the grocery store entryways, gawking at girls and shooting dice with the old heads for their pocket change. I wasn't too crazy about being back in the neighborhood, but I was glad to be home with the people I knew and loved. Jere came back to the car handing me a bottle of Snapple fruit punch.

"Do you want to stop and see Ma or no?" I snarled at him, my brother was real cute because he knew damn well my mother was the last person I needed or wanted to see.

"No, I don't want to see your mother!" I responded flippantly.

Jere rolled his eyes at my attitude. "Shenelle, please do not get this twisted. I love you to death and you know whenever you need me I got you, but you need *our* mother for assistance when you get into these men issues. If they putting their hands on you then you call me, other than that..." Jere's face got serious and he sensitively coaxed, "I really wish you two would stop acting so damn stubborn and just talk to each other. Ya'll doing too much harboring and life is too precious for that." He looked at me as though I was supposed to comment. When I didn't and kept looking at the road ahead, he got aggravated.

"You know, you might get mad at what I'm about to tell you, but you already know me. I ain't afraid to put your ass in check. You're acting just like her, Shen, and that's why you and moms can't get along because ya'll remind yourselves too much of each other. You might want to correct yourself now while you're still young and cute before you end up the way she is today." I flared my nose at what Jere said because I took it as a slap in the face. He noticed my facial expression and changed his voice to a softer tone.

"Sis, you really need to get back in contact with Moms. I'm sure she would like to hear from you." I curled my lips. Jere was always good for making things sound sweeter than what they really were to keep the peace within the family, but when it came to our mother, I knew better.

"Yeah, okay," was the response he got from me.

"Shenelle, I hope you know I ain't always going to be around to save you whenever you get into some drama. What if I wasn't around then what would you do? Who would you call?" I hated when people I loved said things like that. It scared me.

"Jere, I'm not worried about that. You're going to be in my life forever until we grow old and die. You're a good dude. What could possibly happen to you?" We pulled up in front of his building. Jere unbuckled his seatbelt and opened his side of the door when he said, "You never know, anything could happen."

I grabbed my luggage from the back seat and walked into the lobby of the building. As we waited for the elevator, a girl who entered from the staircase saw Jere and smiled. "Sup, Jay-P!" I observed her and could automatically tell she was feeling my brother. I was able to detect that because whenever I was around Jere, any girl who saw him always had that same yearning, lustful look on their face.

"What's good, Ma," Jere replied. The girl flung her long, synthetic, ponytail to the side looking like a life size bratz doll. She had on a tight white *Juicy Couture* shirt that made her breast play peek-a-boo, halfway covering her wash board tummy and a pair of black leggings.

"How you been? How are your wife and kids?" While the girl asked my brother questions, her eyes were fixed on me. I sensed she wasn't going to go about her business until she found out who I was. Jere tried hard to keep himself from focusing on her appearance and stood watching the electronic numbers on the elevator count down as he spoke.

"Chilling! Everybody's good. How's school?" The girl simply sighed as if everything with her was normal.

"Lyndsey, this is my lil sister Shenelle. Sis, this is Lyndsey. She lives in the apartment under us?" The girl stretched out her hand and it took everything in me not to laugh when I saw the expression of relief on her face. I shook hands with her and the elevator opened.

"Aw'ight Lynz, take care and tell Ms. Grier I said hello."

"Aw'ight! Nice meeting you, Sis. Later ya'll!" The girl put an extra twitch in her walk as she exited the building. I got on the elevator after Jere and began to tease his ego.

"So big bro, I see you still got that magic."

"What magic?" He played it off like he didn't get my drift and I harmlessly mushed his shoulder. "Oh, don't even front like you don't be wetting up these chicks out here, Jere."

"Shen, get outta here! That girl's a couple years younger than you. In fact she just made eighteen. Her mother runs a daycare from their crib and watches the kids for us."

"That's wassup!" We got off on the third floor. When we walked in the house, my little niece came running towards us.

"Daddeeee," she excitedly squealed.

"Aye, lil mama!" Jere picked her up and started playfully biting her pudgy cheeks. She busted out laughing and I giggled at the scene. It took me back to when my father used to do the same thing to me whenever I would run to him walking in the house from work.

"Miah, look whose here. Say hi to Auntie." She eagerly reached over to me and I took her from his arms.

"Hi, Auntie!"

"Hey My-My, look how big you got." I smothered her cheek with kisses.

"I'm four," she said holding up four of her little fingers, sounding all happy. I was amazed at how much she looked like me at that age. Her nose, eyes, pouty lips, and even her big bushy pigtails, was a resemblance of me. She was definitely Jere's twin. I dropped my bags in Miah's room and went into Jere's bedroom to greet his wife and my nephew.

"Hi, Taye." I gave my sister- in- law a hug and kiss.

"Hey girl, how's everything been with you?" she asked. I already knew she was aware of my mishaps, maybe not the full extent, but I was sure Jere told her some things. Even though I loved her dearly like a sister, I kept my personal life limited for my own good reasons.

"Everything's been cool and you?" Jere who was sitting on the bed next to her frowned his face as if to say, *"Stop front'n"*. I rolled my eyes at him.

"The same goes for me," Lataya said. My nephew began to squirm and fuss waking up from his nap. I picked the baby up from his crib and cooed as I danced with him in circles.

He smiled, airing out his toothless gums. I peeped Jere watching me.

"What?"

"Don't get any ideas, Sis. Wait as long as you can." There was no doubt in this world that I loved children. They were the most stress free and happiest souls alive and being around them made me happy, but I wasn't in any hurry to be responsible for one.

"Jere, please!" He put his hands up. "Hey, I'm just making a statement."

"Would you mind if I take the kids out tomorrow?" Jere looked at me as if I had asked a stupid question and Lataya's face lit up as though she could really use a break.

"I guess that's a yes."

I called my girls and let them know where I was. They'd been trying to reach me since I left Virginia. Each one of them was pissed off and barked on me for not calling them first before I left. I didn't explain to them my reason for leaving right in the middle of the school semester. I just told them I would talk more with them when I got back to school. I had all of my professors email my work, so I wouldn't fall behind. Since Thanksgiving break was around the corner, I decided I would stay with Jere and his family until the holiday break was over. Darryl called me several times and I forwarded all of his calls to my voicemail. He had already left me ten messages. I listened to a few of them and he sounded so worried and concerned. I was surprised he wasn't flipping out about the mess I created in his house. I didn't call him back and turned off my phone. I informed my girls not to tell him a thing. I wanted his trifling ass to agonize over my sudden disappearance. Then I would deal with him and give him a piece of my mind once I was back on campus. For the remainder of the night, I played with my nephew and watched a Disney movie with my niece after I braided her hair. By the time midnight hit, I was a goner.

I got the kids up early in the morning. I used Jere's car and took them to F.A.O. Schwarz where they could have fun and I bought them a few toys. I played with them in the park a little and conversed with a girl who was around my age with an infant son. We talked while the kids swung on the swings. I listened to her talk about her wild life as a struggling single mother and how the father of her child wasn't worth shit. She explained how her mother wouldn't help her and watch the baby so she could look for employment. Whatever money she did get was from public assistance and child support. She had to give her mother half of that just so she could have a place to stay. I felt the girl's pain because her crazy life story wasn't so much different from my own. I was reminded of that saying… when you think you're going through tough times, there's always someone out there going through worse. I offered to buy her and her son some ice cream since the weather was dry. When I was about to pay the ice cream man for my order, I heard someone call my name. I looked through the crowd of people and didn't see anyone I knew.

Chapter 16

Thanksgiving came quick. I did a lot of running around with Lataya and helped her cook for the family gathering she and Jere planned. By five in the evening, over twelve dishes were made and six different desserts were baked. It looked like the feast I used to help my mother prepare. At the end of the day, after putting a burn up in that kitchen I was exhausted. I freshened up and drank a red bull for energy to be able to socialize with everyone. When I got to the living room, most of the guests who showed up were all Lataya's relatives and friends.

Jere had only a small amount of his close friends there with their kids. At first I wasn't going to ask him, but I had to know if he invited our mother over. He said he had tried calling her, but she didn't answer and I took that as God having mercy on me. The house was already full of more people than it was intended to hold, when the doorbell rang. Jere opened the door and just like that, my joy was stolen. My brother Timothy walked in with one of his skeezers. I looked on as Timothy gave Jere some dap and gave Lataya a hug and kiss. He looked at me and his eyes widened.

"Shenelle, what up!"

"Tim," I replied flatly and left the living room. I joined the children who were occupied in my niece's room, watching *That's so Raven*. A second later, Jere came in.

"Yo, Shenelle, let me holler at you for a minute," We went into his bedroom and he closed the door.

"Sis Look, I know you and Tim had ya'll quarrels in the past, but on the real. You got to let all that stuff go and put it behind you. Come on, it's Thanksgiving, family day and we are all family, so cheer the hell up and mingle with your brother like you mean it." I stared at Jere for a minute, telling him with my eyes that even though his speech was well put, I still wasn't feeling it.

"Please, do it for me, your big brother." He poked out his lip pleading. I rolled my eyes and smiled.

"Thank you," he said and kissed me on the cheek.

"Only because it's you, Jere."

He chuckled. "It's all good though, Sis. I don't know what it is, but something's gonna change you two. One day ya'll gonna get along, just watch!" I looked at Jere like *"Yeah aw'ight!"* and walked out in front of him to the living room.

Everybody was enjoying themselves and having a great time eating, talking and drinking. It was a blessing that after a few hours passed; no one had gotten too drunk and was making a fool of themselves. Once it started to get late, half of the crowd had taken their bagged up plates and went on home. The others stayed behind and indulged in more liquor, bringing up old annoying stories. You know how when everything is going sweet and there's always that one person who ruins everything? Well that person was my brother Timothy; he obviously had too much to drink.

He even left out to spark up a blunt a couple of times and was so high you might as well had considered his head a hot air balloon.

"So lil, Sis, what's really good with you? I hear you stepping low and screwing married men now, what's up with that?" Everybody looked at me and I scowled at Jere. He stared at Timothy with his drink paused at his mouth. His jaw was twitching and he looked like he wanted to rip Tim's face off. For the first time ever, I wanted to slap the black off Jere for telling my business and to the worst of my enemies. All I needed was for my problems to get back to my mother and have her spreading it through family like she always did.

"Tim, what I do is none of your fucking business! What you need to worry about is checking your balls out with all these girls you be screwing. I'm surprised it hasn't rotted and fallen off by now. Nasty ass!"

The girl who Timothy brought to the party snapped her head over at him. "All these girls! What does she mean by all these girls? And why is everybody calling you Timothy? I thought your name was Thomas!" Timothy was now glaring at me with an ill grill.

"You see, that's why Moms don't like your ass now because you's a stupid bitch. I should've let her strangle your ass to death that day when I pulled her off you!" Right when I sprang up from my seat about to choke Timothy's Adam's apple from his throat, Jere hopped in front of him and punched him in his mouth causing him to hit the floor.

"Yo Jay, what the fuck you hit me for?" Tim said with blood trickling from his mouth. Ever since we were kids, Jere had always beaten Timothy in a fight. Both of my brothers were over six feet tall, but Jere was built like a Spartan opposed to Timothy's slender frame. It was easy for Jere to grab Timothy by his collar, lifting him clear off the floor and pulling him towards the door in half of second.

"Because, your ass is fucking drunk Tim and you really need to leave my house right about now!"

When Jere opened the door to throw him out, Timothy blocked the doorway with his hands hollering, "This is that bullshit, Jay! Everything was all gravy until that little brat was born. We used to be happy and we still would've been if Dad wasn't beasting to have a daughter on his jock like Shenelle was!" Everybody who was already baffled by the scene, gasped at what Timothy said and I was halfway out of my wits. Jere scuffled with Timothy, trying to push him out the door and I could hear my nephew crying from the bedroom. Timothy was still screaming in the hallway.

"You know I'm right, Jay! Ma was going to abort Shenelle until Dad begged her not to and because you wanted a little sister! I don't know what it is between you and Dad that ya'll needed this bitch to be around!" With that said Jere pounced on Timothy and pounded him. I went into my niece's room, leaving the Cain and Abel fight. My niece was widely awakened from all the racket.

"Auntie, where you going? Don't leave, I love you," she whined and I broke down crying. I knew out of all people I heard tell me they loved me, coming from my niece, it was real. I wished I could've taken her with me and move into a big house with all the other people who loved me genuinely and we could all stick together as a family. I grabbed my bag, went over and kissed my niece on the cheek.

"Auntie loves you too, My-My," I said between sobs.

"You have good parents who love you and you must listen to them, okay. Do everything they say. Don't ever be like your auntie, be better okay!"

"Kay!" she cried. I hugged her one last time.

"Be good, Miah." Hearing her cry was ripping me apart as I left the room. In the living room the cops were there asking Lataya questions and anyone who would answer. I didn't see Jere or Timothy around when I walked out the door. I heard Lataya scream my name and I ignored her. One of the policemen tried to stop me, but I kept going. I walked past the nosey neighbors who were feening to find out what was going on and pressed the elevator button hard, breaking off the tip of my acrylic nail. When the elevator opened up, Jere walked out with spots of blood on his shirt and I hoped it was a sign that he had beaten Timothy unconscious.

"Shenelle, where are you going? You ain't gotta leave. Tim is gone; the cops arrested him for disturbance."

"Jere, I have to go! I can't stay here! I want to go back to campus. I'm sorry; I should never have even come." Jere took my bag out of my hand. "You're not going anywhere!"

He walked towards his apartment and I pulled at my bag, trying to take it from him. "Jere, I want to leave. Please just let me go!" I lost control of my crying by then. I was so sick of the drama and wished I would just die, so I can be free already. I couldn't be happy nowhere I went. Jere grabbed my forearm pulling me with all his strength, overpowering me.

"Shenelle, I said you're not going anywhere. You're staying here like you were supposed to until it's time for you to leave. You got to stop doing this. You got to stop running away every time there's an issue you don't want to deal with. You need to be stronger than that. There's going to be problems everywhere you go and you're going to have to learn how to handle them like an adult." I kept crying as Jere talked and we were now in his bedroom.

"You are not the only person in this world who goes through fucked up shit. We all go through it. Nothing that happened tonight was your fault. It was my fault. I shouldn't have said anything to Tim. He asked why you were here during the school semester and I told him everything without thinking and I apologize for that. My bad!" Though Jere should've kept what I told him to himself, I didn't put blame on him. Timothy didn't have to blast my business and humiliate me like that.

"Tim was just being an asshole tonight. He was drunk, so don't believe anything he said. Mom and Dad did want you, they just had their own personal issues and it really didn't have anything to do with you." If Timothy ever told the truth in his life, it would be about anything negative people said pertaining to me and nothing else. He was one out of many who lived to hurt my feelings. Jere playing the good, big brother role was just sparing my feelings by withholding the truth.

Jere gave me a hug. "Sis, I know you're tired. Go to bed and get your mind off of tonight." Without any questions, I did exactly that because I really did need to sleep. All of the crying had given me a tension headache and to be up, still thinking about the mess that went down would've just made it worse. I slept in Jere's bedroom by his kindness and he and Taye took the pull-out couch. The last thing on my mind when my eyes closed was how I left Virginia to get away from the drama down there. I get to New York, just to end up dealing with family drama and still had to go back to Virginia to deal with probably even more drama. I've come to think that when I was created, drama was all I was destined for.

During the rest of the vacation, I kept inside the apartment and didn't do much of anything. What happened at the Thanksgiving party destroyed my sense of comfort, making my stay in the Bronx miserable. Jere and his wife tried everything they could to get me to lighten up and do things with them and the kids, but to no avail. My brother Timothy was at central bookings and was ordered to stay there for two weeks for disturbing the peace and having marijuana on him. I was still heated at him for the big performance he put on, embarrassing me and Jere. I knew Lataya's friends and family who were there, had millions of wild thoughts and opinions about us by the time they went home that night.

Jere drove me to the airport on an early Sunday morning. He was trying to make conversation with me, but I wasn't speaking. He parked the car in front of the airport. "Shenelle, turn around and look at me!" I turned to him with watery eyes. I wasn't mad at him, I was mad at the world. I was tired of all the problems I was going through, no matter what I would do to avoid them. I was tired of how I wouldn't do anything to anyone, try my best to stay out of other's way, but still was like a magnet for drama. It seemed like people went out of their way to make me feel uncomfortable and I couldn't take it anymore.

Jere shook his head and used his knuckles to brush away my tears. "Sis, don't let people bring you down. When you do that, you give them power over you. Power they might not know exists when they're not even around you. You've got to learn how to brush things off your shoulder and keep it moving. Save all of those tears for something serious." I used the crumpled up McDonalds napkin I found in my pocket to dry the overflow of my angry tears.

"I love you, Shenelle. Dry your eyes!" He reached over and put his hand under my chin, lifting it. "And keep your head up!"

I gave Jere a long hug. I hated I had to leave him. I was considering for a brief second, transferring my credits to a CUNY school to finish off there and stay close to him and his family, but I knew he wouldn't allow that. Like our father, Jere had always been keen about me finishing school and making a name for myself. I wasn't going to disappoint his faith in me. I got out of the car and took my luggage from the trunk. I told him I would call when I got to campus and went on to board my plane.

***

I made it back to campus in exactly three hours. When I went into my dorm, Natari wasn't there. I hadn't called my girls to let them know I was arriving. I wanted to surprise them. I kept my clothes packed in my suitcase and went to Alicia's old dorm room to see if they were in there. Right before I knocked, the door opened and Hannah came walking out. When she saw me her eyes bucked out of her head. She jumped onto me giving me a big hug. It felt good receiving affection from someone. My friend didn't know, but a hug did a lot for me at that moment. I smiled, surveying Hannah's hair that was braided in free styled cornrows.

"I'm so happy to see you, girl! It feels like it's been forever. Are you okay? Is everything good with you?" To leave my drama from New York right where it was, I replied, "Yeah I'm good. Where are the girls?"

"They're in the cafeteria. I just came to wake the other girl up to see if she wanted to eat with us." After Alicia moved out, a new girl moved in and took her spot. I didn't know too much about her, but from what I heard, she was another quiet one who stayed in her own world.

"I don't know what's up with people acting so anti-social these days," Hannah said as we were walking together. "Oh, and I'ma let you know now, Darryl has come by mad times looking for you, but we didn't tell him anything. Did something happen between you two, because he seemed highly upset?"

Hannah rambled on while I became tight at the remembrance of the situation that had me running back to the Bronx. When we walked through the entry door of the cafeteria, I spotted Darryl standing, talking to another student. I told Hannah to keep walking to her table while I went over to give Darryl what I owed him. Once I reached his back, I tapped him on the shoulder. He turned around and I right hooked him in the face. He put his hand over his eye, staggering into the guy he was talking to. Everybody guffawed as I exited the cafeteria. I was too angry to even want to sit with my girls anymore. I went back to my dorm room. Darryl was right on my heels, pushing my door open when I tried to slam it. He gripped my arm, mad as hell wanting to wring my neck.

"Shenelle, what is your problem? Why the hell did you hit me and why did you jack up my crib like that?" I snatched my arm from him and was about to hit him again when Natari and the rest of them ran into the room. The first one that stepped to his face was Alicia, and she shoved him.

"Darryl, what the fuck did you do to her? I knew you were the reason she left. What did you do?" Natari was pulling Alicia from out of Darryl's face when Rondell came running in.

"Alicia back up, what are you doing? You're pregnant!" He was holding her back. Everyone was talking at the same time trying to figure out what was going on. Other students started to crowd into my room. Darryl and I gazed at each other, both of us vexed. Everything was getting way out of hand, more than I bargained for in one week. All of the commotion was driving me so crazy, I screamed out like a mad woman.

"Everybody, out! This is between me and Darryl! Please all of ya'll, GET OUT!!!!" Everyone got quiet. The girls and Darryl were all flabbergasted. Everyone slowly dispersed, one by one and I waited for my room to clear out. Natari told me to get her from Hannah's room if Darryl was to try anything funny. I gave her the okeydoke and nicely asked her again to leave. Once everyone was gone, I locked my door, turned to Darryl and slapped him. He grabbed my hands and I tried to pull myself from him. I wanted to give him more of an ass kicking, but he shook me up.

"Stop hitting me, Shenelle!" he said angrily, gritting his teeth.

"What the hell is wrong with you, girl?" I pulled my hands from his and backed away from him.

"Go ask your wife what the hell is wrong with me!" I would never forget the look that etched on Darryl's face when he found out his secret had been revealed.

"Shenelle, I could explain."

"Then please explain! Explain why you underhandedly made me into your fucking mistress!" Darryl lowered his eyes to the floor, still uneasy about being caught.

"You lied to me, Darryl! You looked me right in the face and lied to me!" I picked up one of Natari's sneakers that was by her bed and threw it at him, aiming for his head. He ducked out of the way.

"Shenelle, it's not really what it looks like."

"So then tell me? What does a lying, cheating, married man really look like?" Hearing myself say those words made me think back to my father's actions when he was cheating on my mother... Always working late, keeping his phone off at certain times, suspicious notes and phone calls. My nose flared at the thought when I realized all of the pinpoints seemed to fit Darryl.

"Shenelle, yes I am married, but I don't want to be with her." I sucked my teeth because that's what all cheating men say when they're caught in a lie.

"Right now, we're not together. She knows I want to get a divorce and every time it becomes a topic, she always gets angry. Shenelle, getting a divorce is not a hop, skip and jump. It's a long and hard process."

"Why are you divorcing your wife? Because of me? I'm not a home wrecker, Darryl. I wouldn't have given you the time of day if I had known you were married." Darryl looked guilty and he needed to feel that way, because the way he played the whole thing out was wrong.

"Babe, I know. That's why I didn't tell you anything. I didn't want you to think you were violating things because you weren't and you're not now..." Darryl stopped talking for a brief second and then went the extra mile to enlighten me.

"Shenelle, way before you and I even met, I was going to end things with my ex. I realized getting married was a mistake. I was only eighteen; I really wasn't ready and was just being young and dumb. She was my first love, so at the time when I married her, it felt right because I thought I was going to be with her forever. Now that I regret it, I just want to do the divorce thing and move on from her." My heart was telling me to believe Darryl, but in my mind the situation still seemed too shady.

"Darryl, how did she get my number?" I tested him to see if he would at least tell half of the truth and admit that he saw her recently. He huffed like he really didn't want to give in on the details that would further explain his dirty little secret.

"She goes to school back in New York and of course I've been keeping in contact with her. Every once in a while she would come here to visit me and stay at a hotel and I will go see her." I waited for him to get to the part of how she got my number. While he talked, I took a glance at the purple bruise that was rising on his cheekbone. I felt bad I struck pain to his pretty face, but I reminded myself he got exactly what he deserved and I would've done it again if I had to.

"The day you trashed my house, she hit me up to let me know she was in town and I stopped by the hotel to talk to her. She must've gotten your number while..." I cut him off.

"While you were sleeping in her hotel bed after you screwed her!" Darryl's face looked stumped by my comment.

"That's what she told you?" I didn't respond and just glared at him. He rolled his eyes shaking his head. "No Shenelle, I didn't have any type of sexual contact with her. We just had a civil conversation. She asked me if she could use my phone to make a call because her phone was dead, so I let her. She didn't even know about you..." I cut him off again.

"Of course she didn't know. You wouldn't be that stupid to tell her about me, yet I'm supposed to be your *so-called* girl!"

"You are my girl! Look man, you were the last person I called, so she must've stolen your number to start some shit to get you riled up. Shenelle, I'm not in love with her anymore and she thinks she could make me stay married to her, but I'm not going to." My head was pounding; this situation was totally out of my league and wasn't something I needed to be a part of. Even if what Darryl was saying was accurate, it still didn't feel right. To have come from a household that was falling apart my whole life until things finally ended all because of another woman, I just couldn't do it. This wasn't for me and I realized in that moment, Darryl wasn't for me either.

"Darryl, I need you to leave my room. I need you to leave me alone altogether!" He looked at me as if I didn't know what the hell I was saying, but I meant every word. I had already been through too many disappointments and was determined to make no more room for any others.

"What do you mean leave you alone altogether?" Darryl sounded offended.

I walked past him to my door and opened it. "I mean I don't want anything to do with you. I'm done with you! I'm sorry I even met you! Now get the fuck out of my room! NOW!" Darryl stood there for a minute, obviously pissed that I was dropping him. He walked toward the door, turning to me before exiting.

"Aw'ight, but you're not going to get rid of me that easy, girl. I'm going to come back for you and don't take that the wrong way." When he walked out, I slammed the door. I threw myself on my bed and for the rest of the day let my pillow absorb my tears. It seemed like everybody in this world was screwed up and I was so confused about who was real or fake. It had come down to the point where if I had to cut off everybody to keep myself from feeling disheartened, then I was willing to do exactly that.

***

I was coming from classes when my stomach started to do flip flops. I tried to get to my dorm but didn't make it. I hurled my lunch, embarrassing myself in front of students passing by. It had been a month since I last saw my period. This time I didn't ignore it. I drove to a pharmacy immediately to purchase a pregnancy test. I took the test in the pharmacy bathroom and just as I thought, I was pregnant.

"You are fourteen weeks," said the nurse from the school medical clinic. I sighed. It was crazy how whenever I ended a relationship and was trying to get over a guy, I wound up in the same predicament. I sadly slithered off the exam table like a snail.

"Are you okay, Ms. Patterson? You seem upset. We have a counselor here if you would like to talk to someone?"

"No, I'm alright. Thanks." I clutched my purse and walked out of the clinic.

I sat in my car and called Alicia, telling her the news. She was cool about it, even though she wasn't feeling Darryl at the moment. She was now six months into her pregnancy and was expecting a baby girl. I stopped by her house and sulked for a while. She was trying to tell me not to stress over the issue and that Darryl and I was just going through a mild storm. But it wasn't just about Darryl; it was my life in general. It always seemed that when things were going good bad things happened, and nice things always happened to pop up at the wrong times. Was this God's way of trying to tell me something? I was dying to know what it was and what it had to give. When I got back to my dorm, I walked in to find Natari taking a nap. I tiptoed to my bed, so I wouldn't wake her. Natari, who had always been a light sleeper whenever she wasn't drunk, turned over. "Hey, girl!" She squinted her eyes, barely able to see because the sun was half down and the room was dark.

"Are you alright?"

"Yeah I'm good. I just want to get some sleep." I kicked off my black ballet shoes and laid down. Natari sat up and turned on the floor lamp that was in between my bed and hers and stared at me awkwardly. I stared back. The light put a glow on her face. I always thought Natari was so pretty. When she wasn't hostile, acting like a wild banshee and her face was tranquil, she could really put herself on a bracket that was higher than Iman and Tyra Banks put together. We eyed each other without words and I watched as she looked like she wanted to say something, but was fighting it. She dramatically blew out a loud breath of air.

"You're gonna be pissed at me, but I feel as a true friend I have to tell you this." I tried not to express my bothersome feelings through my face when my heart sank, ready to face yet another dilemma. "Shenelle, I knew that Darryl was married." I popped up out of my relaxed position, ready to pop off at the mouth at her for not telling me that information sooner.

Natari put her hands up for me to hold it back as she explained herself. "I didn't tell you before because I heard it from another person and didn't know if it was true. I'm sorry, Sis, I just didn't wanna tell you anything and get things twisted." I was so tired of people supposedly not telling me things, pretending they were protecting my feelings. What made them look bad, was that I wasn't anywhere near dumb and knew when someone was hiding something for their own benefit. At times it made me wonder if people did certain things just to see me suffer at the end of the day. My body, mind and spirit was too through with dealing with anymore issues, so I remembered what Jere told me and brushed it all off my shoulder.

"It's cool, Nat. I'm not mad." I laid back down with the means of ending the night with that understanding. Natari looked a little surprised by my response and smiled.

"Well, thank you for not biting my head off," she said jokingly. I smirked, and rolled over to go to sleep and she turned off the light.

I made an appointment for an abortion the following week. I had no intentions on ever telling Darryl about the baby. I just wanted to get the thing out of me and move along with my life. I hadn't spoken to Darryl in a couple of months since I'd broken things off with him. I had the school dean ban him from my dormitory and I changed my number so he couldn't call me. I would be lying if I said I didn't miss him like crazy, but I had to be strong enough to distance myself from him. Darryl sent pink roses and snickers miniature bars, which he knew was my favorite candy to my room to get my attention. I found out he would pay some young boy, more than likely a freshman to deliver them to me. For his trouble, I told the boy to give the flowers and candy to his love interest, secret crush or whoever, as long as he kept anything that came from Darryl away from me.

I spoke to Jere just about every week and he even surprised me by making a trip down one weekend with his family to visit me. He was upset that I was irresponsible and allowed myself to get pregnant, but he didn't criticize too much. The latest news on my brother Timothy, aside from him being locked up for the catastrophe that day at Jere's house, he ended up getting six months at Rikers Island for not paying child support. He also had to do another year for violating his parole. To make matters worse, he done got the skeezer he brought to the thanksgiving party pregnant. It was just sad all the way around because he was only going to be a deadbeat dad for the third time. Jere and I barely knew Timothy's other two children and could only pray that the mothers would let go of their grudges against him, so we could see our two nieces again someday.

Chapter 17

*I was running down the street. It was dark outside in the boondocks. I ran and ran until I saw a light and I tried to make it there, but I fell down. He turned me over and put the gun to my temple. His eyes were cold as he yelled, "Open your mouth!" I was so scared I pissed my pants; warm fluid spread down my thighs. I wouldn't respond to his request. I was willing to die. I heard the click of his gun and closed my eyes right before he could squeeze the trigger...*I felt my body being shaken and I heard someone say my name over and over.

"Shenelle... Shenelle, wake up!" When I awoke, Natari was staring down at me and my clothes felt wet.

"Shenelle, are you okay? You were talking in your sleep." I stared back at her, clueless at where I was and she cradled my face. "Damn! You're sweating like a muva, girl!" I sat up and felt a sharp pain in my abdomen.

"I think I peed on myself," I said. Natari pulled the covers back and in the middle of my bed was a big spot of blood. Natari gasped. "Oh my god! Shenelle, you're bleeding! I'm calling the ambulance!" I grabbed my stomach when I felt sharper pain erupt and more warm liquid released from me. I started crying when the pain went from being severe to unbearable. It was four 0'clock in the morning. I was trying to get out of the bed when blood continued to stream. My pajama bottoms went from the color pink to dark red.

Hannah came running into my room after Natari alerted her about my situation.

"Shenelle, don't move the ambulance is on its way." In less than ten minutes, I was being put onto a gurney by two medical technicians. As I was being hauled out, so many eyes of many different faces were staring at me. They were probably wondering in their minds, how one girl could go through so much hell in the duration of four years. I felt ashamed and covered the white sheet over my head to make me feel like I'd disappeared.

It wasn't too long after the D&C procedure when I awoke. I could feel cool oxygen air blowing through my nostrils. The sleep felt too damn good. If it wasn't for the anesthetics wearing off, I would have stayed asleep forever. Natari was the face I saw again, looking down at me. "Hey you, it's about time you woke the hell up!" I was hardly alert to endure her sarcasm.

"I'll be right back! I'ma let the nurse know you're awake." Natari left the room and doubled back with a nurse. The nurse removed the nasal cannula from my nose and I propped myself up. I looked over at my tray and inspected the food. I didn't see anything I liked, so I pushed it to the side and just drank the small plastic cup of apple juice.

"Alicia is on her way. She's bringing you breakfast," Natari said. I looked at the clock and it was almost time for classes. "Nat, it's 7:15. You can go to class, I'll be alright."

"I'm not worried about it. I want to make sure you get out of here. I'm going to give you a ride back to campus since

Leesh can't drive." The door to my room opened and Alicia walked in with Rondell. Alicia came up to me and hugged me, crushing my chest with her protruding belly. She looked at me with a fretful face.

"Girl, I swear you're going to give me a heart attack one day with you going through all these gotdamn emergencies." She handed me a brown paper bag. I opened it and was mad happy when I saw my most preferred breakfast, a supreme omelet. It contained cheese and every vegetable and meat that the earth offered with a side of home fries, and a container of orange juice. I looked up at Alicia smiling and she smiled back; she knew my wishes all too well.

An hour after I ate, I was discharged and given a prescription of antibiotics. At my request, I was also given a letter recommending I stay on bed rest for a week, just so I wouldn't have to go to class and deal everyone's enquiring stares. The note didn't stop the dean from questioning me though; it was inevitable that a white man would want to know why such a young black woman would get embattled with so much drama. I kept the conversation brief and told him if I had control over my deck of cards, my life would be a whole lot different.

I'm sure he thought my response was a smart ass comment to keep the conversation from dragging, but truth be told, that was the realest answer I could've given him. In the end, he did exactly what I wanted him to do. He laughed it off, shook my hand and sent me along my way. I gave my brother Jere a courtesy call to let him know all the updates. He felt bad about my misfortune, but was glad I was alright. Classwork came about wonderfully and I was able to get everything done in peace, while secluded in my room. I was looking to finish up on my finals in time and then I would skedaddle, leaving all of my adversities behind.

***

It was two more months before graduation, and to say I was elated was an understatement. I was so beasting to leave I packed the majority of my stuff, keeping just the remaining months' worth of outfits in my closet. I was laying on my bed, talking and listening to music with Natari when someone knocked on the door. Neither one of us were expecting anyone. Hannah was out with her honey and Alicia was doing the mommy thing now with her newborn, so we didn't know who it could be. Curiosity made me get up and open the door. It was Darryl. We just stared at each other in complete silence. If my instincts told me he would be behind the door, I wouldn't have opened it. Seeing Darryl face to face made whatever negative thoughts in my mind about him become extinct.

"Oh, hell no!" Natari shouted. She stopped from painting her toenails and rushed up at my side.

"Darryl, what the hell are you doing here? I thought you were banned from here. Shenelle, isn't he banned?" Natari sounded paranoid for my safety. Darryl was just standing there staring at me, looking drop dead gorgeous in a charcoal gray business suit.

"I need to speak to Shenelle." His eyes never left me as he spoke to Natari. I was debating with myself whether I should let him in. I wanted to be tough and tell him to kick rocks, but my insides were screaming for him.

Natari moved in front of me and started pushing him. "Uh no, you need to leave! You need to raise your trifling ass up outta here now!" Darryl made a funny face at her. "Ma, look. First of all, don't touch me! Second of all, I didn't come here for you; I came for Shenelle and if she wants me to leave then I'll leave. Other than that, shawty, you need to back up off me!" Even when he was serious, he sounded sexy. I wanted to smile, but I held it in. I had almost forgotten how much his testosterone level turned me on.

"Hold up! Who the hell do you think you're talking to?" Natari said, getting all up in his face. "You don't know who you're messing with. You could get cut, my dude!" Once I saw things were about to get heated, I woke up from my daze on Darryl.

"Nat, it's okay. He could come in." She looked at me like I was crazy.

"Shenelle, are you serious? You're going to kiss this man's ass after he played you the way he did? See, this is why you always getting screwed over, because you always give these dirty dogs second chances they don't deserve." Now I shot her a funny look because she really needed to rethink what she said to me. *I always give dirty dog second chances...yeah right!* Darryl looked from Natari acting a fool, back to me and smiled. It overwhelmed me, but I still fought to suppress my smile. When I didn't say anything, Natari sucked her teeth and waved her hand in the air.

"Whatever, Shenelle! You can't say I didn't try to protect you." She moved from in between us, slipping on her flip flops and left the room, cursing Darryl under her breath as she passed him. He snorted at her attitude.

"Can I come in?" I moved to the side and he walked in.

"Darryl, what do you want and how did you get in here?" He smiled a sly smile. "Shenelle, I know VA better than you do. I got connects. I told you that you weren't getting rid of me that easily." He might've been right, but he must've forgotten I had connects too and that was family, right down in Richmond. I crossed my arms over my chest with a solemn look on my face to let him know I was still mad at him.

"You are aware that you're trespassing, right?" He sneered and replied, "No I'm not, girl. If I had broken in then I would be considered trespassing, but you let me in." Damn, this dude was too smart for his own good. I dropped my arms at my side, giving up the verbal battle and walked over to my bed.

"I heard about the baby, Shenelle; was it mine?" I couldn't believe he would have the audacity to ask me that and it really made me wonder if he had somebody stalking me. I snarled at him.

"Who else's would it have been?"

"I don't know. I just asked considering you didn't tell me about it." I was stupefied because he did have a point.

"How did you find that out anyway? Darryl, you better not have nobody following me around!"

"Negative! I told you before, I'm not like that. I have friends here on campus. You might not realize it, but you've become notorious at this school." I felt overcome. My gut instincts were right all along; I was the news headline at VSU. It only took one snowflake to start an avalanche and sadly, I was that snowflake. Just about all my life, I was well known without even trying to be.

"Darryl, what do want?"

"I want you, babe. I came to get you back so we can rekindle what we had." My throat muscles tightened. I really did miss him. Sometimes I even cried myself to sleep at night because I was so used to falling asleep in his arms, but I would never tell him that.

Darryl took off his blazer and without asking, tossed it on my bed. He released a breath of air and as he spoke, his words flowed to me like poetry. "Shenelle I'm sorry, I should've told you the truth. I felt that since I was here and my ex is where she is, I didn't need to say anything. I just wanted to live my life; I wasn't trying to hurt you." He sounded sincere, but I couldn't just pretend that this chick wasn't a factor, because after all she was his wife.

"What about your wife? What about her being hurt?"

"Why does it matter to you how she feels?"

"Darryl, I'm still a woman and I am not about wrecking anyone's home. She obviously still wants to be with you."

"Don't worry your pretty little head, girl. She's no longer our concern. I just came from court and we're getting a divorce." I wondered how he made that happen. When Darryl's wife called me, she acted so sure that they breaking up couldn't be possible. I wasn't even going to bother asking any question. I just secretly took in the glory.

"Well, how do I know you're telling me the truth this time?" He reached into his back pocket and tossed a letter on top of his jacket and I picked it up. It was crystal clear he was telling the truth, but I was still nervous for my heart's sake. How did I know he wouldn't do something slick again? I also wondered out of all the girls Darryl could've had on this earth including the ones who wanted him at school, what was so special about me that it would prompt him to leave his wife.

"Darryl, why me… Why do you choose me?"

"Because you're the one I want to be with. I love you, Shenelle. When I first told you I wanted you to be mines, I meant it." Even though he said those three famous words, I didn't want to dive back in, head first and end up drowning again.

Darryl opened his arms for me to hug him. "Come here, babe. I know you want to do this with me and I want this." I still didn't move from two feet away from him. I've heard people say if looks could kill, they would be put ten feet under and I could believe it. Darryl's superb looks, and the fact he had me so sprung to the point where I couldn't even form my mouth to tell him no, was killing me. I hadn't realized that tears had arose and fallen until I tasted the saltiness at the corners of my lips. Darryl started walking towards me and after every step he took, I inched away.

"I don't want to get hurt," I said through my tears.

"I love you, girl. Don't worry! You won't get hurt because I don't want to hurt you. All I want to do is give you the world and make you happy; happier than you've ever been." After a few more minutes of pondering, I gave into him. I walked over and buried my head into the curvature of his chest, a place where I felt safe. Darryl held onto me like he wouldn't let me go if his life depended on it.

"You have my heart," he whispered.

I could smell his cologne and it hypnotized me every time. I was so in love with the man it was sickening. Darryl telling me he loved me meant a lot to me. He said it first as I anticipated, but his actions spoke louder than his words. So he saying the words wasn't what did the trick for me. It was the divorce letter, similar to the one I discovered on my mother's bedroom floor years ago. That itself spoke volumes. Not only did it mean that Darryl's wife was now history, but it told me that he loved me in writing.

Chapter 18

I huffed in exhaustion after I said all that my brain could muster. Dr. Mayes was staring at me wide-eyed and it was well into the night. I looked at the time on my cellphone, it was after nine. I can't believe I'd been rambling for that long, but then she did ask a lot of questions. Darryl called several times, probably wondering if I had gotten lost on the way home. I was sitting in Dr. Mayes office for over four hours and was ready to go.

"Well Shenelle, we've really hit home on a lot today, haven't we?" I raised my eyebrows in accord. "Yes, we really did."

"But, I sense we're not done yet," she said and I shook my head. "Nope, not even close!" What I told Dr. Mayes was just the beginning of my story for real and I still was nowhere near getting to the crazier stuff.

"Okay, so can we meet next week, same time, same day?"

"Same day is fine, but five thirty would be better for me."

"Five thirty it is, see you then."

As soon as I walked out, I called Darryl. He was working late *as usual*, so I arranged to pick him up from the subway in Soho, since I wasn't too far away. I took every short cut on the road to get there faster and got there in no time. I saw Darryl standing by the bus stop a block before the train station. I honked the horn, then got out and switched seats.

"What's up, girl?" He pecked me the lips.

"Damn, you were with the therapist for a minute. You must've had a lot to say, huh?" Darryl curled his lips and made a face as if to query, *what the hell did you have so much to talk about?* I completely overlooked his gesture. "Darryl, please do not start this tonight. I'm too tired!"

"What? I didn't even say anything." He chuckled.

"Yeah, but you're making stupid faces and I know what they mean," I said, rolling my eyes at him.

"Don't read too much into it, baby. We cool." He stopped at a stop sign and smiled at me.

"Come here, Mama." He reached over, grabbing my chin. I leaned in and we kissed passionately. He always did that whenever he sensed I was aggravated and his charm on me never once botched. When I drew from him something made me look at the back seat and I did a double take as he started driving again. I back tracked my memory to when I picked Darryl up and noticed that something was missing. I looked to the front in between us and knew I wasn't bugging out. I could see Darryl watching me from the corner of his eye and he turned to me, taking his focus off the traffic ahead of us.

"What's wrong? What are you looking for?"

"Darryl, where's your backpack?" When Darryl first started his job, I bought him a backpack as a gift. It was a black, buttery leather, Orvis bag and he loved it very much. Ever since he started his job, he never came home without it. I gazed at him, trying to study his face for any suspicious signs, but all I got was a shrug of the shoulders.

"What are you worrying about it for?" he asked. My gaze turned into a scowl. What Darryl didn't know was after all the years we'd spent together, I'd taken note of whenever he used that line. He always said it to reverse the topic to me, a loophole to give himself more time to come up with a lie. Men, when they know something strange about them has been exposed, every question was answered with a question. While there are some men who have far better game and may not do that, mine was one who did. Seeing my screwed up face, Darryl altered his approach.

"I left it at the job, Shenelle." I looked at him puzzled. "Why?"

"Because I felt like it. Is that a problem?" Instead of smacking his lips off for being a smart ass, I turned my attention back to the highway. I let the whole thing go to avoid a tit for tat session with him that would lead to a heated argument I didn't need. After all my talking with the therapist about my life and not trusting men, I just couldn't stomach Darryl's shifty motives tonight.

My gut instincts were telling me that Darryl was possibly up to something again. I couldn't exactly put my finger on it, but I wasn't going to stress it either. From the turmoil my life had been in, I was perfectly sure that whatever he was doing in the dark would soon come to light and sooner than he probably thought.

Chapter 19

I was on my way to see Dr. Mayes for our scheduled appointment. I left work later than usual and was in a hurry. I didn't have to borrow Darryl's jeep this time. Over the past week I bought a new car and it hurt like hell to spend the few grand I paid for it. But I can't even lie; it felt good to be driving my own car again. When I arrived on the street where the therapist's office was located, I looked at the time on my dashboard and had ten minutes to be at her door. I parked my car and damn near ran to the elevator. When the elevator doors opened on Dr. Mayes' floor, it was five thirty on the dot and she was the first face I saw.

"Ms. Shenelle, how are you doing? You're right on time." We walked in her office and I was surprised to find a small table set up with light refreshments. There was bottled water, an electric liquid dispenser of coffee, cocoa and hot water for tea. There was a small platter of meat, cheese, and crackers, and a host of grapes. I looked over at Dr. Mayes in complete awe.

"You did all of this for us?"

"Yes, I know we have a lot more to discuss today and since you're my last patient, I wanted to make sure you were comfortable. So whenever you're ready just help yourself." I turned my phone off and sat down.

"Thank you, Dr. Mayes," I said in appreciation for her consideration.

"My pleasure. How was your week?" Besides treating myself to a new car, my week wasn't all bad. Knowing how I always ended up going through something dramatic, I just eventually learned to expect it and each day was just another day and time.

"It was pretty good." Dr. Mayes smiled as though she'd gotten the best news of the day. She got her pen and pad from her desk and positioned herself comfortably in the club chair in front of me.

"Great, well you look like you're about ready to start and I'm ready. So, take it away…"

Chapter 20

(2006)

It was the big day! The crew and I graduated and we were all very happy. Alicia's family, my brother Jere, his wife, Natari's grandmother and even her mother, all came down to see us get our degrees. I was amped up and couldn't stop smiling when my bachelor's degree in Journalism was handed to me. Beyond all the calamities I went through at college, it had all become irrelevant and I was moving on. I met Darryl's parents and their spouses and he introduced me as his girlfriend. Darryl's mother was already beautiful and finely sculptured in pictures, but was much more stunning in person. As for his father, Darryl was precisely his image; just think of Darryl as an older, chunkier man with salt and pepper hair. His younger brother, Dante was cute as a button and looked just like his momma with his wavy hair, pecan skin and small stubby nose. Darryl's parents seemed like very sweet, well-rounded people. By talking to his father, I could see where Darryl got his persona from.

I introduced Darryl to my brother Jere and sister-in-law. Jere at first wasn't all that thrilled with meeting him because of what happened between us the year before, but I begged him to give Darryl a chance. Everybody makes mistakes! It didn't even take Jere that long to warm up to Darryl and he ended up really liking his style. As a matter of fact, I always said to myself Darryl had certain ways about him that reminded me of Jere. When Latoya met him, she waited till no one was paying attention and gave me my props for having such good taste. I saw how her eyes glinted when she first saw him, but there wasn't no fronting on it. My baby was really that freaking gorgeous.

During the last hour, when we were all celebrating at the alumni banquet, I broke the news to everyone that I was officially moving in with Darryl. My brother just looked at me disapprovingly and Darryl's parents didn't have much to say. His mother was more so on the, *"Are ya'll sure ya'll really wanna do this?"* end, and his dad really didn't seem to care. Before we all parted ways, Jere pulled me to the side to have the one on one brother and sister talk.

"You know you wild'n, right?" I turned my nose up at him.

"What do you mean?"

"Shenelle, just last year you were crying about him being married and now you're moving in with the dude?" He was obviously annoyed at my decision.

"Jere, I don't know why you're acting like I haven't told you that he's not married anymore. He and I agreed last year's drama was last year. Now we just want to do us and move on." Jere was just staring at me cockeyed with anger and not even trying to understand where I was coming from.

"Bro come on, you lived your life and now you're married with two beautiful kids. What makes you think it can't be the same outcome for me some day?" He mellowed down his fit once he realized I had real dreams and goals for my relationship with Darryl.

"Sis, I'm not refuting that. I'm just saying you just got your degree. You should do you and focus on your career. Don't emotionally depend on homeboy to give you what you want and think that you need."

"Oh, Lawd!" I cried out in irritation. I was not about to let anyone ruin my day with their lecturing. I don't know how I let it totally slip my mind. Although Jere was my sibling and not my father, he still carried a lot of our father's wisdom. Also he was a father raising a daughter of his own, so I guess it made sense for him to feel he should tell me how to live my life even though I was my own woman. I knew he meant well, but I really wasn't down for hearing all that, not on graduation day. Jere took a deep breath as though he was giving up a losing battle and grabbed me in an embrace, kissing me on the cheek.

"You know what? I'm not even going to trip, Sis. You're grown, so I can't tell you what to do. I just hope that if shit was to hit the fan, you would know how to stand on your own two feet." I grinned at him to lighten his mood.

"Fo'sho! As you always said when I was a little girl, I'm a Patterson and I have tough skin!"

Jere chortled, knowing the certainty of our family vows. "I'm glad you remember, girl. Be easy, ya heard, and keep your head up!"

I smiled.

"Got you!"

***

There was still a little bit of sunlight when Darryl and I got home from the banquet. He told me to wait outside while he went in the house. He had me waiting for so long, I was becoming impatient and started to drive down to Alicia's house. She and Rondell decided to stay where they resided in the neighborhood since it was convenient for them. They were considering moving back to the city, but thought it was best to wait until their daughter was at least five years old. In the beginning, the original plan was Alicia and I would graduate from VSU, and then move close to the city somewhere like New Jersey and become roommates. As we saw, life had other plans. Alicia was happily married and a mom; I was shacked up and in love.

"Babe, you can come in now." I walked in and all of the lights were off. Candles lit up the hall pathway to the bedroom and the song "Butta Love" by Next was playing from the stereo.

"Darryl, what did you do?" I asked all mystified.

"Girl, just follow the yellow light and stop asking questions." He laughed, moving my hair to the side and kissed the nape of my neck. On the door of the bedroom spelled out in colorful alphabet magnets said, *Welcome home!* I blushed and turned the knob entering in. The whole room was candle lit and leaning against the two big pillows were three huge teddy bears, each with a long stemmed rose tucked in its arm and branded onto their cotton stuffed hearts said, I love you. When Darryl and I got back together, after he divorced his wife, I didn't stay at his place. We started back dating slowly and I stayed on campus. The whole wife thing freaked me out, so I wanted to keep away from his premises for a while.

"Wow, this is all beautiful, boo."

"There's still more, babe. Undress and come to the bathroom." He left the room and I took off my dress. I kept my slip and stilettoes on and sashayed to the bathroom. Darryl was standing next to the candle decked tub that was filled with bubbles and rose petals were sprinkled on top. It was a beautiful setting.

"Aw shit, you kept your heels on. I like that!" He cited.

"I'll only do this for you, baby," I seductively replied. He wrapped his arms around my waist and kissed me. The rest of the night was passionate and romantic and wore me the hell out.

For the next two years of our relationship, everything was going perfect. Blessings were coming left and right for both of us. When I first graduated, I did a four month internship working as an editorial assistant for a company that issued school magazines. I also worked at a public middle school as the library receptionist for backup to keep my money flowing. Once I was done with the internship, I was hired at the company to work permanently, but I still kept my job at the library just to be able to stack up. Darryl got a nice gig working as a Juvenile Justice Specialist at the Detention Home School of Richmond since he had his degree in Political Science. Darryl and I hadn't made any plans on moving from our townhouse and were good sticking with saving our money for other plans in the future.

While my relationship and everything else was doing fine, Natari who got her degree in teaching choreography, was having a hard time finding employment in that field. She had to settle on working as an intake clerk at the public assistance office and was not too happy about it. She also wasn't getting along so well with her grandmother. After she graduated, she moved back into her grandmother's home with no intentions of finding a place of her own until she was able to afford a house. Just as I already said, her grandmother was very old school and although Natari was a grown woman, a lot of things didn't fly with Ms. Willis. Natari didn't have a curfew or anything like that, but her grandmother wasn't trying to have her bring her boyfriend Shawn over all the time and spending the night was out. Then she expected Natari to pay her four hundred dollars rent every month. Natari's grandmother was Negro strict and she stuck to her rules firmly. Alicia's family life was all good. She didn't work right away after graduation. Since she had their infant daughter, her husband suggested she stay home and take care of the baby while he worked. Alicia didn't have much family in Virginia. Most of them were from North Carolina, so it wasn't like she was going to have somebody to watch the baby while she was working. Her husband Rondell had family right in Petersburg, but he wasn't too familiar with them and wouldn't even think to trust them around his child.

***

In the year 2009 around Christmas time, Darryl and I found out we were expecting. We were both excited, but Darryl was going overboard. I wasn't even two months yet and he was talking about opening up a bank account for the child's college fund. I didn't believe in rushing to plan anything big and thinking too far ahead. After I experienced the first miscarriage, I always kept in the back of my mind that things were liable to happen at any given moment. Ten weeks into my pregnancy; I was taking a shower when I felt sharp pains in my belly and blood came gushing out profusely. Thank God Darryl didn't work that day and was there to keep me from having a panic attack because I was terrified.

Here again, I went through another hospital visit and another scraping, but this time I was devastated. It plagued my mind if struggling to bear a child was my fault, because it seemed ever since I had that abortion back in high school my pregnancies weren't succeeding. I began to feel if children weren't designated for my future, then I rather God just put my reproductive system on a pause. That way I wouldn't get pregnant at all and have to keep going through such gruesome incidents. Physically I recovered well and Darryl helped me get through the emotional pain. Instead of complaining, we just accepted it and left it up to God to decide what the future would hold as far as having children were concerned.

Aside from the blessings, I hated my life sometimes because when it rained, it poured. The way it worked was when one bad thing happened, a series of other bad things spiraled right behind it. I was coming home from work when I noticed the front door of my house was slightly open. I didn't think Darryl was there because I regularly came home before him. I got out of my car and looked around to see if I saw anyone. I didn't like being caught up in odd situations, so I was hesitant to walk in the house and got back in the car. I didn't know if someone crazy would run out and then I'd have to drive off quickly or run over them. Better yet, I wasn't sure about what I might've found when I walked in. I called Alicia since she was usually on her way home from her job by six 0' clock. She answered on the first ring.

"Hey Sis, what's up?"

"Leecy, I think someone is in my house. My door is cracked open,"

"For real! Aw'ight, I'm on my way!" Not long after she hung up, Alicia pulled up in her get fancy Lexus. I smiled when I saw her through the rearview mirror, looking all sophisticated in a pin striped business skirt suit. My girl and I had come a long way from the skin tight jeans and tank top wearing, little hoochie mamas we were as teenagers. Now we were two young career women. At times I couldn't even get over that *Ms. Loud Mouth Gutsy* Alicia was somebody's momma and somebody's wife.

"Hey, Lady!" I said when she walked up to me and we hugged. She looked over at my door and shook her head. She was just as tired as I was of the funny stuff that was constantly happening in my life.

"Shenelle, are you sure you're not some secret assassin or something because you always got some strange shit going on in your world?" she jokingly said.

"Shit, who are you telling?" We were about to walk in the door, when she stopped suddenly.

"Hold on! Let me go get my switchblade out my purse." As she walked to her car, I noticed she had one of her pumps on one foot and an Air max sneaker on the other.

"Sis, don't forget to change into your other sneaker." I thought about how funny she would've looked trying to fight while she was slipping and sliding in her one shoe, but that was something most working women did when they were driving. It made me check my own feet to see if I had both of my sneakers on just in case I needed to scrap. She came back towards me with her pressed and curled hair pulled into a ponytail.

"Alright chick, let's do this!" We walked in and crept with our blade in our hands. Since it was my house I took the lead and turned the living room light on. We both gasped when we saw everything disordered and thrown about.

"Oh shit, ya'll been robbed!" Alicia screamed.

The first thing I did was run in the bedroom to my custom made jewelry box and all of my jewelry was gone except for the costume pieces; I was tight. The jewelry that was sacred to me, my chains, bracelets, rings and earrings that had been given to me as gifts from my father, and from my mother as pity presents whenever she did something screwed up to me and wanted to make up for it, were all gone. My diamond bezel watch and other gifts that Darryl bought me, his silver Rolex, his earrings and a Cuban link bracelet with the matching chain was gone as well.

The mattress was flipped over. Someone poured bleach all over the comforter set and throw pillows that was tossed on the floor. Both of our flat screen TV's and the stereo system from the living room was stolen. I looked through my drawers and closets. Some of my designer shoes I wore for special occasions and some I hadn't even worn yet were stolen. My black fur coat was gone and that was just a knock off for the time being, but still that shit was not cheap. Somebody straight up disrespected me and Darryl. I hyperventilating out of anger and I was two seconds away from flipping the hell out. Alicia called the cops and they were there trying to get answers that I couldn't give them when Darryl came home. He looked around and his face was bamboozled.

"Shenelle, what the hell happened in here?" he asked rushing over to me. I threw my hands in the air stressed out.

"Darryl, I don't know. When I came home the door was opened and the house looked just as it does now." It was discovered that the back door was broken into. The detectives were there trying to find finger prints and DNA, but nothing was found. They've questioned neighbors and bystanders. I hoped someone seen anyone suspicious coming from our house or lurking around the area, but no one saw a thing. No one else's house was broken into either. All that the cops could do was write a report and put it on file until something came up for further investigation. While I could've thought some relentless crack head burglarized us, it was obvious that someone had it out for us and planned the robbery, but neither Darryl nor I had a clue on who could've done such of thing. The more the mystery was in the air, the more agitated I became.

What was bugging me out was how the hell someone could just raid our house and walk out with two big TV's and no one spotted that. Somebody on the block had to know something, or maybe they were just haters and robbed us themselves. I sat on my couch trying to hold back my water works, so that I wouldn't wail in front of everyone and look pitiful. All of the stuff I cherished and thought I would have forever was history and I could never get them back. Alicia rubbed the small of my back to comfort me as she stayed through everything and tried to say some encouraging words to calm me down.

"Shenelle, I know you're upset, but whoever did this obviously needed ya'll shit more than you guys did. Screw them assholes; you and Darryl have good jobs and everything that they stole could be replaced." Alicia reminding me that I had a good job to replace my things didn't make me feel too much better. She didn't understand the full degree of my hurt and why my things meant so much to me. My jewels were momentums that kept me connected to my parents.

Alicia might've been the baby in her family, but she wasn't the only girl, so she didn't have the luxury of getting anything she wanted like I did. While she was growing up, everything had to be equal and divided among her and her sisters, so that none of them would feel left out. Once her husband Rondell heard of the disarray, he came over to the house. By then he and Darryl were basically blood brothers. He hung out at the house much more than Alicia did and all we would do was swap positions with each other. He would come by my house to see Darryl to have their homeboy time and I would be driving on my way to see Alicia, and vice versa between her and Darryl. They helped us clean up the house while their next door neighbor watched the baby. After midnight and a few drinks, they went home leaving behind all their love and sympathy. Darryl was visibly upset about everything, but managed to handle it as he did every time something went wrong.

I jumped in the shower hoping to wash away my fury and he joined me trying to console me. I buried my head in his chest, letting my tears mix with the droplets of water that was spraying onto his skin as he held me. Emotionally I was a sucker when it came to disruptions. I lived through them, but I hated going through them.

"Why is this happening to us?" I asked Darryl.

"I don't know babe, sometimes things just happen, but we'll be alright. We can't let small stuff like that bring us down." I was so glad I had a man who was tough while walking through fire, because Lord knows that it sure as hell burned me out.

***

I walked into my job an hour earlier to organize some material my boss left on my desk and water her plants. After working for the high school magazine company for a year, I sought other employment and worked for the Daily Press Newspaper Company in Richmond as a junior editorial assistant. I had long quit my side job at the school library and started doing some freelance writing for extra money. I loved my job at the Press, but like most places, there was that cocky, uppity someone who got on your last nerve because they were higher up than you on the job. Her name was Madison Smith. She was the Editor-in-chief and a hefty, African American, middle aged Richmond native.

I didn't know what was up with this chick or more like who put a stick up her ass, because every morning she came in with an attitude as though the red carpet was supposed to be laid out for her whenever she walked through the door. She and I did not get along. I guess you can say she was my boss because she was two notches up from me and I was her co-editor's assistant, but let me tell it. Robert Logan, a Caucasian man and the founder of the whole organization, was who I considered my boss. Screw that chain of command stuff. Somehow Mrs. Smith felt that because she was old enough to be my mother, I was supposed to succumb to her arrogant bullshit, but not I. See, I was the type of person who had been through a lot of shit and didn't intend to take any other shit from anyone.

When I left my mother's house, I always kept in my mind that if I could graciously walk out on the woman who birthed and raised me, because I was tired of her crap, everyone else was no exception and could kick rocks with sore feet for all I cared. So this lady, whenever she saw me would walk past me, rolling her eyes with an attitude. Most of the time, I didn't even look at her and that seemed to tick her off even more. She and I have been bumping heads since the day we first met and the rival sustained.

I was sitting at my desk, typing a document when she strutted past my cubicle smirking. I ignored her. After dealing with my mother and her antics for so long, I was already used to those types of things. She came by my cubicle again, stopped and watched me. I looked up from my computer at her and didn't utter a word, trying to figure out how I could help her.

"Don't mind me. You can continue on with what you are doing. I'm just doing my rounds and checking up on ya'll. Make sure you bring the paper to my office when you're done," she said in a haughty tone. I continued typing my article and shook my head out of anguish. I couldn't stand testy people, especially when they were middle-aged, menopausal women.

I tried my hardest not to let her stuck-up attitude take me to a place where I didn't want to go. What got me was that she was a married woman, and I saw her washed up version of Uncle Ben-husband when he came to the job one day to bring her lunch. He seemed like a nice old man; probably the type that spoiled his grandkids rotten. Then going by how old and stale cigarillo smelling he was I could tell he couldn't have been laying down the pipe at home. Maybe after he'd been smoking and choking on one to satisfy his nicotine habit, but not close to satisfying his wife. As we all know, when a woman isn't getting none, she is spastic stricken daily.

Towards the end of the day, Mrs. Smith felt to come out of her character towards me. The old bat tried to give me a homework assignment for the weekend. She stated some lame excuse that since she liked the way I proofread and documented things, she wanted me to go over this thick stack of articles. I had to proofread the whole thing, type it out correctly and then put it on a flash drive so I could print and have it on her desk when she arrived Monday morning. I gave her a look that said she must've been stupid if she thought I was crashing my weekend off from work for her bull. Not that I couldn't have had it done by that night because the work was so easy to me, but I wasn't going to give her the power to think she could make me do whatever she wanted. I had to stand up to her. I told her that it couldn't be done and for her to leave the work on my desk. I would be in on Monday and have everything taken care of by lunchtime. When I left her office, the broad got crazy and followed me to my cubicle calling herself barking on me.

"You know what, young lady? You must not know where you stand at your position, but let me remind you. I am your boss and when I tell you to do something, you must do it!" At first, I wasn't going to feed in to her because I knew arrogant people fed off of others reactions to make them feel superior, but I was tired of this broad's shit. I barked on her big ass right back and much louder than she did.

"Well you know what with your old, miserable ass, I'm tired of your shit! You must not know where you stand at your position, but let me remind you that you do not sign my gotdamn paycheck nor do you pay my gotdamn taxes, so you need to get up out my face! Leave the paperwork on my desk and I would have it done on Monday!" She and everybody were looking at me like I was psycho. They were all shocked because I was normally a sweet, quiet girl and when I popped, it came unexpected. She screamed at me, pointing her finger in my face.

"That's it, Ms. Patterson! You're finished! I am calling Mr. Logan right now and I guarantee you will not have a job on Monday!" I sucked my teeth and walked to the elevator, going down to the parking lot. I wasn't the least bit worried about her threat. I was one of the best editorial assistants the Daily Press Company had. Ms. Aileen Lane who was the co-editor and in charge of me, she loved how I worked and I knew she would put in a good word for me in regards to Mr. Logan. I mean come on, I was her assistant and on more than one occasion, she brought me breakfast. I just wished she was in the office and not out on sick leave.

Chapter 21

"Girl you good, cause I would've been slapped that old bumpkin!" Natari said. The girls and I were out on our habitual chill time, sitting in Starbuck's. I told them about the dispute that went down at my job and they weren't even amazed. They knew the feeling because everybody had that person at their job that targeted them and other people, whether it was to provoke them or they pretended to be their friend just to get into their business and gossip to other workers and spread rumors. These individuals were usually the ones who didn't have anything better to do in their own life.

If the provoker was a woman, she didn't have no man, no kids and was a loner who went home to her cat or dog. If she was married and had kids, she was regretful of it and was miserable when she went home. Her husband or baby-daddy was probably a bum who couldn't maintain a job, yet cheated on her like a dog and had no respect for her. Her kids were affectively spoiled, bad as ever and depended on her for everything, stressing her out. Then of course the single mother, the woman who's unhappy, tired and undesirable and thinks she knows everything, but usually perceptive about nothing when it comes to herself.

If the provoker was a man, no woman probably wanted him, so the only way he could let out his blue ball frustration was by picking on the humble people who didn't pay him any attention. Either that or he was once a lowlife everybody despised who finally got on his feet. He found an area that made him successfully stand out, and now was cocky as hell.

"For real, I couldn't deal with that shit every day. Shenelle, you might have to start walking around with a tape recorder in your pocket from now on," Alicia said.

"Darryl already suggested that. We have one in the house, so I' ma use it. That's if I hopefully still have my job." Hannah waved off my comment.

"Shenelle, you still have your job. I've seen your work and anyone who keeps getting promoted the way you do; it's not easy for any company to just get rid of them like that." Hannah worked at a women's shelter as a clinical social worker and was engaged to her beau of four years, Nicholas. He had a fantastic job working at Virginia Medical Center as a pediatric nurse and working towards getting his doctorate. He was an excellent partner to Hannah and I was happy for her.

"Yeah, I guess that's true."

"So, did you and Darryl ever find out who robbed ya'll?" she asked.

"Nope and it's pretty much all water under the bridge now. There's no way that Darryl and I are getting our stuff back, so we don't even talk about it." They all nodded their heads in an understanding notion. In as quick as a week, Darryl and I replaced all the electronics that were stolen. There's something about life that when you cry about your misfortune when it happens, you end up recognizing your blessings later on. All of the stuff that was taken from us, right under our noses was upgraded right in front of our faces. Our TV's were bigger and more extravagant and the stereo was beautiful. The sound system had much more clarity. We changed the springer mattress to a Tempurpedic, the foamy kind that adjusts to your frame and it felt like heaven. My savored jewelry was still a wrap, but I appreciated all that God had allowed to be renewed in the end. I finished off the last drop of my vanilla bean frappuccino, ready for the next destination.

"So, what's the next move ladies, is it going to be reruns at my house or movie night?"

"Screw all of that! Let's do the club tonight!" Natari said. Alicia and Hannah sucked their teeth.

"Um honey, you must forget that I am a married woman and a mom, so I can't be doing that stuff no more," said Alicia. I smirked because the flipside to that was Alicia's husband wasn't going to allow it even if she begged him. Rondell although he was in his twenties, he was a little old school when it came to his woman or should I just say he was straight up domineering. He wouldn't let Alicia do anything and if he did, it was after he'd carefully thought it through.

"I think a movie is a good idea, let's check out that new Tyler Perry flick," Hannah said. We all looked at each other and agreed. I pulled some money from my purse to pay for my part of the bill.

"Come on ya'll, let's go catch it while it's still early."

We got our tickets at the Hoffman Center and had a good laugh and cry watching the film. I have always been a big fan of Tyler Perry's Madea plays and movies. They put me in a great essence. At first Natari tried to drag us to the Regal Stadium down in Richmond, but I crossed that out real quick. I didn't need to be dealing with no nagging heifers and scoundrels, pushing people and skipping lines. Yet as the fire streak burned its way gradually through my life, trying to dodge the drama on any scale was impossible.

When the movie was over, the girls and I stood outside the theater talking about the flick, when I noticed this girl was grilling me. I flashed a funny look at her because she was just staring at me ice cold like I did something to her. Her face didn't ring any bells to me, so I knew I didn't know her. A part of me wanted to walk up to the chick and ask her if she had a problem, but I left her be because I wanted to end my night on a positive note. I excused myself from the girls, puffing on their cancer sticks and went back into the theater to the ladies room.

There weren't many people in the restroom when I walked in, just a woman changing her child's diaper, and another washing her hands. Before I handled my business, I checked the voicemail Darryl left saying he was going to be home late since he was hanging out with the guys. The bathroom was silent for a while, so I knew that the other women vacated. While I cleared out the well, I heard someone come into the bathroom and I could've sworn I heard the latch to the door lock. I could hear the woman's heals click as she walked from one stall to another until she reached mine. She stood there in front of my door and I saw her peeking through the slight opening to identify me. I tried to tell myself to calm down as I felt apprehension kicking in. I had already flushed the toilet and just stood there opposite her. I took a deep breath, mentally preparing myself to rumble.

"Miss, why the hell are you standing in front of my stall?"

"Nothing, I'm waiting for you to finish so I could use it. That's if you don't mind." I kept standing there trying to figure this chick out before I faced her.

"There are plenty of other stalls. Why can't you just use any one of those?"

"I like this one better, it's cleaner," she said hissing her teeth. I was getting pissed off and was just ready to do whatever I had to do to get the woman to fall back off me. So I unlocked the stall and yanked the door open, locking eyes with the crazy broad. Just looking at her dead, dark eyes, I knew that something wasn't all there with her, but it didn't worry me at all. Crazy recognizes crazy and based on what I knew about myself, it had been a fact for a very long time that I wasn't all there either and was probably way more demented than she was. I stood there glaring right through her pupils.

"Miss, do I know you or do you know me because I'm not going to play this crazy hostel shit with you all night!" She threw her head back and chuckled from my impudence, I continued to stare at her, fuming. I hoped her laugh felt good because she really didn't know; I wasn't the one to mess with. She inched up closer to my face and said angrily, "Yeah I know you. You're the bitch who got my man sent to fucking jail, claiming he tried to rape you. Does the name Gary sound familiar to you?" When I heard the name *"Gary"* all of the organs in my body fired up. I didn't know where this woman came from after so many years.

"I didn't claim shit! He did try to rape me!"

"You're a fucking liar! We were engaged and he wasn't like that! He was faithful to me and now thanks to you, my son won't see his father for the next six years!" I didn't care for her pity story; it was all because of that mofo why I was going mildly insane.

"Okay and all that ain't my problem, so what the fuck is your point?"

"The point is, bitch! I'm going to kick your ass!" She shoved me and I fell backwards against the toilet. I manhandled her skinny little ass to the floor and pulverized her. I have to admit, the girl may have been a bag of bones, but she wasn't no frail thing. We thumped and I could hear people who more than likely were my girls, banging on the door, trying to get in. I shuddered as she vigorously pulled my hair. I had her head mushed onto the cold tiled wall. I felt my scalp pulsate and blood surge up. Tears welled into my eyes from the agony and she wasn't intending to let go.

"I hate home wrecking bitches like you! Ya'll always screw things up for women who want a happy home like me!" she whimpered as she continued to tug on my hair. I didn't want to do it, but I had to do it. I reached to my back pocket for my switch blade and right when the door to the bathroom busted open, my knife came slicing down the woman's face. If she only knew the truth of what her so-called faithful man did to me, and the damage it put me and my loved ones through. The five inch gash I put on her face was only out of mercy otherwise it would've been her throat. I watched as she held her left cheek and blood oozed between her fingers.

"I'm not a fucking home wrecker! Maybe if women like you did your jobs right at home, then there would be lesser assholes like your man screwing up the lives of women like me!" Alicia and the rest of them ran up to me. They looked at the girl in horror with their mouths hanging wide open.

"Shenelle, what the hell?" Alicia said. She kept looking back and forth from me to the girl. The usher was helping the girl put a towelette on her wound.

"Shenelle, what the fuck went on in here and who's this girl?" Natari asked. I too angry to speak. Alicia examined my head at what probably was a nasty injury. The cops arrived and I told them everything. The girl was taken to the hospital to get her face stitched up. She couldn't press any charges against me since she was the one who caused the conflict. The dumb broad was so distraught over her baby daddy's verdict that she openly admitted to confronting me, so my actions were considered exactly what they were, self-defense. I pressed charges on her and filed for an order of protection, so I wouldn't have to see her again. I refused to go to the hospital and the girls followed behind me driving home.

***

Alicia was cleaning up the scarring on my head and Natari was putting ointment on the scratches on my face when Darryl, Rondell and a few of their friends walked in. He scanned over the scars on my face. "Babe, what happened now?" I sighed and shook my head. If I had all of the answers to why jacked up things constantly swung my way, I would make things easier and let everyone know ahead of time, so I wouldn't have to hear that same question all the damn time.

"Apparently to some psycho bitch, she's a home wrecker," Hannah said. Darryl's face looked panicked. "A home wrecker? Who the hell said that?"

"The estranged ex-girlfriend of Gary, the rapist. Turns out the broad is just as loony as he is and a stalker like him too. She followed Shenelle all the way to the bathroom, locked them in and called herself confronting her," Alicia replied. I watched as Darryl's face warmed over a little as though he was relieved about something. I couldn't hold my tongue at his suspicion any longer, so I called him out on his conduct.

"Darryl, what is wrong with you? Do you know something I don't?" I asked annoyed. Everyone looked at him and he replied offensively, "Shenelle, what are you talking about?" I know he was mad I put him on the spot in front of everybody like that, but I was tired of things popping up out of the blue. Somebody needed to tell me all I needed to know a.s.a.p.

"I'm just asking, as a matter of fact I'm going to ask everybody in this room. Who the fuck else is out to get me. I want to know so I can prepare myself now. So if anybody knows anything, I suggest everybody to speak the hell up because I'm giving ya'll tonight to do it." I announced that out loud as I stood up and gazed at all of them. They all looked at me like I had lost my mind and I nearly had.

"Sis, you're bugging out right now. I think you should seriously go to bed and get some sleep. It's getting late anyway." Alicia was standing in front of me holding my face.

"Shenelle, really she's right. You're losing it girl. You know everybody here wouldn't let anything happen to you and would tell you if we knew anything," Natari said, standing next to Alicia.

"Yeah, we love you, Shenelle. I hope that you know that." Hannah said from the couch. I understood the girls' input, but in my recollection everybody who has claimed they loved me had damn sure hurt me or lied to me. I snatched my face out of Alicia's hands.

"Yeah, that's what they all say!" I said as I plopped myself down on the couch next to Hannah and concealed my face into my hands. She rubbed my back and I could sense everybody's empathetic eyes on me. Everybody has a story. I knew I wasn't the only one, but how I was feeling at that moment, I could've bet my life my story had to be one of the worst ever.

"Everyone, I think ya'll should go home now. Thanks for all your help. It's appreciated." I heard Darryl say. All our friends said their goodbyes and made their promises to call, then left as a group. I looked up at Darryl standing in front of me. His face looked plain, but I could imagine that he thought I was losing it, just like Natari said and what everyone else might've thought. Sometimes I wondered if he ever thought of dipping out on me because my life was so encircled with drama.

"You need to chill out, babe. We're going to go through our trials and errors, that's life. I know it gets hardtop deal with sometimes, but you're letting it get the best of you and I hope you don't let it take you out." I wiped away the stream of my tears and asked, "You would leave me before that happens, right?" Darryl swallowed the detectable lump in his throat.

"No mama, not now and not ever. I just don't want you to leave me." I took his extended hand and he pulled me off the couch and into his arms.

"You really are loved, Shenelle. One day you're going to realize that even if I can't be the one to prove it to you. Let's go to bed!" Other than the five or six people who said they loved me and have done their best to show it, for some reason I felt that there could be somebody else who would really prove it.

***

Monday morning, back at work I had to have a meeting with Mr. Logan, Ms. Lane and Mrs. Smith concerning the face-off from Friday. It didn't go on for that long because just like I figured, Ms. Lane had my back. Mr. Logan was courteous to the fact that everyone was susceptible to having an intensified moment. Of course I didn't walk out without a verbal warning, Mrs. Smith was still higher up than me and I had to respect her. She too walked out with a verbal warning because higher than me or not, respect was respect. According to Mr. Logan, everybody deserved it and there were no special accommodations. For the rest of the day the big hussy had the nerve to have an attitude with me. I knew it was because she was just mad things didn't go her way. All she wanted was to see me get penalized, so she could feel right.

From then on she kept going with her little antics, the sucking of her teeth and mumbling under her breath whenever she came around me. That was her scheming way of challenging me, so I could go off again and get myself fired, but her attempts were powerless and I continued to ignore her. I eventually gave up on the plot to tape record her since she never really said anything. In every situation, there comes a time when someone cuts the cake and something has to be done.

I was walking past her, going towards my cubicle when the burly broad purposely bumped into me, almost knocking me clear to the floor. All of the paperwork that was stacked in my hands scattered all over the place. She gave a phony ass apology and my adrenaline rush was tempting me to knock her lights out. My co-worker James, a young white guy who looked like he might've been a nerd all throughout his school days, but was visibly handsome came and helped me gather my papers.

"Don't worry, Shenelle, I saw what she did. I'll vouch for you and let Ms. Lane know as soon as I see her."

"Thanks James, I appreciate that, but you really don't have to. It's not needed." His face became puzzled.

"Why wouldn't you want me to help you? You know that if somebody doesn't step up at your defense and tell Ms. Lane about what Mrs. Smith is doing to you, she's going to keep doing it." I smirked at his benevolence even though his point was accurate.

"No she won't, eventually something is going to make her stop, so I'm not worried about it and neither should you. But really thanks for your concern."

"Alright, but if anything else occurs and you need me to say something for you, I'm here." I smiled again.

"Thank you, now get back to work before she sees you talking to me and start attacking you next." He nervously started looking around hoping Mrs. Madison didn't see us.

"You know, you're probably right about that." I raised my left eyebrow at him.

"I do know I'm right about that, and you're too nice of a guy, so please get back to work!" He didn't say another word when he made his way back to his cubicle.

***

I'd just got off from my lunch break and was catching up on some of my paperwork when I heard the loud mouth of the fat lady sing six cubicles away. While everyone stopped what they were doing to focus on what she was raving about, I kept focusing on my work and didn't pay her any attention, but then she sought it out when she stopped at my desk screaming, "You know, little girl, you really have some major issues. I know it was you who bummed up my car!" I looked at her in shock.

"Mrs. Smith, what are you talking about, I bummed up your car how?" I had to hold my laugh in when I realized I was catching the Virginian twang and had been since I resided there, she snarled.

"Don't play with me, young lady! I know it was you. It wouldn't be anyone else but you." I gazed at her and we had an audience because everyone was entranced by the scene. I stood up crossing my arms against my chest and decided to get sarcastic, hoping it'd send her rage to the top.

"Well, what makes you think that? Why would you believe I would do something to upset you? I mean it's not like you do things to me to make me feel a certain way, right?" My eyes briefly glanced over at James and he grinned. Mr. Logan and Ms. Lane were heading our way and Mrs.

Smith's back was turned towards them, so she didn't know it. I hoped like all hell she would say something to blow her own spot, so that Mr. Logan would hear her and get rid of her.

"I know that it was you because..." She suddenly stopped herself and I anxiously pried.

"Because what?" She just stared at me and I stared at her breaking a sweat, dying for her to slip up. She yelled, "You know, God don't like ugly and he fitting to handle you. Just watch!" I know she didn't just use that line with all the dirt she was doing. Before I could give her an unreligious piece of my mind, Mr. Logan stepped in and it was clear he was fired up because his face was tomato red.

"Would you two stop it? This is a place of business and this behavior is very unprofessional. I want both of you in my office, right now!" Mrs. Smith and I strolled silently behind him and Ms. Lane. When we entered his office, he shut the door and got to talking.

"Now I don't know what it is with you two, but you guys are getting out of hand with this fiasco and it has to stop immediately, or I'm going to terminate the both of you. Mrs. Smith, you will be the first to go without any recommendation." Mrs. Smith's face looked slighted when Mr. Logan threw that bombshell at her.

"Mr. Logan, somebody messed up my car and I know that it was her sitting right there!" She pointed at me. Mr. Logan looked at her with no sign of astonishment on his face.

"Why would you automatically assume it was her? Did you see her do it?" Mrs. Smith huffed and replied quietly, "No, I didn't."

"So, then you cannot blame her." The whole time I remained quiet. All of this was a waste of my sweet time, but it was killing my work hours, so I wasn't mad. Mr. Logan let out a breath of exasperation and looked at Ms. Lane who was shaking her head in disgust, and then he swiftly concluded the meeting.

"I don't want any more out of you two. Both of you are my best employees and I do not want to have to let you guys go, but I will if this nonsense continues. Mrs. Smith, from now on if there are any problems concerning Ms. Patterson, do me a favor and let Ms. Lane deal with her. Am I understood?" I looked over at Ms. Lane. She smiled at me and nodded. Mrs. Smith and I both agreed and were about to leave Mr. Logan's office when he asked me to stay behind.

"Yes, Mr. Logan!" His blue eyes studied me like there was something to find on my face.

"Tell me the truth; did you do anything to her car?" I looked Mr. Logan right in the eyes and replied, "Sir honestly No, I don't even know what she's talking about." He nodded his head in acceptance.

"Okay, back to work!"

Mrs. Smith never really stopped aggravating me. She curbed it down some, but she obviously just couldn't help herself. The following month she eventually turned her major provoking on to another person. The person was also a young female, a newbie, shy and an intern. Mrs. Smith had to find out the hard way that she was screwing with the wrong person. The girl turned out to be Mr. Logan's niece and one day she recorded Mrs. Smith getting rowdy with her on her cellphone and Mrs. Smith was fired no less than five minutes later without recommendation, just like Mr. Logan promised.

I heard she shed tears when she got the news and walked out with a box of her things and a sad puppy dog face. I took a sick day that day, so I wasn't there to see it. I got a call from James since he was the one who escorted her off the floor. I wasn't the type to wish anyone to lose their job because everyone needed to eat and keep the bills paid, but I didn't feel sorry for her ass either. One thing I would always remember about Mrs. Smith is that she was right about the last thing she said to me, God don't like ugly. Some people loved to speak that line and it was always the people who were like Mrs. Smith, however when it was on them they seemed to take it for a joke. But God really doesn't like ugly and instead of Him demonstrating that to me like she swore He would, He flipped her words and confirmed it to her.

Chapter 22

My twenty sixth birthday came around quick. The girls got together and threw me a big birthday bash at a club called "The Cave" down in Virginia Beach. It was off the chain and the hostesses there were friendly and engaging. Darryl and I wore the same colors; I wore a strapless sky blue mini dress with royal blue high heeled sandals and royal blue costume jewelry. Darryl looked all GQ in a Royal blue, silk, short sleeved button up shirt, off white slacks and royal blue dress shoes. I let my hair flow, whipping it back and forth as I danced.

It was a big surprise when I saw my brother Jere and Lataya there. They joined me with the crew on the dance floor and a professional photographer took millions of pictures. The food was scrumptious and to say that there wasn't enough liquor to make the place into a distillery would be the lie of the century. As I partied I didn't stop to pray that nothing crazy would go down and ruin my day, but when the girls brought out my three tier birthday cake covered in chocolate fondant, I made sure to put in a wish.

"Alright Shenelle, make a wish and a good one girl cause you deserve it," Alicia said holding back my hair as I stood over the flamed blue candles.

"Okay ya'll be quiet now, I want to be focused and make this turn real." Everyone laughed. I closed my eyes and took a whole minute to ask God to grant my wish of a stress free night and blew the candles out. Everyone clapped and cake was being passed around. I didn't see when Darryl trailed off and I heard his voice over the microphone.

"Eh ya'll, listen up. This moment is for someone who is very special to me, my number one, my love, and my heart." I stared at him on the stage and gleamed while everyone expressed their emotions in muffles. My brother Jere grabbed my hand and lightly squeezed it. I could tell in his smile that he was happy for me.

"Shenelle, come up here baby," I was reluctant acting all shy; I always hated being put on blast even when it was for a good cause. My friends and my brother were pushing me and telling me to go up and when I was about to, Darryl just stepped down.

"Gosh-lee girl, I hope you break out of this shyness one day and stop fronting because you really ain't that shy." He wrapped his arms around my waist and slipped me the tongue in front of everybody. I interrupted our kiss, breaking into laughter when I spotted my brother scrunch his face and turn his head from us. I playfully nudged him on the shoulder.

"Oh please Jere, like I've never seen you and Taye lip locking before. You remember back when you used to bring her over to Mom and Dad's house how ya'll were." Lataya agreed and he chortled.

"Yeah but still, you're my baby sister man, Chill!" We all laughed and he said to Darryl while we were still in each other's arms, "Yo, behave yourself my dude until you take my sister into a private room." I smacked my lips at my brother's comment with his over protective ass.

"No doubt, man!" Darryl chuckled, they gave each other a pound and Darryl turned back to me, pecking me on the lips.

"I love you, Shenelle!"

"I love you too, Darryl." He had the MC play our song we loved to dance to, Usher's song "Yeah" and we grooved together. For the rest of the night as I wished, everything went well without any shambles. I got nice gifts and two thousand dollars in a card that my friends and family all chipped in. As usual I got something nicer and surprising from Darryl when we got home. Somehow he found one of my pieces of jewelry I thought was stolen. It was my fourteen carat gold x and o bracelet with my birthstone I had gotten from my parents for my thirteenth birthday. Darryl had it cleaned and it looked spanking new like it had never been touched. He didn't want to tell me where he found it and explained he wanted to save it for my birthday and when I saw it, I almost fainted. I couldn't even think of how to reward him for such a nice gesture, but I didn't close out the night with him feeling unhappy.

***

The smell of something burning woke me out of my sleep, I looked at the clock and it was almost four in the morning. I looked over at Darryl and he was in the dead zone. The smell was repugnant and I quickly rolled off my side of the bed and put my slippers on. I walked out to the living room and was knocked on my butt when I heard an explosion that shook the house. Glass shattered from the window because of the force and I screamed. The scene was so graphic and the sound was so loud it felt like I was in a Baghdad war zone. Darryl ran out of the room.

"What the hell was that?"

"I don't know." We could see the blazing light from flames in the living room.

"I' ma go check, stay right here." Darryl put on a shirt and his sneakers and as soon as he opened the door the sweltering heat hit me as if a dragon had blown a whistle. When I saw the raging fire, I couldn't believe my eyes as I unconsciously walked closer.

"Oh my gosh, my car!" I ran outside against Darryl's instructions and he was pushing me back as another sound reverberated.

"Shenelle, I told you to stay in the house."

"Darryl, my car is on fire! We have to put it out!" I tried to push him out of the way and run back outside. He pulled me towards the bedroom.

"Let go of me, Darryl!"

"Shenelle, what do you think you could possibly do, stomp the fire out with your feet? Stop and let me call the fire department." I heard the sirens of fire trucks and police cars coming up the block and I broke into tears. My car was the only thing I had left from my father and it was the grand prize to all of the other things he had given me. Screw not having the luxury of my own transportation, that wasn't important. My car was the number one object I made note to cherish forever and that too was now in a fireball and gone. I watched the firemen watered down my baby with the hose and I pouted at the sight of the metal skeletal that was left of it. That right there was it and I completely went off. I stormed around the house, cursing the air and punching the wall. I wanted to hit somebody; I wanted to break something. I was getting so tired of everything going wrong and I didn't know what to do.

"Shenelle, calm down," Darryl said trying to stop me from wilding out and I angrily pushed him.

"Don't tell me to calm the hell down dammit! Look at my car! It's gone! Somebody fucking torched my car!" Darryl was looking at me transform into a maniac as the minutes passed. I grabbed a picture from the wall and threw it across the room.

"Shenelle, stop!" Darryl was holding my arms and I hauled away from him and ran towards the door. I wanted to see if my real car was still there and if this was all just a nightmare. When I put my hand on the doorknob, Darryl pulled my hand off and I screamed at him with fire in my eyes.

"Darryl, you better get the fuck off me and let me see what's going on outside!" Darryl was still holding me, trying to keep me from going outside.

"Shenelle, you're not going to see anything different than what you saw before." He saying that caused me to seize my hand from him and smack him. He looked at me stunned and I released myself from him and ran out of the door. The crowd of damn near the whole avenue was standing around in their gowns, jammies, and robes talking amongst each other. I was too through.

"Ma'am, do you know whose car this is?" one of the officers asked. I shot him an eerie eye.

"It's in front of my damn house! Who's car do you think it is?" Darryl rushed out of the house and took hold of me like I was a toddler.

"Officer, it's her car and this is our house."

"Do you know who did this?" another officer asked. I looked around at everyone and at the news reporters standing on the strip of our block recording the whole thing. I ran back inside the house before Darryl could answer the officer's question and hurled the garbage can across the hall. I screamed out in anger and wanted to destroy everything of mine my eyes laid on, at least this way I could be the first one to do it. I emptied out my drawers and closets and carried a bunch of my clothes, making a pile in front of the bedroom door. I got the gas lighter from the kitchen and was about to burn them up when Darryl walked in the house and looked at me like he knew I was crazy.

"Shenelle, what are you doing?"

"What does it look like I'm doing? I'm getting rid of all my things so that nobody else could get to it." I looked at the pile of clothes and thought about the news reporters filming my humiliation to be broadcasted on national television. Then to think, I would've had to go back to work at the Press and possibly review my own story as an article for the public to read. That's when it hit me that this last situation was the deal breaker for my life in the state of Virginia. I was a little calmer when I looked at Darryl.

"As a matter of fact, I'm packing my things and I'm leaving. I cannot live here anymore. I'm going back to the city to live with my brother until I find my own place." I turned my back to him and walked to the closet to pull out my suitcase.

"Shenelle, you can't be serious," he said stepping in front of me.

"I am dead serious, now move!"

"Shenelle, you know that I'm not going to let you just leave like that. Come on let's go back to bed." I knew this dude couldn't be for real to think I was going to be able to sleep after what I witnessed a half hour before.

"NO! I'm not going to bed I am out of here. You can stay if you want to!"

"How are you going to leave town without a car?" Since he went there, I went there and slapped him so hard I knew he saw stars. I went and dragged my suitcase out of the room and he yanked it out my hand. I was tired of fighting.

"Alright Darryl... screw all of this! I'll just go with the clothes on my back and have Alicia drive me to the airport in the morning. Goodbye!" I hurried towards the door in a spaghetti strap night tee and jammie shorts and Darryl was after me. He lifted me up, moving away from the front door. I was yelling at him to put me down. We were in the bathroom when he locked the door and stood in front of it.

"Darryl, let me out!"

"No man! I'm tired of you running away every time something goes wrong, you're a quitter! When are you going to learn how to just hang in there and rock it out?" Hearing Darryl call me a quitter hurt because it meant he hadn't acknowledged that I had taken all I could bear. I've gotten into fights, arguments, dealt with theft and now arson. After a while there is but so much one person can take.

"I'm tired of rocking it out! There's a point when enough becomes enough and if you think you're tired, you really don't want to be in my shoes right about now, bruh. Now please move so I can leave. I do not want to be here." Darryl stared at me and shook his head.

"Shenelle, please! Stick this out. It's not the end of the world." I was so frustrated that I punched the bathroom mirror. It cracked and so did I. At times I didn't understand what everybody wanted me to do. All I ever wanted was peace and no matter what, I could never find it. I knew Darryl didn't want me to leave him. I knew that a lot of people I'd left probably didn't want me to leave them, but what else was there to do when you feel like you're going through so much agony, and nobody seems to understand the way you need them to? Darryl pulled me towards him to comfort me. I didn't want to be consoled, I just wanted to have my moment and scream; let it all out. No matter how pitiful my situation was, I hated being pitied at times because all it did was make me feel more helpless than I already felt, so I jerked away from him.

"Darryl, I'm okay. Let me go over to Alicia's and I'll come back in the morning." He went into the medicine cabinet and took out an Advil p.m. capsule from the bottle and put it in my mouth.

"Babe, take this and let's go back to bed. Please give me a month. I'll put in a two weeks' notice at my job and I promise I'll get us out of here." My mind was still telling me to leave, but I would've been fooling myself to believe I wasn't totally exhausted. I swallowed the pill dry and splashed some tap water from the faucet into my mouth to chase it down.

***

A month and some change later Darryl and I moved from our town house back to New York. Fortunately for Darryl, his supervisor knew someone in New York who knew someone, so he was able to be transferred to another detention facility with a good recommendation. I didn't even put in a two weeks' notice at my job. I just called Mr. Logan and had a discussion with him regarding my situation. Expectedly, he already knew the story. It was actually front-page in the newspapers, so everybody and their momma knew. Mr. Logan also gave me a good recommendation. He tried to meddle a little bit to understand why I had to leave town for something that minor. I gave him no information and just kept my own understanding of my issues to myself. Ms. Lane was upset with me for resigning. I felt bad too because I for sure would miss her. The only one who really did understand was my co-worker, James and he wished me well. I promised him and Ms. Lane I would keep in contact with them and they would never be forgotten.

Darryl and I didn't move to Castle Hill, my hometown. Instead we moved to a one bedroom apartment in Harlem. It wasn't bad. I actually felt it was a little better than the Bronx, but I didn't plan on living there for long and was looking to be making bigger moves soon. Alicia and her husband hated that we left them in Virginia all by themselves, but they weren't too mad because they were also ready to leave and were making the arrangements to do just that. Natari who was on ends with her grandmother moved up to the city right behind us and rented a room with her boyfriend Shawn until they could find something stable. She was lucky enough to land a job as a case worker at the public assistance office in Harlem, which was good because they paid a few thousand dollars more than what she was making in VA. Hannah was good money with her circumstances in Petersburg and because she was an outgoing person, her staying in VA wasn't a threat to our friendship with her. We knew she would come to the city and visit us any time she could.

I didn't find employment as quickly as I thought I would. After living in Virginia for so long, I forgot all about the recession and the unemployment rate in New York. Next I found myself wondering if I'd made a completely stupid move by leaving Virginia. Constantly thinking about it was becoming a glitch, so I removed my mind off it to keep from kicking myself every day and made do with my new circumstances. I signed up for public assistance, temporarily. I went to Natari and she pulled some strings. When I left the building, I walked out with two hundred dollars in food stamps and I only had to pay four hundred dollars for my eleven hundred dollar rent. I was able to get away with that because Darryl and I weren't married, so it was easy to just lie and say we weren't together anymore considering his name was on the lease. The part I hated was going to the EVR appointments and dealing with those trying to make me work for a small monthly paycheck. Darryl loved the new standards. He didn't mind paying the seventy percent deducted rent and never having to come out of pocket for food. He had never really been a big fan of Natari, but he sure warmed up to her after that solid she did for us.

In the meantime, I started back doing some freelance writing and sold myself to public schools, writing columns and posts in magazines. I enrolled at Hunter College to pursue my Master's degree in Journalism. I thought one day I could possibly own my own magazine company geared towards struggling teens. After living in the suburbs for some time, it wasn't easy readjusting to the ghetto; the gun crimes, drug addicts and everything else. Although it wasn't like the same things didn't happen at other places. The best thing I loved about being back home was I got to see my brother Jere frequently and was able to spend the weekends with my niece and nephew. I bought another car with some of my money I had saved. It wasn't anything spectacular, just something to get me around while I went to school and had the kids with me. Things definitely weren't the way they were when I was in Virginia, but at least I had the basics. I had a roof over my head, food, and mobile transportation, so I couldn't complain. Life may not have been exactly the way I wanted it, but it was copacetic and to me that was better than the worst.

Chapter 23

The following year, I was halfway through my mission of getting my Master's degree and couldn't wait until it was accomplished. I still hadn't found a permanent job, but was doing some temp work as an editor for The New York Times. Suddenly as it always seemed to bloom from left field, blessings came through. Darryl got promoted and became the Assistant Director of the detention facility and walked into an additional ten more grand to his annual salary. Soon after that, I was hired to work permanently for the Times. A few months later, I was promoted and became Senior Editor. When I got the news, I was over joyed but humbly accepted it until I got to the ladies room and fell to my knees, thanking God.

"See Sis, what did I tell you? I told you that you were going to be doing big things one day. Now look at you! You're doing almost better than me, I'm proud of you!" Once I told everybody the good news, my brother Jere set up reservations at the "Lobster House" in City Island to celebrate. All of the usual crew was there with me. Alicia had moved back to New York in a two bedroom apartment in Castle Hill, so that she could be close to her parents. She and Rondell had another daughter a year and a half before and it was good for them to be back around their families. Hannah also took time off from her job to drive from VA to share the moment.

"Jere, you're doing big things too. Look at you! You just bought a house in Pennsylvania with a big backyard. I'm more than proud of you. Shoot, I'm jealous!" I said playfully. Jere worked as an accountant and over the years he progressed wonderfully. He worked for everyone from major stock brokers to celebrities and was making money on top of money. He wasn't exactly rich yet, but his ass was paid.

"Don't worry though, babe. We'll get there too someday soon," Darryl said and I smiled at him.

"Aye, Dee? You might have to tell her that a million times before she believes it," Jere stated and we all laughed.

"Well, She-She? How does it feel to be boss lady now? That's what I'm going to call you for now on, boss lady!" Alicia said, considering I've climbed the latter of starting out as an assistant to now becoming an overseer of the assistants.

"It feels good, girl. I could dig it!" I replied delightfully. The whole time while we celebrated, I noticed Natari hadn't said much and seemed to be a little on the outs.

"Nat, are you okay? Why are you so quiet?" She looked at me and gave a phony smile.

"Yeah I'm cool. I'm happy for you, Shenelle. Congratulations!" Alicia flashed me a look that said Natari was on her hating mode again, but I didn't pay any true mind to it. If anything, I felt for her. She'd been struggling with trying to reach her goals in life. She still hadn't been able to land a choreography gig and was stuck working at the welfare office. She finally got her own apartment, but was paying a grip on it all by herself because her relationship with her boyfriend Shawn was on and off. Ever since they left Virginia where he was born and raised, he was having trouble finding a steady job. He was coming from working at a factory with no other employment history and was beginning to drive Natari crazy due to his own stress. All of her issues left her no other choice, but to step on the worst road and start dancing at this club out in Brooklyn as a side hustle to keep the bills paid.

"Well ya'll, I have another announcement to make." Everyone was quiet and giving me their attention.

"I'm pregnant! Ya'll going to be aunties and uncles." I watched as Darryl's drink almost fell out his hand from astonishment and everybody else's face glimmered.

"Oh my God, I'm going to be an auntie! Well it's about damn time! Now your nieces can have somebody to play with!" I looked at Alicia funny because her daughters had more than enough cousins to play with from her sisters. She caught my glare and stuck her middle finger up at me.

"Shut up! You know exactly what I mean," she said and I chuckled. Darryl was sitting next to me, stroking my stomach. "Wow, I'm going to be a dad." Hannah, Jere's wife Lataya and Natari said their congratulations. My brother blurted out, "Aw'ight Sis, that's what's up, but when's the wedding?" I sucked my teeth. Why did he have to take it there?

"Soon, man," Darryl said to him and then he looked at me smiling.

"Real soon."

My first prenatal visit was wonderful. To see the instantaneous movements of the little person I carried was a moment to remember. It was too bad Darryl couldn't be with me because he had to work. I was riffing about it in the beginning, but had no other choice but to understand. Now that Darryl was one of the big guys, he had bigger work responsibilities. I received the first sonogram picture of our little peanut and send it to his Blackberry. I wasn't far along yet for my belly to show, but I was further than I had ever been. I smiled whenever I passed any woman with a bulging baby bump and imagined what the experience would be like. The comfort level at my job was soothing, especially comparing to what I went through at the Daily Press. There didn't seem to be anybody miserable and it was all a peaceful atmosphere. One of the head editors was a bi-racial male; his name was Alexander Joseph Carter.

Since the day we met, we got along perfectly. We became so close that we even gave each other nicknames. I called him A.J. and he called me Nelly, my name was more like an anecdote since we both liked the singer Nelly Furtado. The majority of the workers were males and to me that was always a plus because the less females the less drama. The coordinator of the business, Mr. Frances, he was like another Mr. Logan and what I dug about him was that he was very zealous and made his colleagues feel like they were a part of big a happy family. We never had to buy breakfast in the morning. Every day there was coffee, donuts and bagels waiting in the break room. I was happy that life made its way back on a swell path and I hoped to God every single day it remained that way.

***

Alicia and I got together and took my niece, nephew and her kids to Chuck E. Cheese. We sat at a table in front of the pinball play net where the kids were and did our usual catching up. She reached her hand over and gently rubbed my slightly swollen belly. "So, mommy-to-be, how have things been going so far with the pregnancy?" she asked all cheerfully.

"It's been cool no problems. I take it one day at a time, thanking God that there's no mess." I self-confidently stated.

"Amen to that!" Since Alicia had her first child she dedicated herself to going to church and practicing the works of the Lord. She wasn't no holy modified saint, not to get that twisted. She would tell a person that with the quickness, but she still was very much a child of God.

"How are things going with you and Rondell?" Her painted happy face turned into a frown and she rolled her eyes.

"We're Alright!" I picked up in her body language that something wasn't right in her household and she just wasn't telling me. I was a little offended, for as long as Alicia and I had been friends, we've never kept secrets from each other no matter how bad it was.

"I don't know, Sis; your facial expression is telling me something different. Now talk to me, what's up?"

"Shenelle, it's really nothing you don't already know. Rondell is just who he's always been and as much as I love him, I'm starting to get tired of him and his bullshit high and mighty ways. I mean, I know that as a wife there's this whole thing of letting your husband be the man who runs things and I should be submissive but…" Alicia huffed letting the stress ease on out.

"Girl I can't breathe, everything must be his way. It's a shame that back when we were in VA he didn't even want me to work and I had to move out so he would give in. I'm glad I do have a job now because the way things are going, the debates and the ultimatums, it is wearing me out." I shook my head. I remembered the whole jump off between Alicia and her husband.

Alicia called me in the middle of the night crying. She was parked outside of my house with her then two year old daughter strapped in a car seat and two suitcases packed. She waited until Rondell was asleep to make her move and was talking about driving all the way to New York by herself. The situation made me want to kick Rondell's ass for even putting her in that state of mind. I couldn't let her delirium cause her to do something so stupid like drive over three hundred miles through the sticks after midnight with an infant. So I begged Darryl to switch places with her for a while. Alicia stayed with me while Darryl stayed with Rondell until things got back in order between them.

Their situation had even caused fuse between Darryl and I because he wasn't with the arrangement of staying with Rondell and out of his own house, but Alicia didn't have anywhere else to go. Darryl knew that if Alicia left town, I would have drove to NYC with her leaving him and everything else behind. All I could say is the arrangement didn't last but two days. Whatever man rage or verbal admonishment Darryl cast down on Rondell, worked. Within the following week Alicia found her dream job and was working without a negative word or threat out of him.

"So, what exactly are you saying? You're thinking about leaving him?" She gazed at me with a sad face.

"I don't know. I don't want to, but I just don't know." I let out a loud breath. All the time I've known Rondell, I also hated his ways, but I couldn't deny he was an excellent father and loved Alicia and their children with all his heart. So to agree with Alicia that she should consider leaving her husband after being with him and taking his crap for more than a decade, that wouldn't be right. I spoke to her softly, so she wouldn't think I was taking his side but just wanted to help her understand what she signed up for.

"Sis, you knew how Rondell was before you married him. What made you think that things would be different now?" Her unhappy tears rolled and she quickly wiped them away.

"Maybe I thought as we got older, he would change. But after the kids were born, he just got worse. Very worse!" Alicia's statement made my stomach flutter. I looked over at the kids to make sure they weren't in earshot, leaned in closer to her and whispered, "Alicia, has he been putting his hands on you?" I was relieved when she vigorously shook her head.

"Hell freaking no! I wish that mofo would! He's blocked our accounts so I can't take out any money when I need it. If I do need money, I have to ask him for it. He checks my cell phone to see who I have called. He even knows the passcode to my voicemail. I can't even take a bathroom break for too long without him wondering what I'm doing. Hell, if I was crazy, I'd think the fool times me when I take a shit." It was only because she was serious why I didn't break out into laughter in her face and just shook my head again.

I didn't know what else to say. Everything that Alicia said sounded like Rondell's doings to me. I don't know why she thought he would change. Now I wasn't married to the man, I barely had any type of connection with him other than he just being my best friend's husband. Even I saw back when we were teenagers that there was not a spark in him that said he would be any different now than what he was then. But this was the thing, when a woman becomes too visually attracted to a man on the outside; it blinds her from virtually seeing him for who he is on the inside. When she finally does see it, it is always a little too late.

"Sis, you always pray for me, so I'ma pray for you and your marriage. Even if Rondell never changes, he's what God created him to be and remember you took the vows as his wife. So, for better or worse and to death do ya'll part, right?" She sighed, flaring her nose at me because she knew I was making a point, a point that she didn't want to hear.

"Come on Leecy, you would never leave or turn your back to me and ain't I crazy?"

"Hell yeah, your ass is crazy!" We both giggled.

"But you love me anyway and Rondell deserves the same treatment, you think?"

"Yeah true that, what the hell he is my husband," Alicia looked over at the kids.

"And my children's father who they love to death!" She looked back at me grinning.

"We're going to work it out. Thanks for your help, Sis... She-She!" She grabbed my hand and I caringly squeezed hers. I cracked myself up sometimes how I could give my friends advice and make their day better, but when it came to giving myself advice it was an automatic fail.

***

Another prenatal appointment and Darryl wasn't around again. This time he had a meeting to attend and swore that it was mandatory to be there, so Alicia accompanied me to hear the baby's heartbeat for the first time. It sounded like tiny water waves and it made my eyes water to know that my child was very much alive and well. From the time I was a little girl, I always wanted a baby boy. Since I didn't click with females like that, I didn't really care for raising one.

"Ms. Patterson, would you like to find out the gender of your baby?" I thought about it for a second and realized I rather it be a surprise.

"No, I want to wait until the end." The practitioner smiled.

"Good choice!" She wiped the slimy gel substance off my pelvic area and handed me the sonogram. I was euphoric. I have seen many sonograms, but never my own and it really made me feel like a parent already. Alicia beamed as she looked at the picture with me all excited.

"Screw that! I want to know what you're having." When she was about to go to the nurse I quickly yanked her arm. If I'd yanked any harder, I would've pulled her shoulder clear out of the socket.

"Uh-uh, no you're not!"

"Damn She-She, it's really that serious?"

"Uh yeah! If I'm going to be surprised, that means you are too and everybody else." She smacked her lips.

"Girl, I can't stand you right now, you know I hate suspense. But alright, it is your baby, so I'll wait."

"Good, thank you!" With both of her children, early in her pregnancy Alicia had tried any tactic and baby quiz to determine the sex of them. I used to tell her whatever God had settled for her was what it was going to be. She anticipated girls and I guess God knowing her heart, gave her two beautiful daughters.

I went home and found Darryl sitting on the couch. He had a smile on his face and I looked at him skeptically wondering what it was for. He was home earlier than I expected and that was unusual. I noticed an envelope was on the coffee table, I sat down next to him setting my own envelope with the sonogram in it onto the table. I leaned over and greeted him with a kiss.

"Hey, what's with the smile?"

"Baby, with all of the good things that's been going on I have a lot to smile about." I smiled with him because he couldn't have been more right. He picked up the envelope to hand it to me; I picked up my envelope and traded so we could open them at the same time. I opened his envelope and practically rolled out of my seat when I pulled out a check for forty thousand dollars.

"Darryl, where did you get this and what is it for?" He was still smiling down at the sonogram when I asked the question.

"It's the money for our new home. I've been saving up. That's why I've been working so much overtime." I was in awe. For a minute I had been wondering if he'd been doing dirt instead of actually working. I was pleased when my suspicions were turned into joy.

"When could we start packing?" I said eagerly and he rubbed my belly bump.

"Relax, baby girl! I didn't want you to do too much movement, so I already did most of the packing. The guys are going to help me do the rest." I wiggled my forefinger for him to bring his handsome face to mine and kissed him long and slowly. From all the problems I had ran into, I never thought I would see this day. It was like my dream was coming to life. Every night before bed, I prayed for a miracle and I thanked the man upstairs for the umpteenth time that he heard me and answered.

Chapter 24

Less than two weeks later, Darryl and I moved into a two and a half bedroom, two bath, detached condominium in Jersey City. It resembled a single-family house and was gorgeous. Our street was clean and beautiful; I felt like I was at Hampton VA again. The master bedroom was the biggest I had ever seen. It had its own bathroom and a balcony where you could view the Hudson River and New York skyline. The other two rooms were just as wonderful and what they called a half room was a joke on us because it was average size. I chose to make that room, the baby's room and the other bedroom, a guest room. The first room I decorated was my little angel's room. Since the gender wasn't yet revealed, I painted the room in turquoise with wall decals of swans and cygnets swimming in a lake. I put in a glider rocking chair with a foot bed, so I could be comfortable when breastfeeding. So many other things were added that it made the room into a prodigious nursery. I was so impressed with my work that I started to think I should switch my career from an editor to a home interior designer. The whole condo was phenomenal, completely decorated by *moi* and I didn't waste any time showing it off to my friends.

I wouldn't say I threw a house warming party because Darryl and I already had everything we needed. I just invited everyone over for a get-together. Our kitchen was big and fancy and I loved to cook, so I was in a hurry to christen it. I prepared all the foods that black people loved and my pregnant ass craved for.

"Sis, this place is off the chain. You really did your thing in here, but I ain't even surprised. I remember how you did your old room back at your parents' house," Alicia said. When I was a teenager my parents allowed me to paint my room. I painted it powder pink rose and decked it out with pink and white drapes, bed set and all. Despite who I really was as a person, my room was the only place that made me feel like Alice in Wonderland.

"Why thank you!" I gleamed.

"Girl, you're about to have Rondell and I quit house shopping and buy a condo." Jere's wife and the girls were sitting with me at the dining table snacking on banana cheesecake, while the guys were in the living room watching a basketball game and talking junk. I couldn't stop smiling. I was proud of all of my accomplishments and my friends' accomplishments. I was really proud of Natari. Since she was so unhappy with her job working for the government, Alicia, Hannah and I encouraged her to fill out applications for the civil service positions. She did and scored so high that she was placed as one of the top candidates on a list of five different positions. She was hired to work for the police department in the city as a general officer. She was so ecstatic that she cried and we all cried with her. It felt a little awkward in the end because Natari really wasn't the sensitive type, but we all laughed afterwards. We all knew this was a blessing from the great man upstairs. When God stepped in when you least expected it, He had the power to bring out unexpected emotions.

"So Shenelle, you and Darryl are making all of these big moves. Do I hear wedding bells soon? I want to be matron of honor," Hannah said and I saw the look Alicia gave her. Late in the previous year, Hannah got married to her husband Nicholas and had this big lavish wedding at Niagara Falls. When she asked me to be the maid of honor it surprised the heck out of me. I didn't see that coming at all really since Alicia was the one who met her first and they were so close. Alicia didn't even trip over it and was cool just being one of the bridesmaids, but with me it was a different story.

"I don't know, but right now I just need to drop this baby and a few pounds before I think about a wedding." I patted my stomach that was now the size of a basketball and thought about it. I knew that having a baby out of wedlock wasn't the best thing, but I wasn't begging or rushing to get married. I wanted to be married, that was without question, but I knew there were essentials to being a spouse and I wasn't too sure if I had what it took to commit to them. I knew I only had one key thing down packed and that was being loyal to one person. After experiencing so many disappointments, I was now scared to death of any other form of failure happening such as a divorce. So as far as marriage was concerned, I left it up to God to decide when that would happen. For the rest of the night, we all danced and played different kinds of games from adult games to board games. We made homemade virgin and spiked pina coladas. My friends knowing how I liked to get my drink and my two steps on, they made sure to pester me as they sipped their drinks while I settled with the virgin stuff and Kool-Aid punch. It was cool though; they were being protective and having fun, so I couldn't even be mad at them.

When the party was over, Darryl and I relaxed on the balcony and watched the lights sparkle from the city. I laid on his chest while he cradled my tummy, something he had grown very fond of doing. Everything felt perfect. I had a bomb home, a wonderful, handsome man, money in the bank and a bundle of joy on the way. I had all the things I dreamed of and was happy with my life.

"Darryl, you know you're sort of my hero, right?" I watched his face blush.

"Am I really? You think so?" I kissed his chin.

"Yes, you don't believe so?" He slightly shrugged his shoulders, still grinning.

"I'm just playing a role, babe. As long as you're happy, I'm happy." I smiled.

"I love you, Darryl."

"I love you too." He kissed my forehead and then said, "We're good." I rested my head back on his chest and closed my eyes. I was more madly in love with Darryl than I was before. He'd done a lot to make my heart warm over. He was like my night and shining armor. He gave me the world and made me happy like he promised. A man that could make his woman happy was every girl's core desire, whether or not she has gone through rough times.

***

"Hey, Nelly-Nelle!" I heard a very familiar baritone voice say. I looked up from my desktop and my colleague A.J. was standing at my door. "Hey, come in and have a seat," I said as I sent out an email to one of the editorial assistants. A.J. and I would stop by each other's office every now and again to chat. He was really cool. I didn't have any male friends I could talk to and I felt I could talk to A.J. about anything. I didn't have to limit what I wanted to say out of courtesy. Sure I had a brother and a boyfriend, but when it came to having a male friend you could be around, speak freely and he didn't expect anything from you. Well… the feeling is much different. He walked in with a red gift bag in his hand.

"I'm not going to hang around too long cause I have a lot of work to do. I just wanted to give you this." He handed me the bag. I smiled when I pulled out a yellow crocheted jumper, hat and bootie set. I put it up to my belly, envisioning what my son or daughter would look like in it. I was five months and had a little more time before I could throw a baby shower. This was the first gift I had gotten from anyone.

"My mother made it. She used to love to crochet and hasn't done it in a while. I gave her the idea so she could do something she enjoyed." I appreciated that. A.J. always talked about his eighty year old mother; how she used to be an outgoing woman, until she was diagnosed with

Alzheimer's disease. He moved her in with him and took care of her. A.J. was the middle child between two sisters. You would think the daughters, especially the oldest one would take the initiative to care for her ailing mother since that's what most daughters did, but they both were married and dedicated to their own lives. I could tell by the way A.J. talked about his mom that she was his first love.

While some men would have a picture of his family or his love interest sitting on his desk; the picture that sat on A.J.'s desk, framed in gold was the green eyed, olive skinned brunette woman who birthed him. I never liked momma's boys. For a time, I thought they were annoying how they smothered their mommas. After being around A.J., I learned he didn't just love his mother, he cherished her. Sometimes I guess depending on what kind of person his mother is, a man could really go all out of his way to show how much he appreciated her. That was one form of it though, it was another form when it was the mother who acted like her son was her everything and couldn't stand to see him cling to any other woman, but her. I've seen plenty of lifetime movies about jealous mothers and in my opinion it was just downright sick.

"Aw, thank you, A.J. This is very nice."

"No problem, I hope you have a boy. I feel you'd be a great mom to him." I smiled. His words made me feel good.

"See you later!" He walked out. I could understand why he was as sweet as he was. It was true, good women raised good men and for that they deserved to be cherished.

At lunch time I shared a pizza pie with A.J. and told him about the warm-up party I had over the weekend. For a split second, I realized I was actually being rude because he was my friend and I hadn't invited him. He reminded me of that and playfully acted like he was hurt. I felt bad, but he didn't seem too bothered and brushed the subject off talking about something else. From the many conversations we've had, I always wanted to bring up the topic of why he wasn't married, but never had the nerve. I didn't want to pry into his personal life, but A.J. was so damn gorgeous and as sweet as he was, I couldn't understand why at the age of thirty five he wasn't settled down. He definitely wasn't gay because I've seen how he acknowledged women. All of the women at our firm talked about him in the staff lunch room. I've even observed how they made frequent stops to his office to purposely ask questions about their work they already knew the answers to.

What I found strange was how they seemed to forget to come to me first since that was chain of command. It really was no big deal to me. I personally thought the more they stayed out of my face, the better. Plus I already knew what the deal was. A.J. knew what it was too because he would joke about it with me whenever we would link up. He mentioned how much he hated women who threw themselves at him and they sure did that. One of the women even had the audacity to come up to me in the copy room and asked if I was dating him. I assumed she was trying to figure out why I wasn't wearing a ring on my finger to indicate I had a man, but yet turned up pregnant. I didn't answer her nosy question and walked away leaving her to herself with her suspicions. The other women gave me ugly looks and hard stares, but I didn't give two shits about them. I actually loved the attention because they made me feel more relevant than I cared to be. A.J. was just my dude and I didn't even look at him like that. Basically, he was like my brother from another mother.

I was back in my office when I felt some mild cramping in my lower abdomen. The pain wasn't enough to alarm me, but it was enough to make me feel paranoid. I called Darryl to get his opinion on whether I should check up on it or not, but his voicemail came on. I called his assistant and she said he wasn't in his office. I asked her if he even came into work at all and the little brat told me she didn't want to disclose that information. I slammed the phone down on her before I said something smart and rubbed my stomach to soothe the cramping. I decided after a while to leave work early to see my doctor.

"Everything looks normal, Ms. Patterson. Your baby is fine and healthy. The fetus just grows rapidly in this trimester and your uterus is stretching to make room for his or her little body. So it's nothing to worry about." I blew out a sigh of relief.

"Whenever you feel this way again, just drink a nice hot cup of tea or take a warm bath, it usually helps," she suggested.

"Thank you, Dr. Sal."

"You're very welcome. If you want, I can put you on bed rest so you wouldn't have to be so mobile. Sometimes excessive movement can cause pre-term labor. You'll be able to relax during the remainder of your pregnancy." I took a few seconds to decide. I loved working, but I didn't mind taking some time off. That way I could work from home, do my schoolwork online and catch up on my shows. All that was looking great.

"Yes, that would be nice!" I waited while she wrote out my slip and swung back to my office to drop it off with the boss. After that I went on home and called the girls and told them to come over after work.

***

Darryl didn't come home until three in the morning. I tried to force myself to stay up until he got in, but due to the hormonal fatigue, I didn't hold out past eleven 0'clock. I heard him as he went into the bathroom to take a mighty long shower, gargle after he brushed his teeth and move around to change into his pajamas. I could smell the scent of his body wash get stronger as he crept to the bed. When he laid down and put the covers over him, I turned over towards him.

"Darryl, where have you been all day?"

"What are you talking about? I've been at work all day," he replied wearily.

"Really? Well that's not what I heard. I called your job today because your phone was off and I was told you weren't in your office."

"Babe, what makes you think all of my work is performed in my office?" he asked flatly with his back still turned to me. I felt my body temperature strike up with anger and I sat up.

"That's just it! I don't think all of your work is being *performed* in your office. I think your ass is putting in work somewhere else where you're not supposed to be."

"Yeah, aw'ight! Whatever you say, girl. Go to sleep please," he sarcastically remarked. I pulled the covers back and off of him, throwing it on the floor.

"Shenelle, what are you doing?" He bellowed frustrated. I walked over to his side and turned on the lamp.

"Darryl, you need to stop screwing with me and tell me what's going on." He sat up and rubbed his hands over his sleepy face, huffing and puffing.

"Since when do you have to work until three in the damn morning?"

"Shenelle, it's a live-in facility. Its open around the clock and I'm required to be there at any time." I rolled my eyes because I was not falling for that. I didn't think a bunch of boys at the detention center needed that much attention.

"You're lying!" I said raising my voice to a higher pitch.

"Shenelle, stop with the yelling while you're carrying my seed!" Darryl's eyes were red and puffy like he hadn't slept in days. I toned my rage down to be rational with him.

"Darryl, I know you're doing more than just working. You got to be. Now just tell me. Are you screwing someone else?" I stood there and waited for Darryl to answer. I wasn't a dummy. I knew men and I knew Darryl. Men loved to have sex and I can't front. Ever since I found out I was pregnant, I have deprived Darryl of sex because I didn't want anything to disrupt my pregnancy. It didn't matter if the doctor said it was safe, I still didn't trust it.

"No, I am not screwing anyone else. That's just your brain overworking itself again. Now get back in the bed because the baby needs its rest." Darryl grabbed the comforter and snuggled back in the bed. It really ticked me off how he dismissed my concerns so easy and it was only because I was pregnant that I didn't try to slay him. Instead of arguing with him anymore and stressing myself out, I ended the dispute with one last statement.

"You know what, Darryl? Cool! Since you like coming in the house at three a.m., then you won't be allowed into this house until six a.m. How about that? And I will change the damn locks if I have to." He smacked his lips and before he could say anything, I left the room and locked myself in the guest room. I hoped that whatever Darryl was doing was worth it because as far as I knew it wouldn't be once he lost me.

***

A few days had gone by since our argument and instead of Darryl coming home at any time in the morning; he turned around and didn't come home at all. I would call him to try and understand what his issue was, but we would always end up arguing and cussing at each other. All of a sudden he had this new, snobby attitude and only wanted to discuss matters concerning the baby's well-being. Other than that, it seemed as though he really didn't give a damn about me and my well-being. He hardly called to see how I was doing. I wasn't used to Darryl acting so nasty like that towards me, so I knew he was doing something shady. He didn't even want to tell me where he was staying and kept ignoring the question when I asked. I had to threaten to pack up my things and leave in order to get information from him. He admitted he was staying with his mother and stepdad in Harlem. I didn't believe him, but I wasn't going to waste anymore precious time fooling around with his games. I just focused on my baby's health and arrival. I did what I planned to do while I was on extended maternity leave and worked on some articles from home and studied for my upcoming exams for school.

"So you and Darryl are on ya'll bullshit again, huh?" Alicia asked.

"Yeah, unfortunately," I replied rolling my eyes in disgust. She and Natari came by and brought over some Popeye's chicken and was hanging out with me.

"What the hell happened now?" Natari asked and I just shrugged it off; I didn't even want to explain it and get riled up. "I don't get it with ya'll two, it's like one minute ya'll Romeo and Juliette, and then the next minute ya'll Mr. and Mrs. Smith." We all giggled.

"But you know that's how couples are when they get all caught up with each other. It happens," Alicia said.

"I'm not even stressing it. Darryl wants to act like that then forget him. It's about me and mines right now." I rubbed my belly. I'd taken notice that the baby wasn't as active as it should've been. Only once in a while I would feel a kick or two.

"Good, I like how you're thinking, Sis. Screw all the men right now and all that negative energy because while we cry about them, they're not thinking about us," Alicia proclaimed.

"I'll drink to that," I said as I took a swig of my ginger ale.

"Same here, Sista!" Natari said as she drank from her Smirnoff wine cooler and we all turned our focus back to watching *the bad girls club*.

    With Darryl not in the house, it felt a little lonesome, but it was a good thing I knew how to entertain myself. I actually enjoyed my, me-time. I hadn't had the time to do that for a few years due to working and all. I began purchasing books from a website online and started back on my reading. It helped a lot at keeping my mind off my problems. Each day I woke up was plain and simple. If I wasn't at one of the girl's house, they were at my house. When I was just relaxing by myself, I would whip up something in the kitchen to last all week and the TV or a book was my friend. One Wednesday, for whatever reason I was in the mood to do some cleaning. It seemed very bizarre to me because my house was sparkling clean as I kept it. There just might've been a strand of hair and some dust on my hard waxed cherry wood floor. I swept and mopped and then I hopped in my car and drove to the mall. I picked up a new set of shower curtains and mats to do my bathroom over for the fourth time in almost a year.

About two hours or so later, I was in a middle of taking a nap when I thought I heard someone enter my front door. I was mad and really didn't care for being bothered with Darryl, but my heart did get a little excited at the thought he had stopped by to see me. I didn't get up from my bed to greet him. I wanted him to come to me. When five minutes passed and not a soul entered my room, I got up and went to the hallway. I called out Darryl's name, but didn't get an answer and I felt the baby squirm as I moved toward the staircase. I saw that his black pair of Timberlands was laid out on the stairs. I knew they weren't there when I came home from the mall, so that meant he had to have come in.

"Darryl!" I yelled out again and still no reply. *"Lord, why does he play these stupid games!"* I mumbled to myself. I heard a noise like a door creak and I checked all of the rooms; first the bathroom, then the guest room and the baby's room, no one was there. I removed the boots from the stairs and went back into my room and turned my cellphone on to see if Darryl might've called and left a message, but the only messages I received were from Alicia and Jere.

I was going to call Darryl, but I figured since he wanted to be a bum and just come by and leave without speaking to me, then I wasn't going to give him the satisfaction of my worry. I was speed dialing Jere's number when suddenly I heard glass shatter in my hallway. I jumped up from my bed and rushed out to the hallway. I saw the picture Darryl and I recently took shattered at the top of the steps. It was an eight by twelve professional photo of Darryl cradling my growing belly. I had it hung on the wall in the nursery. I was so stunned at what I saw that it didn't cross my mind to check around again to see who threw it. The special moment captured in the picture and the feeling of missing how happy we were made me bend over and pick up the broken frame. The next thing I remember, I felt myself get fiercely pushed and I went tumbling down the stairs. Everything after that was oblivion.

***

When I opened my eyes, I saw the paramedics pushing me swiftly on a stretcher. I felt extreme pain in my stomach and throbbing in my right arm that brought tears to my eyes. I knew something had to be going wrong with the baby. My body was moved from the stretcher to a hospital bed in the intensive care unit. I asked the nurse what they were doing to me. I didn't realize Darryl was at the hospital and could hear him cussing at the doctors, telling them he was the father and needed to be in the room with me. A moment later he was allowed in and rushed to my side. I cried hysterically, asking him what was going on and what they were going to do. Darryl couldn't even talk. He also was overwhelmed with the situation. His eyes were tearful and his face was flustered. I screamed as I felt more excruciating pain rush through my spine. I yelled out for Darryl to help me.

"I'm sorry, this is all my fault," he whispered in my ear. I didn't know what he meant, but I was in too much pain and confusion to ask him. The nurse stood over the doctor as she spread my legs open and probed at my belly. She stuck her latex gloved fingers into my birth canal.

"She's eight centimeters dilated," the doctor said to the nurse.

"Ms. Patterson, I know this is painful, but I need you to push okay. Push as hard as you can." I nervously looked at Darryl and then back at the doctor.

"No, it's not time! It's too early! My baby is going to die! I don't want my baby to die!" The doctor looked like she was trying to keep her own emotions in order and sympathized with my condition. "I know ma'am, and I'm so sorry for your loss, but you're in labor, so you have to push, okay?" Whether I wanted to or not, I was forced to push because another contraction came. I pushed and pushed while I squeezed Darryl's hand. The pain was so unbearable that even though I didn't want my baby to come out, it was a mass relief when it did.

I looked down at my son as Darryl held him; he was wrapped securely in a blue hospital blanket with a hat topped on his little head. He wasn't a full term baby, yet he was still so adorable and I could make out his tiny features. He looked just like his daddy from the shape of his head, down to his little toes. He was supposed to be named after him and be coming home with us, but he wasn't. I spoke with a priest and signed the death certificate. I really went in a slam when the nurse took my son away to be sent to the morgue. Darryl kept apologizing as I cried on his shoulder. I hated everyone at that moment. I hated myself and I hated Darryl. I was angry at God because I felt he hated me. I felt God thought I deserved nothing that would mean a great deal to me, nothing I desired most in this world.

Chapter 25

I was sent home the following day with my arm in a sling from my bone being broken in two places and a print out of my son's footprints. I didn't want any photos of him because they would've been too depressing. I was closed in and silent during the ride home from the hospital. Darryl didn't have much to say either and could barely look me in the face. I asked him how I got to the hospital. He explained he came by the house to see how I was doing and found me sprawled out on the floor. I told him how I thought he'd stopped by beforehand because his boots on the stairs and the picture thrown down in the hallway. His face looked absent and he didn't seem to know what I was talking about.

When we walked in the house, I dashed away from him and went into the bedroom, locking the door. The memory of the scary situation caused me to relapse and I didn't want to be anywhere near Darryl. I was resentful towards him for acting strange and not being there when I needed him. I was mad at him for being selfish and only worrying about himself instead of what was supposed to be important to him. In my eyes, he was the scum of the earth and I hated his guts in a way I never hated anyone not even my worst enemy. I sat on my bed, spaced out with questions for days. I asked God what He wanted from me and what He needed me to do because I obviously wasn't getting it. I felt displaced and miserable and I distanced myself from everyone. All of my friends and family got the news about what happened to me and was ringing my phone continuously. I wouldn't answer to anyone, not even Jere who had come to the house and left a sympathy card with his own encouraging words. He also left pictures that my niece and nephew drew for me, balloons and a big teddy bear. My girls did the same and I gave them the same treatment.

Darryl stayed around and tried to soothe me by making me tea, bringing me my favorite foods and buying me flowers, but nothing was capable of changing the sadness I was feeling. I felt I had been let down by God. I thought once He opened doors in my life they would never close, but somehow these doors would open and then suddenly, they would slam right back in my face. As far as Darryl was concerned, I was having crazy thoughts about him. Whenever I thought about how I was pushed down the stairs and how at first his boots were there, I began to wonder if he actually planned to hurt me. I wondered if he wanted something bad to happen to our child. The tears he'd shed over my son's body became questionable to me. Was it really an act of grief or guilt? Genuinely, my heart went out to him because it was his first time experiencing something so tragic, but I couldn't commiserate with him because I refused to nurse his ego. I felt he needed to suffer in order to understand all he had done and the negligence he made me feel.

What freaked me out most was how our life together would seem flawless and then it would turn into a nightmare. I didn't know what to think, but I knew I no longer trusted Darryl. I didn't even feel secure being around him anymore and asked him to leave. He wanted to stay and tried to convince me he was a nice guy who just badly screwed up, but that was where my cue came from. He screwed up one too many times and I wanted him gone. I told him that he leaving wasn't a suggestion, it was a demand. It wasn't just about my anger, it was about my sanity. Every day I looked at Darryl, I wanted to kick his face in.

If he were to lay next to me there was no telling whether or not I would stab him fifty times in his sleep and end up on a new season premiere of *Snapped*. The add-up to his screw ups were driving me mad and his ass needed to go and leave me the hell alone while he still had his life. I didn't blame Darryl for our son dying, so don't get me wrong. I just held him accountable for the way he treated me while I was pregnant. If anything, I blamed myself. Many times I wondered what would have happened if I'd done things differently. I would think…What if I hadn't gone off on Darryl that night? What if I hadn't bothered to pick up the picture frame? Why hadn't I just called the cops when I suspected someone strange was in my house? All of those thoughts constantly picked at my brain.

***

When the house was cleared of Darryl, Alicia practically moved in to keep me from drifting out of my normal senses. Natari stopped by every day when she got off work and Hannah had taken emergency leave from her job to be there for me. She tried to counsel me, but I wasn't in any mood for it and told everyone not to blow their mind with my grief and to handle their own business. With Alicia, there just was no arguing with her. She took vacation time to be with me. The times when I laid in my bed and cried she was right beside me, crying with me.

Jere and Lataya were also at my aid. Soon my whole house was full of mourners for my loss. I played it smart and waited until Darryl was gone to tell everyone what really happened. In the beginning, they thought I had been clumsy and slipped and fallen. All of them went crazy and wanted to look for Darryl, especially my brother Jere, but I had to let him know that it wasn't entirely Darryl's fault. I couldn't just blame it all on him, because it could've been anyone who pushed me down the stairs. Someone could've been trying to set Darryl up. A police report was transcribed once again with no allegation made towards anyone. My brother Jere was just fed up with my issues and wasn't even trying to be rational. He was in my room with me and we had one of our talks.

"I don't know about this cat, Shenelle. Ever since you met him you've been getting into some weird shit. You sure he ain't involved in drugs or something?" Jere asked, I shrugged and shook my head no to him.

It had crossed my mind before if Darryl could have been involved with drugs, but I couldn't find anything to prove it. Darryl was no doubt a working man. I knew that for a fact because I went with him to the dinner party his colleagues threw for him to celebrate his promotion. I never kept a record of Darryl's income, and he didn't keep track with mine, but I have seen one of his pay stubs he left behind on the dining table after writing out his budget and he was bringing in a substantial amount of cash for a bi-weekly paycheck. It was that reason I didn't bother him too much about working long hours until he started to get cute coming home in the wee hours. I also googled Darryl's name one day and nothing unfamiliar about him came up besides his Facebook and Twitter pages. I had the passwords to both of them and when I checked they were normal and he barely even used them.

"Jere, I can't tell you that I know Darryl's every move because I do not clock him like that, but I'm pretty sure he's not dealing with drugs. Trust me, he's a smart man and has too much to lose for that." Jere curled his lips.

"I don't know, Sis. I don't think I trust that dude and I think you should seriously consider leaving him alone. You're a beautiful girl and you have a good job. I want you to move out of here and come stay with me. You can have the basement for free until you get your own spot and then find someone else. Someone who'll be man enough to protect you." I heard what Jere was saying and felt the sting of the last part. I was thinking about leaving Darryl because of my animosity against him, but then I didn't want to. My heart was too impounded with love for him. Something was telling me to work things out with Darryl, but to fall back from him for a while. I was so confused as tears rolled down my cheeks.

"I love him, Jere."

"More than you love yourself?" he asked.

"No, but enough to want to try and look past all of this." Jere angrily shook his head.

"Aw'ight Sis, do what you will, but I' ma tell you this much. I hope you're being smart about your decision, because the next time he screws up like this, I'm unlocking my safe and taking him out, regardless of what you say." Jere kissed me on my cheek, scribbled a sweet remark on my cast and left my room. My brother Jere was a good man and always has been, but nobody knew him like I knew him. He didn't let anybody mess with his family. My body shook. Darryl and I needed to get some external help to make our relationship right so there would be no more wild mistakes. It's been a while since I've seen that look in Jere's eyes. He wasn't joking and was dead serious.

***

During our four months' time apart, Darryl called sporadically to check in. I didn't always make it apparent that I wanted to talk to him. I realized that when I heard his voice, it sent a bad surge through me. He tried to do the things he always done whenever we were on the outs, like sending all types of gifts to the house to make me feel better and look at him differently. He called one day and insisted we talk about our issues and asked if he could come by. I wasn't really ready to see him, but we needed to figure out what we were going to do about our relationship. He sat there and stared at me while I sat adjacent to him on the couch. He looked like life had taken just as much a toll on him as it did me. If there was one thing for sure about Darryl, it was that he always kept himself well groomed. I could tell he'd been out of it. His hair wasn't cut and was in coiled curls and he hadn't shaved.

"You really didn't want him, did you?" I asked, referring to my beloved son.

"Shenelle, of course I did. If I didn't, then I wouldn't have been happy when you told me you were pregnant. I wouldn't have gotten us this condo." His face look emotionally drained and he had no way of explaining himself or his faults.

"You were never there, Darryl. You missed out on everything, like you didn't even care. Was it really worth it?" Darryl put his head down. He swore there wasn't another woman, but there was. His actions couldn't have made it anymore obvious. There was no use in even asking him about it again because he had already made a bad rep for himself. In other words, he admitting to being with another woman wouldn't have made a difference anyway.

"Shenelle, I messed up. You just have to forgive me, so we can get past this."

"Forgive you?"

"Yes, what's wrong with forgiving?" I glared at him in anger. I hated when people did jacked up things and then asked for forgiveness, expecting everything to go away. It wasn't that simple especially when a heart got broken. The pain of my broken heart and the vision of my son's dead body reminded me of how heated I was at Darryl, and it caused the tears to flow. I picked up the throw pillow I had my back resting on and threw it at him. It smacked right in his face.

"Fuck you, Darryl! I hate your guts!" I got up and walked away going towards the stairway. He followed me. I slapped him and kept slapping him, calling him every bad name I could think of. He didn't seem to want to stop me and just took it all until he finally grabbed both my hands.

"Shenelle, what do you want me to do? I fucked up! I know what I did was wrong, but what do you want me to do?"

"I want you to get the hell out, you selfish bum! I don't even want to look at you, just leave!" I said, and then pulled away from him. My focus wasn't really on Darryl; it was on my son, I wanted him back. I wanted to be able to hold him and rock him to sleep at night. We were supposed to be a family and everything was good until Darryl ruined it with his egotism.

"Get out, Darryl! Please just get out! You're a worthless piece of shit and you don't deserve me. You didn't deserve him!" I said backing away from him. The rage in my blood rose and I wanted to strike at him again till I saw blood, but I knew at the end, it wouldn't change anything.

"Shenelle, I'm sorry. I'll do anything to make this right." I noticed the hurt look on his face. He walked towards me and I took the vase off the dining room table and threw that at him. It missed and hit the wall. Glass, water and roses shattered everywhere.

"Babe, please calm down," he said with his voice cracking, I stood there and all of my emotions flooded. I cried hard and felt Darryl grab my waist and embrace me.

"I'm sorry. I know you're hurt, but you can't let this get you down. We can have another child and put this behind us. I'm willing to do anything... anything to fix this if you let me. Please, just tell me what to do." I cried even harder, I didn't see how he could fix my broken heart. Having another child wasn't going to replace the son I wanted and was supposed to have. I held on to him and he cried with me. It was undeniable there was divine love with Darryl and me, but we had so much work to do to get back what we truly had.

My maternity leave wasn't due for another three months. I was in such shambles that I was physically getting sick from not eating, I barely slept and I pretty much quit school. I pleaded with my co-worker, A.J. via email to take over my articles and have my assistant deal with the edge work, so I would be up to date when I got back to the office. Being a good friend, he took over my assignments with no problem. When he asked me how my pregnancy was and how things were going with my new baby, I shut my computer down. When my mind went to thinking about how my pregnancy should have went along and how my son should have been home, I mentally shut down big time.

My loved ones being around was the only reason why I didn't swallow a bottle of pills to put an end to my pain. Alicia kept recommending I talk to someone and I lashed out at her for even thinking I would do that again. Darryl was encouraging me to talk to someone too if I wanted us to get through our issues. He was willing to do it with me, but suggested I go first since I was the one who was slipping. Everything was getting so bad that I told everyone to leave me alone; I didn't want to deal with anyone. They all fought with me for my strength and I fought with them to back off. To say that I was losing it wasn't even the proper phrase anymore and I couldn't even come up with one.

I shut everybody out and stayed a zombie in my house. Darryl was the only one who was hard headed and kept coming around no matter what I said. He wanted to make sure I didn't do anything crazy. He took all of my knives, sharp cooking utensils and sedatives from the house. He tried to do whatever he could to make me feel better, but it rarely worked. After some time, I realized that being trapped in my house was even more disturbing. All of my thoughts were negative and I kept having flashbacks of the scary situations that happened in my life. It was like everything was haunting me and I started to get these very bad headaches, so I went back to work. I walked in with everybody congratulating me for my bundle of joy and asking how it felt to be a new parent. I played it off and didn't tell anyone the truth. I just hid my pain until I was inside my office where no one saw me crumble.

A.J. was the one who perceived something was different about me and tried to get me to confide in him. I insisted on telling him there was nothing wrong and I kept the door to my office locked, so I wouldn't be bothered. I really bugged out in public one day, when my car broke down on the highway while I was heading home. A lady who felt badly for me called a car tow service and was big hearted enough to drive me across the George Washington Bridge. I took a taxi from there to my house in tears of stress and embarrassment. I could see the African cab driver looking at me perplexed through the rearview mirror. I shot him a look for him to not dare ask any questions. He got the hint and didn't. I was a mess over my troubles. It seemed like every time I thought I had broken the ice to the psychosis in my life, I would turn around and was back in drama again.

***

I sat there looking at Dr. Mayes, using my twentieth piece of Kleenex to absorb my tears. We didn't exchange words right away. I wasn't sure if my last words were completely audible, because I spluttered as I talked. Seeing the sad expression on her face, told me she understood most of what I was saying. I saw a lone tear escape the corner of her right eye and trickle down her cheek. She quickly wiped the tear away. I was surprised. As I thought about all of the things I just told her, I uttered, "I don't know what to do now." She swallowed hard and cleared her throat, fighting new tears from falling.

"You're going to be strong and move on. That's why I'm glad you came here, Shenelle. I do this work because I love helping people and I'm here to help you get through your struggles." My tears were still streaming from despair. She sounded so sincere. I could hear it in her voice she really felt my pain and wanted me to be healed. Dr. Mayes moved from the club chair to the loveseat alongside me. She rolled up the sleeve of my silk, button up shirt. I didn't resist her. She lightly brushed her finger against the bandage that covered a new gash I inflicted on my wrist with a razor.

"Shenelle, you have to stop doing this to yourself because if you don't, one day you just might succeed. I guarantee you, in the end it will not be worth it." Spiritually I knew what she meant by that. I could easily have lied and said I had a minor accident, but she knew the truth. One thing I respected about Dr. Mayes was unlike most people, instead of focusing on what she thought she saw outside of me, she focused on what was happening inside. She understood that my situation was way more than a pity act and I needed help in finding my salvation.

"I want you back here next Tuesday at five thirty, sharp."

"Noted."

When I left Dr. Mayes' office, I got in my car and pulled out of the parking lot. I drove down one block and as I waited at the red light, I noticed a church and heard piano music coming from it. It had been so long since I'd gone to church; I thought I should go in. I turned the corner and parked. It was surprising to me that a church would be open on a Tuesday. Taped to the entrance door was a sign that read *bible study* and I walked inside. The first thing I noticed was synthetic flowers set in each corner of the church. The walls were beautifully painted in indigo blue. The place was nice and toasty. It smelled like freshly brewed coffee beans and gave off a homey feeling like when I visited my great grandparents down south. I took a seat on one of the cushioned benches at the back of the church and skimmed through a hymnbook. I remembered singing from a hymnal many years ago; I struggled because I never really understood how to read musical notes.

One of the deaconesses asked me to move to the front with everyone else, but I refused. The Pastor was reading a scripture on forgiveness and I silently read along with the congregation, Matthew 5:44 *But I tell you, love your enemies and pray for those who persecute you that may be sons of your father in heaven. He causes his sun to rise on the evil and the good and sends rain on the righteous and the unrighteous.* I analyzed what I read for a while. I always knew that forgiveness was a huge topic in the bible and something that was major in the eyes of the Lord, but forgiving was something I was never good at doing and I considered myself a Christian woman. I did look past things in time, but I never really let things go fully. That thought was so heavy on me I didn't realize bible study had ended. The Pastor greeting me is what broke me out of my zone-out moment.

"Hello, my name is Pastor Moore. Welcome to *Worship and Prayer Fellowship.*" He extended his hand and I shook it. The pastor was fairly tall, brown skinned and carried himself respectfully, wearing a suit and tie. He had a bald head with a little gray in his goatee, but his face looked youthful. By the way he spoke, he sounded like he could've been my father.

"Did you enjoy the word today?"

"Yes," I replied modestly.

"What is your name?" I almost gave him fake name. I wasn't trying to get too into the church thing yet, but then I would really be a fool to lie right in God's house.

"Shenelle."

"Shenelle, why do you look so down? You know, I'm available now if you would like to talk." I wanted to talk to Pastor Moore. I wanted to cry and tell him everything, what I was feeling, all that I had gone through and why it has been bothering me for so long. I wanted to ask him why God chose me. I wanted to let it all out and receive a spiritual healing, but I was afraid. I didn't want to be judged and I didn't want to burden him with my sorrows, even if he did offer his ear. Also, I really didn't trust pastors. I grew up in a church, so I knew that some ministers didn't always practice what they preached. I felt that sometimes ministers liked to take your life story and use it against you, coming up with their own philosophies to try and define you. I wasn't trying to be defined, nor did I want to be labeled. I wanted to be helped. I wanted to be delivered. I wanted to be cured, so that all my struggles would diminish, and I wouldn't have to hurt anymore. I wasn't sure if a church could do that for me right now, so I declined his offer.

"No thank you, Sir. I'm okay."

"Are you sure?"

"I'm sure."

"Okay, well I hope to see you back here one Sunday morning. Jesus loves you and so do I. I'll keep you in prayer." We shook hands again and he walked off. I waited till I could no longer see him and I got up to walk out the door. I felt if I couldn't bring myself to talk to the head man then there was no reason for me to sit in his church. On my way out, the same deaconess who asked that I move up a few pews, called out to me.

"Miss, please come again. Pastor Moore is wonderful and this is a great church. God will move you here and you will feel so much better as time progresses."

I didn't reply and she looked deep into my eyes and said, "The devil is a liar and he has absolutely no power over you. You have power over him. All you have to do is keep believing that and you'll succeed." She wrote her name and number on a prayer request slip and gave it to me. She told me to call her anytime I needed to talk. I thanked her and then I left.

As much as I would love to have a church home where I could spread my wings freely without being put to shame, I didn't feel today was the right time to make that decision. I was beginning to feel like God didn't even exist in my world. I stood outside in front of the church, thinking about all the troubles in my life and began to cry again. I felt so under pressure that I didn't know whether I should run back inside the church, fall at the pulpit and pray or to park at the nearest bridge and jump. All I knew at this moment was that I was fed up with my life and ending it was what I wanted to do. I got in my car and thought about nothing other than heading to the bridge that would take me to my final destination.

Made in the USA
Columbia, SC
14 June 2022

61712146R00202